THE GREAT TABOO.

By GRANT ALLEN.

NEW YORK:
A. L. BURT, PUBLISHER.

PREFACE.

I DESIRE to express my profound indebtedness, for the central mythological idea embodied in this tale, to Mr. J. G. Frazer's admirable and epoch-making work, "The Golden Bough," whose main contention I have endeavored incidentally to popularize in my present story. I wish also to express my obligations in other ways to Mr. Andrew Lang's "Myth, Ritual, and Religion," Mr. H. O. Forbes's "Naturalist's Wanderings," and Mr. Julian Thomas's "Cannibals and Convicts." If I have omitted to mention any other author to whom I may have owed incidental hints, it will be some consolation to me to reflect that I shall at least have afforded an opportunity for legitimate sport to the amateurs of the new and popular British pastime of badger-baiting or plagiary-hunting. It may also save critics some moments' search if I say at once that, after careful consideration, I have been unable to discover any moral whatsoever in this humble narrative. I venture to believe that in so enlightened an age the majority of my readers will never miss it.

G. A.

THE NOOK, DORKING, *October*, 1890.

THE GREAT TABOO.

CHAPTER I.

IN MID PACIFIC.

"Man overboard!"

It rang in Felix Thurstan's ears like the sound of a bell. He gazed about him in dismay, wondering what had happened.

The first intimation he received of the accident was that sudden sharp cry from the bo'sun's mate. Almost before he had fully taken it in, in all its meaning, another voice, farther aft, took up the cry once more in an altered form: "A lady! a lady! Somebody overboard! Great heavens, it is *her!* It's Miss Ellis! Miss Ellis!"

Next instant Felix found himself, he knew not how, struggling in a wild grapple with the dark, black water. A woman was clinging to him—clinging for dear life. But he couldn't have told you himself that minute how it all took place. He was too stunned and dazzled.

He looked around him on the seething sea in a sudden awakening, as it were, to life and consciousness. All about, the great water stretched dark and tumultuous. White breakers surged over him. Far ahead the steamer's lights gleamed red and green in long lines upon the ocean. At first they ran fast; then they slackened somewhat. She was surely slowing now; they must be reversing engines and trying to stop her. They would put out a boat. But what hope, what chance of rescue by night, in such a wild waste of waves as that? And Muriel Ellis was clinging to him for dear life all the while, with the despairing clutch of a half-drowned woman!

The people on the Australasian, for their part, knew better what had occurred. There was bustle and confusion enough on deck and on the captain's bridge, to be sure : "Man overboard!"—three sharp rings at the engine bell :—"Stop her short!—reverse engines!—lower the gig!—look sharp, there, all of you!" Passengers hurried up breathless at the first alarm to know what was the matter. Sailors loosened and lowered the boat from the davits with extraordinary quickness. Officers stood by, giving orders in monosyllables with practised calm. All was hurry and turmoil, yet with a marvellous sense of order and prompt obedience as well. But, at any rate, the people on deck hadn't the swift swirl of the boisterous water, the hampering wet clothes, the pervading consciousness of personal danger, to make their brains reel, like Felix Thurstan's. They could ask one another with comparative composure what had happened on board ; they could listen without terror to the story of the accident.

It was the thirteenth day out from Sydney, and the Australasian was rapidly nearing the equator. Toward evening the wind had freshened, and the sea was running high against her weather side. But it was a fine starlit night, though the moon had not yet risen ; and as the brief tropical twilight faded away by quick degrees in the west, the fringe of cocoanut palms on the reef that bounded the little island of Boupari showed out for a minute or two in dark relief, some miles to leeward, against the pale pink horizon. In spite of the heavy sea, many passengers lingered late on deck that night to see the last of that coral-girt shore, which was to be their final glimpse of land till they reached Honolulu, *en route* for San Francisco.

Bit by bit, however, the cocoanut palms, silhouetted with their graceful waving arms for a few brief minutes in black against the glowing background, merged slowly into the sky or sank below the horizon. All grew dark. One by one, as the trees disappeared, the passengers dropped off for whist in the saloon, or retired to the uneasy solitude of their own state-rooms. At last only two or three men were left smoking and chatting near the top of the companion ladder; while at the stern of the ship Muriel Ellis looked over toward the retreating island, and talked with a certain timid maidenly frankness to Felix Thurstan.

There's nowhere on earth for getting really to know people in a very short time like the deck of a great Atlantic or Pacific liner. You're thrown together so much, and all day long, that you see more of your fellow-passengers' inner life and nature in a few brief weeks than you would ever be likely to see in a long twelvemonth of ordinary town or country acquaintanceship. And Muriel Ellis had seen a great deal in those thirteen days of Felix Thurstan; enough to make sure in her own heart that she really liked him—well—so much that she looked up with a pretty blush of self-consciousness every time he approached and lifted his hat to her. Muriel was an English rector's daughter, from a country village in Somersetshire; and she was now on her way back from a long year's visit, to recruit her health, to an aunt in Paramatta. She was travelling under the escort of an amiable old chaperon whom the aunt in question had picked up for her before leaving Sydney; but, as the amiable old chaperon, being but an indifferent sailor, spent most of her time in her own berth, closely attended by the obliging stewardess, Muriel had found her chaperonage interfere very little with opportunities of talk with that nice Mr. Thurstan. And now, as the last glow of sunset died out in the western sky, and the last palm-tree faded away against the colder green darkness of the tropical night, Muriel was leaning over the bulwarks in confidential mood, and watching the big waves advance or recede, and talking the sort of talk that such an hour seems to favor with the handsome young civil servant who stood on guard, as it were, beside her. For Felix Thurstan held a government appointment at Levuka, in Fiji, and was now on his way home, on leave of absence after six years' service in that new-made colony.

"How delightful it would be to live on an island like that!" Muriel murmured, half to herself, as she gazed out wistfully in the direction of the disappearing coral reef. "With those beautiful palms waving always over one's head, and that delicious evening air blowing cool through their branches! It looks such a Paradise!"

Felix smiled and glanced down at her, as he steadied himself with one hand against the bulwark, while the ship rolled over into the trough of the sea heavily. "Well, I don't know about that, Miss Ellis," he answered with a doubtful air, eying her close as he spoke with eyes of evident admiration. "One might be happy anywhere, of course—in suitable society; but if you'd lived as long among cocoanuts in Fiji as I have, I dare say the poetry of these calm palm-grove islands would be a little less real to you. Remember, though they look so beautiful and dreamy against the sky like that, at sunset especially (that was a heavy one, that time; I'm really afraid we must go down to the cabin soon; she'll be shipping seas before long if we stop on deck much later—and yet, it's so delightful stopping up here till the dusk comes on, isn't it?)—well, remember, I was saying, though they look so beautiful and dreamy and poetical—'Summer isles of Eden lying in dark purple spheres of sea,' and all that sort of thing—these islands are inhabited by the fiercest and most bloodthirsty cannibals known to travellers."

"Cannibals!" Muriel repeated, looking up at him in surprise. "You don't mean to say that islands like these, standing right in the very track of European steamers, are still heathen and cannibal?"

"Oh, dear, yes," Felix replied, holding his hand out as he spoke to catch his companion's arm gently, and steady her against the wave that was just going to strike the stern: "Excuse me; just so; the sea's rising fast, isn't it ?—Oh, dear, yes ; of course they are ; they're all heathen and cannibals. You couldn't imagine to yourself the horrible bloodthirsty rites that may this very minute be taking place upon that idyllic-looking island, under the soft waving branches of those whispering palm-trees. Why, I knew a man in the Marquesas myself—a hideous old native, as ugly as you can fancy him—who was supposed to be a god, an incarnate god, and was worshipped accordingly with profound devotion by all the other islanders. You can't picture to yourself how awful their worship was. I daren't even repeat it to you ; it was too, too horrible. He lived in a hut by himself among the deepest forest, and human victims used to be brought—well, there, it's too loathsome ! Why, see ; there's a great light on the island now ; a big bonfire or something ; don't you make it out ? You can tell it by the red glare in the sky overhead." He paused a moment ; then he added more slowly, " I shouldn't be surprised if at this very moment, while we're standing here in such perfect security on the deck of a Christian English vessel, some unspeakable and unthinkable heathen orgy mayn't be going on over there beside that sacrificial fire ; and if some poor trembling native girl isn't being led just now, with blows and curses and awful savage ceremonies, her hands bound behind her back—— Oh, look out, Miss Ellis !"

He was only just in time to utter the warning words. He was only just in time to put one hand on each side of her slender waist, and hold her tight so, when the big wave which he saw coming struck full tilt against the vessel's flank, and broke in one white drenching sheet of foam against her stern and quarter-deck.

The suddenness of the assault took Felix's breath away. For the first few seconds he was only aware that a heavy sea had been shipped, and had wet him through and through with its unexpected deluge. A moment later, he was dimly conscious that his companion had slipped from his grasp, and was nowhere visible. The violence of the

shock, and the slimy nature of the sea water, had made
him relax his hold without knowing it, in the tumult of
the moment, and had at the same time caused Muriel to
glide imperceptibly through his fingers, as he had often
known an ill-caught cricket-ball do in his school-days.
Then he saw he was on his hands and knees on the deck.
The wave had knocked him down, and dashed him against
the bulwark on the leeward side. As he picked himself
up, wet, bruised, and shaken, he looked about for Muriel.
A terrible dread seized upon his soul at once. Impossible! Impossible! she couldn't have been washed overboard!

And even as he gazed about, and held his bruised elbow
in his hand, and wondered to himself what it could all
mean, that sudden loud cry arose beside him from the
quarter-deck, "Man overboard!   Man overboard!" followed a moment later by the answering cry, from the men
who were smoking under the lee of the companion, "A
lady! a lady! It's Miss Ellis! Miss Ellis!"

He didn't take it all in. He didn't reflect. He didn't
even know he was actually doing it. But he did it, all the
same, with the simple, straightforward, instinctive sense of
duty which makes civilized man act aright, all unconsciously, in any moment of supreme danger and difficulty.
Leaping on to the taffrail without one instant's delay, and
steadying himself for an indivisible fraction of time with
his hand on the rope ladder, he peered out into the darkness with keen eyes for a glimpse of Muriel Ellis's head
above the fierce black water ; and espying it for one second,
as she came up on a white crest, he plunged in before the
vessel had time to roll back to windward, and struck boldly out in the direction where he saw that helpless object
dashed about like a cork on the surface of the ocean.

Only those who have known such accidents at sea can
possibly picture to themselves the instantaneous haste with
which all that followed took place upon that bustling
quarter-deck. Almost at the first cry of "Man overboard!"

the captain's bell rang sharp and quick, as if by magic, with three peremptory little calls in the engine-room below. The Australasian was going at full speed, but in a marvellously short time, as it seemed to all on board, the great ship had slowed down to a perfect standstill, and then had reversed her engines, so that she lay, just nose to the wind, awaiting further orders. In the meantime, almost as soon as the words were out of the bo'sun's lips, a sailor amidships had rushed to the safety belts hung up by the companion ladder, and had flung half a dozen of them, one after another, with hasty but well-aimed throws, far, far astern, in the direction where Felix had disappeared into the black water. The belts were painted white, and they showed for a few seconds, as they fell, like bright specks on the surface of the darkling sea ; then they sunk slowly behind as the big ship, still not quite stopped, ploughed her way ahead with gigantic force into the great abyss of darkness in front of her.

It seemed but a minute, too, to the watchers on board, before a party of sailors, summoned by the whistle with that marvellous readiness to meet any emergency which long experience of sudden danger has rendered habitual among seafaring men, had lowered the boat, and taken their seats on the thwarts, and seized their oars, and were getting under way on their hopeless quest of search, through the dim black night, for those two belated souls alone in the midst of the angry Pacific.

It seemed but a minute or two, I say, to the watchers on board ; but oh, what an eternity of time to Felix Thurstan, struggling there with his live burden in the seething water !

He had dashed into the ocean, which was dark, but warm with tropical heat, and had succeeded, in spite of the heavy seas then running, in reaching Muriel, who clung to him now with all the fierce clinging of despair, and impeded his movement through that swirling water. More than that, he saw the white life-belts that the sail-

ors flung toward him ; they were well and aptly flung, in
the inspiration of the moment, to allow for the sea itself
carrying them on the crest of its waves toward the two
drowning creatures. Felix saw them distinctly, and making a great lunge as they passed, in spite of Muriel's
struggles, which sadly hampered his movements, he managed to clutch at no less than three before the great billow, rolling on, carried them off on its top forever away
from him. Two of these he slipped hastily over Muriel's
shoulders ; the other he put, as best he might, round his
own waist ; and then, for the first time, still clinging close
to his companion's arm, and buffeted about wildly by that
running sea, he was able to look about him in alarm for a
moment, and realize more or less what had actually happened.

By this time the Australasian was a quarter of a mile
away in front of them, and her lights were beginning to
become stationary as she slowly slowed and reversed
engines. Then, from the summit of a great wave, Felix
was dimly aware of a boat being lowered—for he saw a
separate light gleaming across the sea—a search was
being made in the black night, alas, how hopelessly !
The light hovered about for many, many minutes, revealed to him now here, now there, searching in vain to
find him, as wave after wave raised him time and again on
its irresistible summit. The men in the boat were doing
their best, no doubt ; but what chance of finding any one
on a dark night like that, in an angry sea, and with no
clue to guide them toward the two struggling castaways?
Current and wind had things all their own way. As a
matter of fact, the light never came near the castaways at
all ; and after half an hour's ineffectual search, which
seemed to Felix a whole long lifetime, it returned slowly
toward the steamer from which it came—and left those
two alone on the dark Pacific.

"There wasn't a chance of picking 'em up," the captain said, with philosophic calm, as the men clambered

on board again, and the Australasian got under way once more for the port of Honolulu. " I knew there wasn't a chance ; but in common humanity one was bound to make some show of trying to save 'em. He was a brave fellow to go after her, though it was no good of course. He couldn't even find her, at night, and with such a sea as that running."

And even as he spoke, Felix Thurstan, rising once more on the crest of a much smaller billow—for somehow the waves were getting incredibly smaller as he drifted on to leeward—felt his heart sink within him as he observed to his dismay that the Australasian must be steaming ahead once more, by the movement of her lights, and that they two were indeed abandoned to their fate on the open surface of that vast and trackless ocean.

CHAPTER II.

THE TEMPLE OF THE DEITY.

While these things were happening on the sea close by, a very different scene indeed was being enacted meanwhile, beneath those waving palms, on the island of Boupari. It was strange, to be sure, as Felix Thurstan had said, that such unspeakable heathen orgies should be taking place within sight of a passing Christian English steamer. But if only he had known or reflected to what sort of land he was trying now to struggle ashore with Muriel, he might well have doubted whether it were not better to let her perish where she was, in the pure clear ocean, rather than to submit an English girl to the possibility of undergoing such horrible heathen rites and ceremonies.

For on the island of Boupari it was high feast with the worshippers of their god that night. The sun had turned on the Tropic of Capricorn at noon, and was making his way northward, toward the equator once more ; and his votaries, as was their wont, had all come forth to do him honor in due season, and to pay their respects, in the inmost and sacredest grove on the island, to his incarnate representative, the living spirit of trees and fruits and vegetation, the very high god, the divine Tu-Kila-Kila!

Early in the evening, as soon as the sun's rim had disappeared beneath the ocean, a strange noise boomed forth from the central shrine of Boupari. Those who heard it clapped their hands to their ears and ran hastily forward. It was a noise like distant rumbling thunder, or the whir of some great English mill or factory ; and at its sound every woman on the island threw herself on the ground prostrate, with her face in the dust, and waited there reverently till the audible voice of the god had once more subsided. For no woman knew how that sound was produced. Only the grown men, initiated into the mysteries of the shrine when they came of age at the tattooing ceremony, were aware that the strange, buzzing, whirring noise was nothing more or less than the cry of the bull-roarer.

A bull-roarer, as many English schoolboys know, is merely a piece of oblong wood, pointed at either end, and fastened by a leather thong at one corner. But when whirled round the head by practised priestly hands, it produces a low rumbling noise like the wheels of a distant carriage, growing gradually louder and clearer, from moment to moment, till at last it waxes itself into a frightful din, or bursts into perfect peals of imitation thunder. Then it decreases again once more, as gradually as it rose, becoming fainter and ever fainter, like thunder as it recedes, till the horrible bellowing, as of supernatural bulls, dies away in the end, by slow degrees, into low and soft and imperceptible murmurs.

But when the savage hears the distant humming of the bull-roarer, at whatever distance, he knows that the mysteries of his god are in full swing, and he hurries forward in haste, leaving his work or his pleasure, and running,

naked as he stands, to take his share in the worship, lest
the anger of heaven should burst forth in devouring
flames to consume him.   But the women, knowing themselves unworthy to face the dread presence of the high
god in his wrath, rush wildly from the spot, and, flinging
themselves down at full length, with their mouths to the
dust, wait patiently till the voice of their deity is no
longer audible.

And as the bull-roarer on Boupari rang out with wild
echoes from the coral caverns in the central grove that
evening, Tu-Kila-Kila, their god, rose slowly from his
place, and stood out from his hut, a deity revealed, before
his reverential worshippers.

As he rose, a hushed whisper ran wave-like through the
dense throng of dusky forms that bent low, like corn beneath the wind, before him, " Tu-Kila-Kila rises ! He rises
to speak ! Hush! for the voice of the mighty man-god ! "

The god, looking around him superciliously with a
cynical air of contempt, stood forward with a firm and
elastic step before his silent worshippers.   He was a stalwart savage, in the very prime of life, tall, lithe, and
active.   His figure was that of a man well used to command ; but his face, though handsome, was visibly marked
by every external sign of cruelty, lust, and extreme blood-
thirstiness.   One might have said, merely to look at him,
he was a being debased by all forms of brutal and hateful
self-indulgence.   A baleful light burned in his keen gray
eyes.   His lips were thick, full, purple, and wistful.

"My people may look upon me," he said, in a strangely
affable voice, standing forward and smiling with a curious
half-cruel, half-compassionate smile upon his awe-struck
followers.   " On every day of the sun's course but this,
none save the ministers dedicated to the service of Tu-
Kila-Kila dare gaze unhurt upon his sacred person.   If
any other did, the light from his holy eyes would wither
them up, and the glow of his glorious countenance would
scorch them to ashes," He raised his two hands, palm

outward, in front of him. "So all the year round," he
went on, "Tu-Kila-Kila, who loves his people, and sends
them the earlier and the later rain in the wet season, and
makes their yams and their taro grow, and causes his sun
to shine upon them freely—all the year round Tu-Kila-
Kila, your god, sits shut up in his own house among the
skeletons of those whom he has killed and eaten, or walks
in his walled paddock, where his bread-fruit ripens and
his plantains spring—himself, and the ministers that his
tribesmen have given him."

At the sound of their mystic deity's voice the savages,
bending lower still till their foreheads touched the ground,
repeated in chorus, to the clapping of hands, like some
solemn litany : "Tu-Kila-Kila speaks true.   Our lord is
merciful. He sends down his showers upon our crops
and fields. He causes his sun to shine brightly over us.
He makes our pigs and our slaves bring forth their increase. Tu-Kila-Kila is good. His people praise him."

The god took another step forward, the divine mantle
of red feathers glowing in the sunset on his dusky shoulders, and smiled once more that hateful gracious smile of
his. He was standing near the open door of his wattled
hut, overshadowed by the huge spreading arms of a gigantic banyan-tree. Through the open door of the hut it was
possible to catch just a passing glimpse of an awful sight
within. On the beams of the house, and on the boughs
of the trees behind it, human skeletons, half covered with
dry flesh, hung in ghastly array, their skulls turned downward. They were the skeletons of the victims Tu-Kila-
Kila, their prince, had slain and eaten ; they were the tro-
phies of the cannibal man-god's hateful prowess.

Tu-Kila-Kila raised his right hand erect and spoke
again. "I am a great god," he said, slowly. "I am very
powerful. I make the sun to shine, and the yams to
grow. I am the spirit of plants. Without me there
would be nothing for you all to eat or drink in Boupari.
If I were to grow old and die, the sun would fade away in

the heavens overhead ; the bread-fruit trees would wither and cease to bear on earth ; all fruits would come to an end and die at once ; all rivers would stop forthwith from running."

His worshippers bowed down in acquiescence with awe-struck faces. "It is true," they answered, in the same slow sing-song of assent as before. "Tu-Kila-Kila is the greatest of gods. We owe to him everything. We hang upon his favor."

Tu-Kila-Kila started back, laughed, and showed his pearly white teeth. They were beautiful and regular, like the teeth of a tiger, a strong young tiger. "But I need more sacrifices than all the other gods," he went on, melodiously, like one who plays with consummate skill upon some difficult instrument. "I am greedy; I am thirsty ; I am a hungry god. You must not stint me. I claim more human victims than all the other gods beside. If you want your crops to grow, and your rivers to run, the fields to yield you game, and the sea fish—this is what I ask : give me victims, victims! That is our compact. Tu-Kila-Kila calls you."

The men bowed down once more and repeated humbly, "You shall have victims as you will, great god ; only give us yam and taro and bread-fruit, and cause not your bright light, the sun, to grow dark in heaven over us."

"Cut yourselves," Tu-Kila-Kila cried, in a peremptory voice, clapping his hands thrice. "I am thirsting for blood. I want your free-will offering."

As he spoke, every man, as by a set ritual, took from a little skin wallet at his side a sharp flake of coral-stone, and, drawing it deliberately across his breast in a deep red gash, caused the blood to flow out freely over his chest and long grass waistband. Then, having done so, they never strove for a moment to stanch the wound, but let the red drops fall as they would on to the dust at their feet, without seeming even to be conscious at all of the fact that they were flowing.

Tu-Kila-Kila smiled once more, a ghastly self-satisfied smile of unquestioned power. " It is well," he went on. " My people love me. They know my strength, how I can wither them up. They give me their blood to drink freely. So I will be merciful to them. I will make my sun shine and my rain drop from heaven. And instead of taking *all*, I will choose one victim." He paused, and glanced along their line significantly.

" Choose, Tu-Kila-Kila," the men answered, without a moment's hesitation. "We are all your meat. Choose which one you will take of us."

Tu-Kila-Kila walked with a leisurely tread down the lines and surveyed the men critically. They were all drawn up in rows, one behind the other, according to tribes and families ; and the god walked along each row, examining them with a curious and interested eye, as a farmer examines sheep fit for the market. Now and then, he felt a leg or an arm with his finger and thumb, and hesitated a second. It was an important matter, this choosing a victim. As he passed, a close observer might have noted that each man trembled visibly while the god's eye was upon him, and looked after him askance with a terrified sidelong gaze as he passed on to his neighbor. But not one savage gave any overt sign or token of his terror or his reluctance. On the contrary, as Tu-Kila-Kila passed along the line with lazy, cruel deliberateness, the men kept chanting aloud without one tremor in their voices, " We are all your meat. Choose which one you will take of us."

On a sudden, Tu-Kila-Kila turned sharply round, and, darting a rapid glance toward a row he had already passed several minutes before, he exclaimed, with an air of unexpected inspiration, " Tu-Kila-Kila has chosen. He takes Maloa."

The man upon whose shoulder the god laid his heavy hand as he spoke stood forth from the crowd without a moment's hesitation. If anger or fear was in his heart at all, it could not be detected in his voice or his features. He bowed his head with seeming satisfaction, and answered humbly, " What Tu-Kila-Kila says must need be done. This is a great honor. He is a mighty god. We poor men must obey him. We are proud to be taken up and made one with divinity."

Tu-Kila-Kila raised in his hand a large stone axe of some polished green material, closely resembling jade, which lay on a block by the door, and tried its edge with his finger, in an abstracted manner. " Bind him ! " he said, quietly, turning round to his votaries. And the men, each glad to have escaped his own fate, bound their comrade willingly with green ropes of plantain fibre.

"Crown him with flowers ! " Tu-Kila-Kila said ; and a female attendant, absolved from the terror of the bull-roarer by the god's command, brought forward a great garland of crimson hibiscus, which she flung around the victim's neck and shoulders.

" Lay his head on the sacred stone block of our fathers," Tu-Kila-Kila went on, in an easy tone of command, waving his hand gracefully. And the men, moving forward, laid their comrade, face downward, on a huge flat block of polished greenstone, which lay like an altar in front of the hut with the mouldering skeletons.

" It is well," Tu-Kila-Kila murmured once more, half aloud. " You have given me the free-will offering. Now for the tresspass ! Where is the woman who dared to approach too near the temple-home of the divine Tu-Kila-Kila ? Bring the criminal forward ! "

The men divided, and made a lane down their middle. Then one of them, a minister of the man-god's shrine, led up by the hand, all trembling and shrinking with supernatural terror in every muscle, a well-formed young girl of eighteen or twenty. Her naked bronze limbs were shapely and lissome ; but her eyes were swollen and red with tears, and her face strongly distorted with awe for the man-god. When she stood at last before Tu-Kila-

Kila's dreaded face, she flung herself on the ground in an agony of fear.

"Oh, mercy, great God!" she cried, in a feeble voice. "I have sinned, I have sinned. Mercy, mercy!"

Tu-Kila-Kila smiled as before, a smile of imperial pride. No ray of pity gleamed from those steel-gray eyes. "Does Tu-Kila-Kila show mercy?" he asked, in a mocking voice. "Does he pardon his suppliants? Does he forgive trespasses? Is he not a god, and must not his wrath be appeased? She, being a woman, and not a wife sealed to Tu-Kila-Kila, has dared to look from afar upon his sacred home. She has spied the mysteries. Therefore she must die. My people, bind her."

In a second, without more ado, while the poor trembling girl writhed and groaned in her agony before their eyes, that mob of wild savages, let loose to torture and slay, fell upon her with hideous shouts, and bound her, as they had bound their comrade before, with coarse native ropes of twisted plantain fibre.

"Lay her head on the stone," Tu-Kila-Kila said, grimly. And his votaries obeyed him.

"Now light the sacred fire to make our feast, before I slay the victims," the god said, in a gloating voice, running his finger again along the edge of his huge hatchet.

As he spoke, two men, holding in their hands hollow bamboos with coals of fire concealed within, which they kept aglow meanwhile by waving them up and down rapidly in the air, laid these primitive matches to the base of a great pyramidal pile of wood and palm-leaves, ready prepared beforehand in the yard of the temple. In a second, the dry fuel, catching the sparks instantly, blazed up to heaven with a wild outburst of flame. Great red tongues of fire licked up the mouldering mass of leaves and twigs, and caught at once at the trunks of palm and li wood within. A huge conflagration reddened the sky at once like lightning. The effect was magical. The glow transfigured the whole island for miles. It was, in fact, the blaze that Felix Thurstan had noted and remarked upon as he stood that evening on the silent deck of the Australasian.

Tu-Kila-Kila gazed at it with horrid childish glee. "A fine fire!" he said, gayly. "A fire worthy of a god. It will serve me well. Tu-Kila-Kila will have a good oven to roast his meal in."

Then he turned toward the sea, and held up his hand once more for silence. As he did so, an answering light upon its surface attracted his eye for a moment's space. It was a bright red light, mixed with white and green ones ; in point of fact, the Australasian was passing. Tu-Kila-Kila pointed toward it solemnly with his plump, brown fore-finger. "See," he said, drawing himself up and looking preternaturally wise ; "your god is great. I am sending some of this fire across the sea to where my sun has set, to aid and reinforce it. That is to keep up the fire of the sun, lest ever at any time it should fade and fail you. While Tu-Kila-Kila lives the sun will burn bright. If Tu-Kila-Kila were to die it would be night forever."

His votaries, following their god's fore-finger as it pointed, all turned to look in the direction he indicated with blank surprise and astonishment. Such a sight had never met their eyes before, for the Australasian was the very first steamer to take the eastward route, through the dangerous and tortuous Boupari Channel. So their awe and surprise at the unwonted sight knew no bounds. Fire on the ocean ! Miraculous light on the waves ! Their god must, indeed, be a mighty deity if he could send flames like that careering over the sea ! Surely the sun was safe in the hands of a potentate who could thus visibly reinforce it with red light, and white ! In their astonishment and awe, they stood with their long hair falling down over their foreheads, and their hands held up to their eyes that they might gaze the farther across the dim, dark ocean. The borrowed light of their bonfire was moving, slowly

2

moving over the watery sea. Fire and water were mixing
and mingling on friendly terms. Impossible! Incredible! Marvellous! Miraculous! They prostrated themselves in their terror at Tu-Kila-Kila's feet. "Oh, great
god," they cried, in awe-struck tones, "your power is too
vast! Spare us, spare us, spare us!"

As for Tu-Kila-Kila himself, he was not astonished at
all. Strange as it sounds to us, he really believed in his
heart what he said. Profoundly convinced of his own
godhead, and abjectly superstitious as any of his own votaries, he absolutely accepted as a fact his own suggestion,
that the light he saw was the reflection of that his men
had kindled. The interpretation he had put upon it
seemed to him a perfectly natural and just one. His worshippers, indeed, mere men that they were, might be terrified at the sight; but why should he, a god, take any special notice of it?

He accepted his own superiority as implicitly as our
European nobles and rulers accept theirs. He had no
doubts himself, and he considered those who had little
better than criminals.

By and by, a smaller light detached itself by slow degrees from the greater ones. The others stood still, and
halted in mid-ocean. The lesser light made as if it would
come in the direction of Boupari. In point of fact, the
gig had put out in search of Felix and Muriel.

Tu-Kila-Kila interpreted the facts at once, however, in
his own way. "See," he said, pointing with his plump
forefinger once more, and encouraging with his words his
terrified followers, "I am sending back a light again from
the sun to my island. I am doing my work well. I am
taking care of my people. Fear not for your future. In
the light is yet another victim. A man and a woman will
come to Boupari from the sun, to make up for the man
and woman whom we eat in our feast to-night. Give me
plenty of victims, and you will have plenty of yam. Make
haste, then; kill, eat; let us feast Tu-Kila-Kila! To-mor-

row the man and woman I have sent from the sun will
come ashore on the reef, and reach Boupari."

At the words, he stepped forward and raised that heavy
tomahawk. With one blow each he brained the two
bound and defenceless victims on the altar-stone of his
fathers. The rest, a European hand shrinks from reveal-
ing. The orgy was too horrible even for description.

And that was the land toward which, that moment, Felix Thurstan was struggling, with all his might, to carry
Muriel Ellis, from the myriad clasping arms of a comparatively gentle and merciful ocean!

CHAPTER III.

LAND ; BUT WHAT LAND ?

As the last glimmering lights of the Australasian died
away to seaward, Felix Thurstan knew in his despair there
was nothing for it now but to strike out boldly, if he could,
for the shore of the island.

By this time the breakers had subsided greatly. Not,
indeed, that the sea itself was really going down. On the
contrary, a brisk wind was rising sharper from the east,
and the waves on the open Pacific were growing each moment higher and loppier. But the huge mountain of
water that washed Muriel Ellis overboard was not a regular ordinary wave ; it was that far more powerful and dangerous mass, a shoal-water breaker. The Australasian had
passed at that instant over a submerged coral-bar, quite
deep enough, indeed, to let her cross its top without the
slightest danger of grazing, but still raised so high toward
the surface as to produce a considerable constant ground-
swell, which broke in windy weather into huge sheets of
surf, like the one that had just struck and washed over the
Australasian, carrying Muriel with it. The very same
cause that produced the breakers, however, bore Felix on

their summit rapidly landward ; and once he had got well beyond the region of the bar that begot them, he found himself soon, to his intense relief, in comparatively calm shoal water.

Muriel Ellis, for her part, was faint with terror and with the buffeting of the waves ; but she still floated by his side, upheld by the life-belts. He had been able, by immense efforts, to keep unseparated from her amid the rending surf of the breakers. Now that they found themselves in easier waters for a while, Felix began to strike out vigorously through the darkness for the shore. Holding up his companion with one hand, and swimming with all his might in the direction where a vague white line of surf, lit up by the red glare of some fire far inland, made him suspect the nearest land to lie, he almost thought he had succeeded at last, after a long hour of struggle, in feeling his feet, after all, on a firm coral bottom.

At the very moment he did so, and touched the ground underneath, another great wave, curling resistlessly behind him, caught him up on its crest, whirled him heavenward like a cork, and then dashed him down once more, a passive burden, on some soft and yielding substance, which he conjectured at once to be a beach of finely powdered coral fragments. As he touched this beach for an instant, the undertow of that vast dashing breaker sucked him back with its ebb again, a helpless, breathless creature ; and then the succeeding wave rolled him over like a ball, upon the beach as before, in quick succession. Four times the back-current sucked him under with its wild pull in the self-same way, and four times the return wave flung him up upon the beach again like a fragment of sea-weed. With frantic efforts Felix tried at first to cling still to Muriel—to save her from the irresistible force of that roaring surf—to snatch her from the open jaws of death by sheer struggling dint of thews and muscle. He might as well have tried to stem Niagara. The great waves, curling irresistibly in huge curves landward, caught either of them up by turns on their arched summits, and twisted them about remorselessly, raising them now aloft on their foaming crest, beating them back now prone in their hollow trough, and flinging them fiercely at last with pitiless energy against the soft beach of coral. If the beach had been hard, they must infallibly have been ground to powder or beaten to jelly by the colossal force of those gigantic blows. Fortunately it was yielding, smooth, and clay-like, and received them almost as a layer of moist plaster of Paris might have done, or they would have stood no chance at all for their lives in that desperate battle with the blind and frantic forces of unrelenting nature.

No man who has not himself seen the surf break on one of these far-southern coral shores can form any idea in his own mind of the terror and horror of the situation. The water, as it reaches the beach, rears itself aloft for a second into a huge upright wall, which, advancing slowly, curls over at last in a hollow circle, and pounds down upon the sand or reef with all the crushing force of some enormous sledge-hammer. But after the fourth assault, Felix felt himself flung up high and dry by the wave, as one may sometimes see a bit of light reed or pith flung up some distance ahead by an advancing tide on the beach in England. In an instant he steadied himself and staggered to his feet. Torn and bruised as he was by the pummelling of the billows, he looked eagerly into the water in search of his companion. The next wave flung up Muriel, as the last had flung himself. He bent over her with a panting heart as she lay there, insensible, on the long white shore. Alive or dead? that was now the question.

Raising her hastily in his arms, with her clothes all clinging wet and close about her, Felix carried her over the narrow strip of tidal beach, above high-water level, and laid her gently down on a soft green bank of short tropical herbage, close to the edge of the coral. Then he bent over her once more, and listened eagerly at her heart. It still beat with faint pulses—beat—beat—beat. Felix throbbed

with joy.   She was alive ! alive !   He was not quite alone,
then, on that unknown island !

And strange as it seemed, it was only a little more than
two short hours since they had stood and looked out across
the open sea over the bulwarks of the Australasian together !

But Felix had no time to moralize just then.   The moment was clearly one for action.   Fortunately, he happened
to carry three useful things in his pocket when he jumped
overboard after Muriel.   The first was a pocket-knife ; the
second was a flask with a little whiskey in it ; and the third,
perhaps the most important of all, a small metal box of
wax vesta matches.   Pouring a little whiskey into the cup
of the flask, he held it eagerly to Muriel's lips.   The faint-
ing girl swallowed it automatically.   Then Felix, stooping
down, tried the matches against the box.   They were unfortunately wet, but half an hour's exposure, he knew, on
sun-warmed stones, in that hot, tropical air, would soon
restore them again.   So he opened the box and laid them
carefully out on a flat white slab of coral.   After that, he
had time to consider exactly where they were, and what
their chances in life, if any, might now amount to.

Pitch dark as it was, he had no difficulty in deciding at
once by the general look of things that they had reached a
fringing reef, such as he was already familiar with in the
Marquesas and elsewhere.   The reef was no doubt circular,
and it enclosed within itself a second or central island,
divided from it by a shallow lagoon of calm, still water.
He walked some yards inland.   From where he now stood,
on the summit of the ridge, he could look either way, and
by the faint reflected light of the stars, or the glare of the
great pyre that burned on the central island, he could see
down on one side to the ocean, with its fierce white pounding surf, and on the other to the lagoon, reflecting the stars
overhead, and motionless as a mill-pond.   Between them
lay the low raised ridge of coral, covered with tall stems
of cocoanut palms, and interspersed here and there, as far

as his eye could judge, with little rectangular clumps of plantain and taro.

But what alarmed Felix most was the fire that blazed so brightly to heaven on the central island ; for he knew too well that meant—there were *men* on the place ; the land was inhabited.

The cocoanuts and taro told the same doubtful tale. From the way they grew, even in that dim starlight, Felix recognized at once they had all been planted.

Still, he didn't hesitate to do what he thought best for Muriel's relief for all that. Collecting a few sticks and fragments of palm-branches from the jungle about, he piled them into a heap, and waited patiently for his matches to dry. As soon as they were ready—and the warmth of the stone made them quickly inflammable—he struck a match on the box, and proceeded to light his fire by Muriel's side. As her clothes grew warmer, the poor girl opened her eyes at last, and, gazing around her, exclaimed, in blank terror, " Oh, Mr. Thurstan, where are we ? What does all this mean ? Where have we got to ? On a desert island ? "

" No, *not* on a desert island," Felix answered, shortly ; " I'm afraid it's a great deal worse than that. To tell you the truth, I'm afraid it's inhabited.

At that moment, by the hot embers of the great sacrificial pyre on the central hill, two of the savage temple-attendants, calling their god's attention to a sudden blaze of flame upon the fringing reef, pointed with their dark forefingers and called out in surprise, " See, see, a fire on the barrier ! A fire ! A fire ! What can it mean ? There are no men of our people over there to-night. Have war-canoes arrived ? Has some enemy landed ? "

Tu-Kila-Kila leaned back, drained his cocoanut cup of intoxicating kava, and surveyed the unwonted apparition on the reef long and carefully. " It is nothing," he said at last, in his most deliberate manner, stroking his cheeks and chin contentedly with that plump round hand of his. "It is only the victims; the new victims I promised you. Korong ! Korong ! They have come ashore with their light from my home in the sun. They have brought fire afresh—holy fire to Boupari."

Three or four of the savages leaped up in fierce joy, and bowed before him as he spoke, with eager faces. "Oh, Tu-Kila-Kila !" the eldest among them said, making a profound reverence, "shall we swim across to the reef and fetch them home to your house ? Shall we take over our canoes and bring back your victims !"

The god motioned them back with one outstretched palm. His eyes were flushed and his look lazy. "Not to-night, my people," he said; readjusting the garland of flowers round his neck, and giving a careless glance at the well-picked bones that a few hours before had been two trembling fellow creatures. "Tu-Kila-Kila has feasted his fill for this evening. Your god is full; his heart is happy. I have eaten human flesh ; I have drunk of the juice of the kava. Am I not a great deity ? Can I not do as I will ? I frown, and the heavens thunder; I gnash my teeth, and the earth trembles. What is it to me if fresh victims come, or if they come not ? Can I not make with a nod as many as I will of them ?" He took up two fresh finger-bones, clean gnawed of their flesh, and knocked them together in a wild tune, carelessly. "If Tu-Kila-Kila chooses," he went on, tapping his chest with conscious pride, "he can knock these bones together—so—and bid them live again. Is it not I who cause women and beasts to bring forth their young ? Is it not I who give the turtles their increase ? And is it not a small thing to me, therefore, whether the sea tosses up my victims from my home in the sun, or whether it does not ? Let us leave them alone on the reef for to-night ; to-morrow we will send over our canoes to fetch them."

It was all pure brag, all pure guesswork ; and yet, Tu-Kila-Kila himself profoundly believed it,

As he spoke, the light from Felix's fire blazed out against the dark sky, stronger and clearer still; and through that cloudless tropical air the figure of a man, standing for one moment between the flames and the lagoon, became distinctly visible to the keen and practised eyes of the savages. "I see them? I see them; I see the victims!" the foremost worshipper exclaimed, rushing forward a little at the sight, and beside himself with superstitious awe and surprise at Tu-Kila-Kila's presence. " Surely our god is great! He knows all things! He brings us meat from the setting sun, in ships of fire, in blazing canoes, across the golden road of the sun-bathed ocean!"

As for Tu-Kila-Kila himself, leaning on his elbow at ease, he gazed across at the unexpected sight with very languid interest. He was a god, and he liked to see things conducted with proper decorum. This crowing and crying over a couple of spirits—mere ordinary spirits come ashore from the sun in a fiery boat—struck his godship as little short of childish. "Let them be," he answered, petulantly, crushing a blossom in his hand. "Let no man disturb them. They shall rest where they are till to-morrow morning. We have eaten; we have drunk; our soul is happy. The kava within us has made us like a god indeed. I shall give my ministers charge that no harm happen to them."

He drew a whistle from his side and whistled once. There was a moment's pause. Then Tu-Kila-Kila spoke in a loud voice again. "The King of Fire!" he exclaimed, in tones of princely authority.

From within the hut there came forth slowly a second stalwart savage, big built and burly as the great god himself, clad in a long robe or cloak of yellow feathers, which shone bright with a strange metallic gleam in the ruddy light of the huge pile of li-wood.

"The King of Fire is here, Tu-Kila-Kila," the lesser god made answer, bending his head slightly.

"Fire," Tu-Kila-Kila said, like a monarch giving orders

to his attendant minister, "if any man touch the new-comers on the reef before I cause my sun to rise to-morrow morning, scorch up his flesh with your flame, and consume his bones to ash and cinder. If any woman go near them before Tu-Kila-Kila bids, let her be rolled in palm-leaves, and smeared with oil, and light her up for a torch on a dark night to lighten our temple."

The King of Fire bent his head in assent. "It is as Tu-Kila-Kila wills," he answered, submissively.

Tu-Kila-Kila whistled again, this time twice. "The King of Water!" he exclaimed, in the same loud tone of command as before.

At the words, a man of about forty, tall and sinewy, clad in a short cape of white albatross feathers, and with a girdle of nautilus shells interspersed with red coral tied around his waist, came forth to the summons.

"The King of Water is here," he said, bending his head, but not his knee, before the greater deity.

"Water," Tu-Kila-Kila said, with half-tipsy solemnity, "you are a god too. Your power is very great. But less than mine. Do, then, as I bid you. If any man touch my spirits, whom I have brought from my home in the sun in a fiery ship, before I bid him to-morrow, overturn his canoe, and drown him in lagoon or spring or ocean. If any woman go near them without Tu-Kila-Kila's leave, bind her hand and foot with ropes of porpoise hide, and cast her out into the surf, and dash her with your waves, and pummel her to pieces."

The King of Water bent his head a second time. "I am a great god," he answered, "before all others save you : but for you, Tu-Kila-Kila, I haste to do your bidding. If any man disobey you, my billows shall rise and overwhelm him in the sea. I am a great god. I claim each year many drowned victims."

"But not so many as me," Tu-Kila-Kila interposed, his hand playing on his knife with a faint air of impatience.

"But not so many as you," the minor god added, in

haste, as if to appease his rising anger. "Fire and Water
ever speed to do your bidding."

Tu-Kila-Kila stood up, turned toward the distant flame,
and waved his hands round and round three times before
him. "Let this be for you all a great taboo," he said,
glancing once more toward his awe-struck followers.
"Now the mysteries are over. Tu-Kila-Kila will sleep.
He has eaten of human flesh. He has drunk of cocoanut
rum and of new kava. He has brought back his sun on
its way in the heavens. He has sent it messengers of fire
to reinforce its strength. He has fetched from it messengers in turn with fresh fire to Boupari, fire not lighted
from any earthly flame; fire new, divine, scorching, unspeakable. To-morrow we will talk with the spirits he
has brought. To-night we will sleep. Now all go to
your homes; and tell your women of this great taboo, lest
they speak to the spirits, and fall into the hands of Fire
or of Water."

The savages dropped on their faces before the eye of
their god and lay quite still. They made a path as it were
from the pyre to the temple door with their prostrate
bodies. Tu-Kila-Kila, walking with unsteady steps over
their half-naked forms, turned to his hut in a drunken
booze. He walked over them with no more compunction
or feeling than over so many logs. Why should he not,
indeed? For he was a god, and they were his meat, his
servants, his worshippers.

CHAPTER IV.

THE GUESTS OF HEAVEN.

All that night through—their first lonely night on the
island of Boupari—Felix sat up by his flickering fire, wide
awake, half expecting and dreading some treacherous
attack of the unknown savages. From time to time he

kept adding dry fuel to his smouldering pile ; and he never ceased to keep a keen eye both on the lagoon and the reef, in case an assault should be made upon them suddenly by land or water.   He knew the South Seas quite well enough already to have all the possibilities of misfortune floating vividly before his eyes.   He realized at once from his own previous experience the full loneliness and terror of their unarmed condition.

For Boupari was one of those rare remote islets where the very rumor of our European civilization has hardly yet penetrated.

As for Muriel, though she was alarmed enough, of course, and intensely shaken by the sudden shock she had received, the whole surroundings were too wholly unlike any world she had ever yet known to enable her to take in at once the utter horror of the situation.   She only knew they were alone, wet, bruised, and terribly battered ; and the Australasian had gone on, leaving them there to their fate on an unknown island.   That, for the moment, was more than enough for her of accumulated misfortune. She come to herself but slowly, and as her torn clothes dried by degrees before the fire and the heat of the tropical night, she was so far from fully realizing the dangers of their position that her first and principal fear for the moment was lest she might take cold from her wet things drying upon her.   She ate a little of the plantain that Felix picked for her ; and at times, toward morning, she dozed off into an uneasy sleep, from pure fatigue and excess of weariness.   As she slept, Felix, bending over her, with the biggest blade of his knife open in case of attack, watched with profound emotion the rise and fall of her bosom, and hesitated with himself, if the worst should come to the worst, as to what he ought to do with her.

It would be impossible to let a pure young English girl like that fall helplessly into the hands of such blood-thirsty wretches as he knew the islanders were almost certain to be.   Who could tell what nameless indignities, what incredible tortures they might wantonly inflict upon her innocent soul? Was it right of him to have let her come ashore at all? Ought he not rather to have allowed the more merciful sea to take her life easily, without the chance or possibility of such additional horrors?

And now—as she slept—so calm and pure and maidenly —what was his duty that minute, just there to her? He felt the blade of his knife with his finger cautiously, and almost doubted. If only she could tell what things might be in store for her, would she not, herself, prefer death, an honorable death, at the friendly hands of a tender-hearted fellow-countryman, to the unspeakable insults of these man-eating Polynesians? If only he had the courage to release her by one blow, as she lay there, from the coming ill! But he hadn't; he hadn't. Even on board the Australasian he had been vaguely aware that he was getting very fond of that pretty little Miss Ellis. And now that he sat there, after that desperate struggle for life with the pounding waves, mounting guard over her through the livelong night, his own heart told him plainly, in tones he could not disobey, he loved her too well to dare what he thought best in the end for her.

Still, even so, he was brave enough to feel he must never let the very worst of all befall her. He bethought him, in his doubt and agony, of how his uncle, Major Thurstan, during the great Indian mutiny, had held his lonely bungalow, with his wife and daughter by his side, for three long hours against a howling mob of native insurgents; and how, when further resistance was hopeless, and that great black wave of angry humanity burst in upon them at last, the brave soldier had drawn his revolver, shot his wife and daughter with unerring aim, to prevent their falling alive into the hands of the natives, and then blown his own brains out with his last remaining cartridge. As his uncle had done at Jhansi, thirty years before, so he himself would do on that nameless Pacific island—for he didn't know even now on what shore he had landed. If the savages bore down upon them with hostile intent, and threatened Muriel, he would plunge his knife first into that innocent woman's heart ; and then bury it deep in his own, and die beside her.

So the long night wore on—Muriel pillowed on loose cocoanut husk, dozing now and again, and waking with a start to gaze round about her wildly, and realize once more in what plight she found herself ; Felix crouching by her feet, and keeping watch with eager eyes and ears on every side for the least sign of a noiseless, naked footfall through the tangled growth of that dense tropical under-bush. Time after time he clapped his hand to his ear, shell-wise, and listened and peered, with knitted brow, suspecting some sudden swoop from an ambush in the jungle of creepers behind the little plantain patch. Time after time he grasped his knife hard, and puckered his eyebrows resolutely, and stood still with bated breath for a fierce, wild leap upon his fancied assailant. But the night wore away by degrees, a minute at a time, and no man came ; and dawn began to brighten the sea-line to east-ward.

As the day dawned, Felix could see more clearly exactly where he was, and in what surroundings. Without, the ocean broke in huge curling billows on the shallow beach of the fringing reef with such stupendous force that Felix wondered how they could ever have lived through its pounding surf and its fiercely retreating undertow. Within, the lagoon spread its calm lake-like surface away to the white coral shore of the central atoll. Between these two waters, the greater and the less, a waving palisade of tall-stemmed palm-trees rose on a narrow ribbon of circular land that formed the fringing reef. All night through he had felt, with a strange eerie misgiving, the very foundations of the land thrill under his feet at every dull thud or boom of the surf on its restraining barrier. Now that he could see that thin belt of shore in its actual shape and size, he was not astonished at this constant shock ; what surprised him rather was the fact that such a speck of land could hold its own at all against the ceaseless cannonade of that seemingly irresistible ocean.

He stood up, hatless, in his battered tweed suit, and surveyed the scene of their present and future adventures. It took but a glance to show him that the whole ground-plan of the island was entirely circular. In the midst of all rose the central atoll itself, a tiny mountain-peak, just projecting with its hills and gorges to a few hundred feet above the surface of the ocean. Outside it came the lagoon, with its placid ring of glassy water surrounding the circular island, and separated from the sea by an equally circular belt of fringing reef, covered thick with waving stems of picturesque cocoanut. It was on the reef they had landed, and from it they now looked across the calm lagoon with doubtful eyes toward the central island.

As soon as the sun rose, their doubts were quickly resolved into fears or certainties. Scarcely had its rim begun to show itself distinctly above the eastern horizon, when a great bustle and confusion was noticeable at once on the opposite shore. Brown-skinned savages were collecting in eager groups by a white patch of beach, and putting out rude but well-manned canoes into the calm waters of the lagoon. At sight of their naked arms and bustling gestures, Muriel's heart sank suddenly within her. "Oh, Mr. Thurstan," she cried, clinging to his arm in her terror, "what does it all mean? Are they going to hurt us? Are these savages coming over? Are they coming to kill us?"

Felix grasped his trusty knife hard in his right hand, and swallowed a groan, as he looked tenderly down upon her. "Muriel," he said, forgetting in the excitement of the moment the little conventionalities and courtesies of civilized life, "if they are, trust me, you never shall fall alive into their cruel hands. Sooner than that—" he held up the knife significantly, with its open blade before her.

The poor girl clung to him harder still, with a ghastly

shudder. "Oh, it's terrible, terrible," she cried, turning deadly pale. Then, after a short pause, she added, "But I would rather have it so. Do as you say. I could bear it from you. Promise me *that*, rather than that those creatures should kill me."

"I promise," Felix answered, clasping her hand hard, and paused, with the knife ever ready in his right, awaiting the approach of the half-naked savages.

The boats glided fast across the lagoon, propelled by the paddles of the stalwart Polynesians who manned them, and crowded to the water's edge with groups of grinning and shouting warriors. They were dressed in aprons of dracæna leaves only, with necklets and armlets of sharks' teeth and cowrie shells. A dozen canoes at least were making toward the reef at full speed, all bristling with spears and alive with noisy and boisterous savages. Muriel shrank back terror-stricken at the sight, as they drew nearer and nearer. But Felix, holding his breath hard, grew somewhat less nervous as the men approached the reef. He had seen enough of Polynesian life before now to feel sure these people were not upon the war-path. Whatever their ultimate intentions toward the castaways might be, their immediate object seemed friendly and good-humored. The boats, though large, were not regular war-canoes ; the men, instead of brandishing their spears, and lunging out with them over the edge in threatening attitudes, held them erect in their hands at rest, like standards ; they were laughing and talking, not crying their war-cry. As they drew near the shore, one big canoe shot suddenly a length or so ahead of the rest ; and its leader, standing on the grotesque carved figure that adorned its prow, held up both his hands open and empty before him, in sign of peace, while at the same time he shouted out a word or two three times in his own language, to reassure the castaways.

Felix's eye glanced cautiously from boat to boat. "He says, 'We are friends,'" the young man remarked in an undertone to his terrified companion. " I can understand his dialect. Thank Heaven, it's very close to Fijian. I shall be able at least to palaver to these men. I don't think they mean just now to harm us. I believe we can trust them, at any rate for the present."

The poor girl drew back, in still greater awe and alarm than ever. " Oh, are they going to land here ? " she cried, still clinging closer with both hands to her one friend and protector.

" Try not to look so frightened ! " Felix exclaimed, with a warning glance. " Remember, much depends upon it ; savages judge you greatly by what demeanor you happen to assume. If you're frightened, they know their power ; if they see you're resolute, they suspect you have some supernatural means of protection. Try to meet them frankly, as if you were not afraid of them." Then, advancing slowly to the water's edge, he called out aloud, in a strong, clear voice, a few words which Muriel didn't understand, but which were really the Fijian for " We also are friendly. Our medicine is good. We mean no magic. We come to you from across the great water. We desire your peace. Receive us and protect us ! "

At the sound of words which he could readily understand, and which differed but little, indeed, from his own language, the leader on the foremost canoe, who seemed by his manner to be a great chief, turned round to his followers and cried out in tones of superstitious awe, " Tu-Kila-Kila spoke well. These are, indeed, what he told us. Korong ! Korong ! They are spirits who have come to us from the disk of the sun, to bring us light and pure, fresh fire. Stay back there, all of you. You are not holy enough to approach. I and my crew, who are sanctified by the mysteries, we alone will go forward to meet them."

As he spoke, a sudden idea, suggested by his words, struck Felix's mind. Superstition is the great lever by which to move the savage intelligence. Gathering up a few dry leaves and fragments of stick on the shore, he laid

them together in a pile, and awaited in silence the arrival
of the foremost islanders. The first canoe advanced slowly
and cautiously, the men in it eying these proceedings with
evident suspicion ; the rest hung back, with their spears
in array, and their hands just ready to use them with effect
should occasion demand it.

The leader of the first canoe, coming close to the shore,
jumped out upon the reef in shallow water. Half a dozen
of his followers jumped after him without hesitation, and
brandished their weapons round their heads as they advanced, in savage unison. But Felix, pretending hardly
to notice these hostile demonstrations, stepped boldly up
toward his little pile with great deliberation, though trembling inwardly, and proceeded before their eyes to take a
match from his box, which he displayed ostentatiously, all
glittering in the sun, to the foremost savage. The leader
stood by and watched him close with eyes of silent wonder.
Then Felix, kneeling down, struck the match on the box,
and applied it, as it lighted, to the dry leaves beside him.

A chorus of astonishment burst unanimously from the
delighted natives as the dry leaves leaped all at once into
a tongue of flame, and the little pile caught quickly from
the fire in the vesta.

The leader looked hard at the two white faces, and then
at the fire on the beach, with evident approbation. "It
is as Tu-Kila-Kila said," he exclaimed at last with profound
awe. "They are spirits from the sun, and they carry with
them pure fire in shining boxes."

Then, advancing a pace and pointing toward the canoe,
he motioned Felix and Muriel to take their seats within it
with native savage politeness. "Tu-Kila-Kila has sent for
you," he said, in his grandest aristocratic air, "for your
chief is a gentleman. He wishes to receive you. He saw
your message-fire on the reef last night, and he knew you
had come. He has made you a very great Taboo. He
has put you under protection of Fire and Water."

The people in the boats, with one accord, shouted out

in wild chorus, as if to confirm his words, "Taboo! Taboo! Tu-Kila-Kila has said it! Taboo! Taboo! Ware Fire! Ware Water!"

Though the dialect in which they spoke differed somewhat from that in use in Fiji, Felix could still make out with care almost every word of what the chief had said to him; and the universal Polynesian expression, "Taboo," in particular, somewhat reassured him as to their friendly intentions. Among remote heathen islanders like these, he felt sure, the very word itself was far too sacred to be taken in vain. They would respect its inviolability. He turned round to Muriel. "We must go with them," he said, shortly. "It's our one chance left of life now. Don't be too terrified; there is still some hope. They say somebody they call Tu-Kila-Kila has tabooed us. No one will dare to hurt us against so great a Taboo; for Tu-Kila-Kila is evidently some very important king or chief. You must step into the boat. It can't be avoided. If any harm is threatened, be sure I won't forget my promise."

Muriel shrank back in alarm, and clung still to his arm now as naturally as she would have clung to a brother's. "Oh, Mr. Thurstan," she cried—"Felix, I don't know what to say; I *can't* go with them."

Felix put his arm gently round her girlish waist, and half lifted her into the boat in spite of her reluctance. "You must," he said, with great firmness. "You must do as I say. I will watch over you, and take care of you. If the worst comes, I have always my knife, and I won't forget. Now, friend," he went on, in Fijian, turning round to the chief, as he took his seat in the canoe fearlessly among all those dusky, half-clad figures, "we are ready to start. We do not fear. We wish to go. Take us to Tu-Kila-Kila."

And all the savages around, shouting in their surprise and awe, exclaimed once more in concert, "Tu-Kila-Kila is great. We will take them, as he bids us, forthwith to heaven."

"What do they say?" Muriel cried, clinging close to the white man's side in her speechless terror. "Do you understand their language?"

"Well, I can't quite make it out," Felix answered, much puzzled; "that is to say, not every word of it. They say they'll take us somewhere, I don't quite know where; but in Fijian, the word would certainly mean to heaven."

Muriel shuddered visibly. "You don't think," she said, with a tremulous tongue, "they mean to kill us?"

"No, I don't *think* so," Felix replied, not over-confidently. "They said we were Taboo. But with savages like these, of course, one can never in any case be quite certain."

CHAPTER V.

ENROLLED IN OLYMPUS.

They rowed across the lagoon, a mysterious procession, almost in silence—the canoe with the two Europeans going first, the others following at a slight distance—and landed at last on the brink of the central island.

Several of the Boupari people leaped ashore at once; then they helped Felix and Muriel from the frail bark with almost deferential care, and led the way before them up a steep white path, that zigzagged through the forest toward the centre of the island. As they went, a band of natives preceded them in regular line of march, shouting "Taboo, taboo!" at short intervals, especially as they neared any group of fan-palm cottages. The women whom they met fell on their knees at once, till the strange procession had passed them by; the men only bowed their heads thrice, and made a rapid movement on their breasts with their fingers, which reminded Muriel at once of the sign of the cross in Catholic countries.

So on they wended their way in silence through the deep tropical jungle, along a pathway just wide enough for three to walk abreast, till they emerged suddenly upon a large cleared space, in whose midst grew a great banyan-tree, with arms that dropped and rooted themselves like buttresses in the soil beneath. Under the banyan-tree a raised platform stood upon posts of bamboo. The platform was covered with fine network in yellow and red; and two little stools occupied the middle, as if placed there on purpose and waiting for their occupants.

The man who had headed the first canoe turned round to Felix and motioned him forward. "This is Heaven," he said glibly, in his own tongue. "Spirits, ascend it!"

Felix, much wondering what the ceremony could mean, mounted the platform without a word, in obedience to the chief's command, closely followed by Muriel, who dared not leave him for a second.

"Bring water!" the chief said, shortly, in a voice of authority to one of his followers.

The man handed up a calabash with a little water in it. The chief took the rude vessel from his hands in a reverential manner, and poured a few drops of the contents on Felix's head; the water trickled down over his hair and forehead. Involuntarily, Felix shook his head a little at the unexpected wetting, and scattered the drops right and left on his neck and shoulders. The chief watched this performance attentively with profound satisfaction. Then he turned to his attendants.

"The spirit shakes his head," he said, with a deeply convinced air. "All is well. Heaven has chosen him. Korong! Korong! He is accepted for his purpose. It is well! It is well! Let us try the other one."

He raised the calabash once more, and poured a few drops in like manner on Muriel's dark hair. The poor girl, trembling in every limb, shook her head also in the same unintentional fashion. The chief regarded her with still more complacent eyes.

"It is well," he observed once more to his companions, smiling. "She, too, gives the sign of acceptance. Korong!

Korong! Heaven is well pleased with both. See how her body trembles!"

At that moment a girl came forward with a little basket of fruits. The chief chose a banana with care from the basket, peeled it with his dusky hands, broke it slowly in two, and handed one half very solemnly to Felix.

"Eat, King of the Rain," he said, as he presented it. "The offering of Heaven."

Felix ate it at once, thinking it best under the circumstances not to demur at all to anything his strange hosts might choose to impose upon him.

The chief handed the other half just as solemnly to Muriel. "Eat, Queen of the Clouds," he said, as he placed it in her fingers. "The offering of Heaven."

Muriel hesitated. She didn't know what his words meant, and it seemed to her rather the offering of a very dirty and unwashed savage. The chief eyed her hard. "For God's sake eat it, my child; he tells you to eat it!" Felix exclaimed in haste. Muriel lifted it to her lips and swallowed it down with difficulty. The man's dusky hands didn't inspire confidence.

But the chief seemed relieved when he had seen her swallow it. "All is well done," he said, turning again to his followers. "We have obeyed the words of Tu-Kila-Kila, and his orders that he gave us. We have offered the strangers, the spirits from the sun, as a free gift to Heaven, and Heaven has accepted them. We have given them fruits, the fruits of the earth, and they have duly eaten them. Korong! Korong! The King of the Rain and the Queen of the Clouds have indeed come among us. They are truly gods. We will take them now, as he bid us, to Tu-Kila-Kila."

"What have they done to us?" Muriel asked aside, in a terrified undertone of Felix.

"I can't quite make out," Felix answered in the selfsame voice. "They call us the King of the Rain and the Queen of the Clouds in their own language. I think they imagine we've come from the sun and that we're a sort of spirits."

At the sound of these words the girl who held the basket of fruits gave a sudden start. It almost seemed to Muriel as if she understood them. But when Muriel looked again she gave no further sign. She merely held her peace, and tried to appear wholly undisconcerted.

The chief beckoned them down from the platform with a wave of his hand. They rose and followed him. As they rose the people around them bowed low to the ground. Felix could see they were bowing to Muriel and himself, not merely to the chief. A doubt flitted strangely across his mind for a moment. What could it all mean? Did they take the two strangers, then, for supernatural beings? Had they enrolled them as gods? If so, it might serve as some little protection for them.

The procession formed again, three and three, three and three, in solemn silence. Then the chief walked in front of them with measured steps, and Felix and Muriel followed behind, wondering. As they went, the cry rose louder and louder than before, "Taboo! Taboo!" People who met them fell on their faces at once, as the chief cried out in a loud tone, "The King of the Rain! the Queen of the Clouds! Korong! Korong! They are coming! They are coming!"

At last they reached a second cleared space, standing in a large garden of manilla, loquat, poncians, and hibiscus-trees. It was entered by a gate, a tall gate of bamboo posts. At the gate all the followers fell back to right and left, awe-struck. Only the chief went calmly on. He beckoned to Felix and Muriel to follow him.

They entered, half terrified. Felix still grasped his open knife in his hand, ready to strike at any moment that might be necessary. The chief led them forward toward a very large tree near the centre of the garden. At the foot of the tree stood a hut, somewhat bigger and better built than any they had yet seen; and in front of the trunk a stalwart savage, very powerfully built, but with a sinister look in his cruel and lustful eye, was pacing up and down, like a sentinel on guard, a long spear in his right hand, and a tomahawk in his left, held close by his side, all ready for action.   As he prowled up and down he seemed to be peering warily about him on every side, as if each instant he expected to be set upon by an enemy.   But as the chief approached, the people without set up once more the cry of "Taboo! Taboo!" and the stalwart savage by the tree, laying down his spear and letting his tomahawk fall free, dropped in a second the air of watchful alarm, and advanced with some courtesy to greet the new-comers.

"We have found them, Tu-Kila-Kila," the chief said, presenting them to the god with a graceful wave of his hand.   "We have found the spirits that you brought from the sun, with the fire in their hands, and the light in boxes. We have taken them to Heaven.   Heaven has accepted them.   We have offered them fruit, and they have eaten the banana.   The King of the Rain—the Queen of the Clouds!   Korong!   Receive them!"

Tu-Kila-Kila glanced at them with an approving glance, strangely compounded of pleasure and terror.   "They are plump," he said shortly.   "They are indeed Korong.   My sun has sent me an acceptable present."

"What is your will that we should do with them?" the chief asked in a deeply deferential tone.

Tu-Kila-Kila looked hard at Muriel—such a hateful look that the knife trembled irresolute for a second in Felix's hand.   "Give them two fresh huts," he said, in a lordly way.   "Give them divine platters.   Give them all that they need.   Make everything right for them."

The chief bowed, and retired with an awed air from the presence.   Exactly as he passed a certain line on the ground, marked white with a row of coral-sand, Tu-Kila-Kila seized his spear and his tomahawk once more, and mounted guard, as before, at the foot of the great tree where they had seen him pacing. An instantaneous change seemed to Muriel to come over his demeanor at that moment. While he spoke with the chief she noticed he looked all cruelty, lust, and hateful self-indulgence. Now that he paced up and down warily in front of that sacred floor, peering around him with keen suspicion, he seemed rather the personification of watchfulness, fear, and a certain slavish bodily terror. Especially, she observed, he cast upon Felix, as he went, a glance of angry hate ; and yet he did not attempt to hurt or molest him in any way, defenceless as they both were before those numerous savages.

As they emerged from the enclosure, the girl with the fruit basket stood near the gate, looking outward from the wall, her face turned away from the awful home of Tu-Kila-Kila. At the moment when Muriel passed, to her immense astonishment the girl spoke to her. "Don't be afraid, missy," she said in English, in a rather low voice, without obtrusively approaching them. "Boupari man not going to hurt you. Me going to be your servant. Me name Mali. Me very good girl. Me take plenty care of you."

The unexpected sound of her own language, in the midst of so much unmitigated savagery, took Muriel fairly by surprise. She looked hard at the girl, but thought it wisest to answer nothing. This particular young woman, indeed, was just as dark, and to all appearance just as much of a savage, as any of the rest of them. But she could speak English, at any rate ! And she said she was to be Muriel's servant !

The chief led them back to the shore, talking volubly all the way in Polynesia to Felix. His dialect differed so much from the Fijian that when he spoke first Felix could hardly follow him. But he gathered vaguely, nevertheless, that they were to be well housed and fed for the present at the public expense ; and even that something which the chief clearly regarded as a very great honor was in store for them in the future. Whatever these people's particular superstition might be, it seemed pretty evident at least that it told in the strangers' favor. Felix almost began to hope they might manage to live there pretty tolerably for the next two or three weeks, and perhaps to signal in time to some passing Australian liner.

The rest of that wonderful eventful day was wholly occupied with practical details. Before long, two adjacent huts were found for them, near the shore of the lagoon ; and Felix noticed with pleasure, not only that the huts themselves were new and clean, but also that the chief took great care to place round both of them a single circular line of white coral-sand, like the one he had noticed at Tu-Kila-Kila's palace-temple. He felt sure this white line made the space within taboo. No native would dare without leave to cross it.

When the line was well marked out round the two huts together, the chief went away for a while, leaving the Europeans within their broad white circle, guarded by an angry-looking band of natives with long spears at rest, all pointed inward. The natives themselves stood well without the ring, but the points of their spears almost reached the line, and it was clear they would not for the present permit the Europeans to leave the charmed circle.

Presently, the chief returned again, followed by two other natives in official costumes. One of them was a tall and handsome young man, dressed in a long robe or cloak of yellow feathers. The other was stouter, and perhaps forty or thereabouts ; he wore a short cape of white albatross plumes, with a girdle of shells at his waist, interspersed with red coral.

"The King of Fire will make Taboo," the chief said, solemnly.

The young man with the cloak of yellow feathers stepped forward and spoke, toeing the line with his left foot, and brandishing a lighted stick in his right hand. "Taboo! Taboo! Taboo!" he cried aloud, with emphasis. "If any man dare to transgress this line without leave, I burn him to ashes. If any woman, I scorch her to a cinder. Taboo to the King of the Rain and the Queen of the Clouds. Taboo! Taboo! Taboo! Korong! I say it."

He stepped back into the ranks with an air of duty performed. The chief looked about him curiously a moment. "The King of Water will make Taboo," he repeated after a pause, in the same deep tone of profound conviction.

The stouter man in the short white cape stepped forward in his turn. He toed the line with his naked left foot ; in his brown right hand he carried a calabash of water. "Taboo ! Taboo! Taboo !" he exclaimed aloud, pouring out the water upon the ground symbolically. "If any man dare to transgress this line without leave, I drown him in his canoe. If any woman, I drag her alive into the spring as she fetches water. Taboo to the King of the Rain and the Queen of the Clouds. Taboo! Taboo! Taboo! Korong! I say it."

"What does it all mean ?" Muriel whispered, terrified.

Felix explained to her, as far as he could, in a few hurried sentences. "There's only one word in it I don't understand," he added, hastily, "and that's Korong. It doesn't occur in Fiji. They keep saying we're Korong, whatever that may mean ; and evidently they attach some very great importance to it."

"Let the Shadows come forward," the chief said, looking up with an air of dignity.

A good-looking young man, and the girl who said her name was Mali, stepped forth from the crowd, and fell on their knees before him.

The chief laid his hand on the young man's shoulder and raised him up. "The Shadow of the King of the Rain," he cried, turning him three times round. "Follow him in all his incomings and his outgoings, and serve him faithfully! Taboo! Taboo! Pass within the sacred circle !"

He clapped his hands. The young man crossed the line

with a sort of reverent reluctance, and took his place within the ring, close up to Felix.

The chief laid his hand on Mali's shoulder. "The Shadow of the Queen of the Clouds," he said, turning her three times round. "Follow her in all her incomings and outgoings, and serve her faithfully. Taboo! Taboo! Pass within the sacred circle!"

Then he waved both hands to Felix. "Go where you will now," he said. "Your Shadow will follow you. You are free as the rain that drops where it will. You are as free as the clouds that roam through heaven. No man will hinder you."

And in a moment the spearmen dropped their spears in concert, the crowd fell back, and the villagers dispersed as if by magic, to their own houses.

But Felix and Muriel were left alone beside their huts, guarded only in silence by their two mystic Shadows.

CHAPTER VI.

FIRST DAYS IN BOUPARI.

Throughout that day the natives brought them, from time to time, numerous presents of yam, bananas, and bread-fruit, neatly arranged in little palm-leaf baskets. A few of them brought eggs as well, and one offering even included a live chicken. But the people who brought them, and who were mostly young girls just entering upon womanhood, did not venture to cross the white line of coral-sand that surrounded the huts; they laid down their presents, with many salaams, on the ground outside, and then waited with a half-startled, half-reverent air for one or other of the two Shadows to come out and fetch them. As soon as the baskets were carried well within the marked line, the young girls exhibited every sign of pleasure, and calling aloud, "Korong! Korong!"—that mys-

terious Polynesian word of whose import Felix was ignorant—they retired once more by tortuous paths through
the surrounding jungle.

"Why do they bring us presents?" Felix asked at last
of his Shadow, after this curious pantomime had been
performed some three or four times. "Are they always
going to keep us in such plenty?"

The Shadow looked back at him with an air of considerable surprise. "They bring presents, of course," he
said, in his own tongue, "because they are badly in want
of rain. We have had much drought of late in Boupari ;
we need water from heaven. The banana-bushes wither ;
the flowers on the bread-fruit tree do not swell to bread-
fruit ; the yams are thirsty. Therefore the fathers send
their daughters with presents, maidens of the villages, all
marriageable girls, to ask for rainfall. But they will always provide for you, and also for the Queen, however
you behave ; for you are both Korong. Tu-Kila-Kila has
said so, and Heaven has accepted you."

"What do you mean by Korong?" Felix asked, with
some trepidation.

The Shadow merely looked back at him with a sort of
blank surprise that anybody should be ignorant of so simple a conception. "Why, Korong is Korong," he answered, aghast. "You are Korong yourself. The Queen
of the Clouds is Korong, too. You are both Korong ;
that is why they all treat you with such respect and reverence."

And that was as much as Felix could elicit by his subt-
lest questions from his taciturn Shadow.

In fact, it was clear that in the open, at least, the
Shadow was averse to being observed in familiar conversation with Felix. During the heat of the day, however,
when they sat alone within the hut, he was much more
communicative. Then he launched forth pretty freely
into talk about the island and its life, which would no
doubt have largely enlightened Felix, had it not been for

two drawbacks to their means of inter-communication. In the first place, the Boupari dialect, though agreeing in all essentials with the Polynesian of Fiji, nevertheless contained a great many words and colloquial expressions unknown to the Fijians ; this being particularly the case, as Felix soon remarked, in the whole vocabulary of religious rites and ceremonies. And in the second place, the Shadow was so rigidly bound by his own narrow and insular set of ideas, that he couldn't understand the difficulty Felix felt in throwing himself into them. Over and over again, when Felix asked him to explain some word or custom, he would repeat, with naïve impatience, "Why, Korong is Korong," or "Tula is just Tula ; even a child must surely know what Tula is ; much more yourself, who are indeed Korong, and who have come from the sun to bring fresh fire to us."

In the adjoining hut, Muriel, who was now beginning in some small degree to get rid of her most pressing fear for the immediate future, and whom the obvious reality of the taboo had reassured for the moment, sat with Mali, her own particular Shadow, unravelling the mystery of the girl's knowledge of English.

Mali, indeed, like the other Shadow, showed every disposition to indulge in abundant conversation, as soon as she found herself well within the hut, alone with her mistress, and secluded from the prying eyes of all the other islanders.

"Don't you be afraid, missy," she said, with genuine kindliness in her tone, as soon as the gifts of yam and bread-fruit had all been duly housed and garnered.. "No harm come to you. You Korong, you know. You very great Taboo. Tu-Kila-Kila send King of Fire and King of Water to make taboo over you, so nobody hurt you."

Muriel burst into tears at the sound of her own language from those dusky lips, and exclaimed through her sobs, clinging to the girl's hand for comfort as she spoke, "Why, how did you ever come to speak English ?—tell me,"

Mali looked up at her with a half-astonished air. "Oh, I servant in Queensland, of course, missy," she answered, with great composure. " Labor vessel come to my island, far away, four, five years ago, steal boy, steal woman. My papa just kill my mamma, because he angry with her, so no want daughters. So my papa sell me and my sister for plenty rum, plenty tobacco, to gentlemen in labor vessel. Gentlemen in labor vessel take Jani and me away, away, to Queensland. Big sea ; long voyage. We stop there three yam—three years—do service ; then great chief in Queensland send us back to my island. My island too far away ; gentleman on ship not find it out ; so he land us in little boat on Boupari. Boupari people make temple slave of us." And that was all ; to her quite a commonplace, everyday history.

"I see," Muriel cried. "Then you've been for three years in Australia ! And there you learned English. Why, what did you do there ? "

Mali looked back at her with the same matter-of-fact air of composure as before. "Oh, me nurse at first," she said, shortly. "Then after, me housemaid, live three year in gentleman's house, good gentleman that buy me. Take care of little girl ; clean rooms ; do everything. Me know how to make English lady quite comfortable. Me tell that to chief ; that make him say, 'Mali, you be Queenie's Shadow.' "

To Muriel in her loneliness even such companionship as that was indeed a consolation. "Oh, I'm so glad you told him," she cried. "If we have to stop here long, before a ship takes us off, it'll be so nice to have you here all the time with me. You won't go away from me ever, will you ? You'll always stop with me ! "

The girl's surprise showed more profoundly than ever. "Me can't go away," she answered, with emphasis. "Me your Shadow. That great Taboo. Tu-Kila-Kila great god. If me go away, Tu-Kila-Kila kill me and eat me."

Muriel started back in horror. " But, Mali," she said,

looking hard at the girl's pleasant brown face, "if you were three years in Australia, you're a Christian, surely!"

The girl nodded her head in passive acquiescence. "Me Christian in Australia," she answered. "Of course me Christian. All folks make Christian when him go to Queensland. That what for me call Mali, and my sister Jani. We have other names on my own island; but when we go to Queensland, gentleman baptize us, call us Mali and Jani. Me Methodist in Queensland. Methodist very good. But Methodist god no live in Boupari. Not any good be Methodist here any longer. Tu-Kila-Kila god here. Him very powerful."

"What! Not that dreadful creature that they took us to see this morning!" Muriel exclaimed, in horror. "Oh, Mali, you can't mean to say they think he's a *god*, that awful man there!"

Mali nodded her assent with profound conviction. "Yes, yes; him god," she repeated, confidently. "Him very powerful. My sister Jani go too near him temple, against taboo—because her not belong-a Tu-Kila-Kila temple; and last night, when it great feast, plenty men catch Jani, and tie him up in rope; and Tu-Kila-Kila kill him, and plenty Boupari men help Tu-Kila-Kila eat up Jani."

She said it in the same simple, matter-of-fact way as she had said that she was a nurse for three years in Queensland. To her it was a common incident of every-day life. Such accidents *will* happen, if you break taboo and go too near forbidden temples.

But Muriel drew back, and let the pleasant-looking brown girl's hand drop suddenly. "You can't mean it," she cried. "You can't mean he's a god! Such a wicked man as that! Oh, his very look's too horrible."

Mali drew back in her turn with a somewhat terrified air, and peeped suspiciously around her, as if to make sure whether any one was listening. "Oh, hush," she said, anxiously. "Don't must talk like that. If Tu-Kila-Kila

hear, him scorch us up to ashes. Him very great god!
Him good! Him powerful!"

"How can he be good if he does such awful things?"
Muriel exclaimed, energetically.

Mali peered around her once more with terrified eyes in
the same uneasy way. "Take care," she said again.
"Him god! Him powerful! Him can do no wrong. Him
King of the Trees! Him King of Heaven! On Boupari
island, Methodist god not much; no god so great like Tu-
Kila-Kila."

"But a *man* can't be a god!" Muriel exclaimed, contemptuously. "He's nothing but a man! a savage! a
cannibal!"

Mali looked back at her in wondering surprise. "Not
in Queensland," she answered, calmly—to her, all the world
naturally divided itself into Queensland and Polynesia—
"no god in Queensland. Governor, him very great chief;
but him no god like Tu-Kila-Kila. Methodist god in sky,
him only god that live in Queensland. But no use worship
Methodist god over here in Boupari. Him no live here.
Tu-Kila-Kila live here. All god here make out of man.
Live in man. Korong! What for you say a man can't be
a god! You god yourself! White gentleman there, god!
Korong, Korong. Chief put you in Heaven, so make you
a god. People pray to you now. People bring you presents."

"You don't mean to say," Muriel cried, "they bring me
these things because they think me a goddess?"

Mali nodded a grave assent. "Same like people give
money in church in Queensland," she answered, promptly.
"Ask you make rain, make plenty crop, make bread-fruit
grow, make banana, make plantain. You Korong now.
While your time last, Queenie, people give you plenty of
present."

"While my time last?" Muriel repeated, with a curious sense of discomfort creeping over her slowly.

The girl nodded an easy assent. "Yes, while your time

4

last," she answered, laying a small bundle of palm-leaves at Muriel's back by way of a cushion. "For now you Korong. By and by, Korong pass to somebody else. This year, you Korong. So people worship you."

But nothing that Muriel could say would induce the girl further to explain her meaning. She shook her head and looked very wise. "When a god come into somebody," she said, nodding toward Muriel in a mysterious way, "then him god himself; him Korong. When the god go away from him, him Korong no longer; somebody else Korong. Queenie Korong now; so people worship him. While him time last, people plenty kind to him."

The day passed away, and night came on. As it approached, heavy clouds drifted up from eastward. Mali busied herself with laying out a rough bed in the hut for Muriel, and making her a pillow of soft moss and the curious lichen-like material that hangs parasitic from the trees, and is commonly known as "old man's beard." As both Mali and Felix assured her confidently no harm would come to her within so strict a Taboo, Muriel, worn out with fatigue and terror, lay down at last and slept soundly on this native substitute for a bedstead. She slept without dreaming, while Mali lay at her feet, ready at a moment's call. It was all so strange; and yet she was too utterly wearied to do otherwise than sleep, in spite of her strange and terrible surroundings.

Felix slept, too, for some hours, but woke with a start in the night. It was raining heavily. He could hear the loud patter of a fierce tropical shower on the roof of his hut. His Shadow, at his feet, slept still unmoved; but when Felix rose on his elbow, the Shadow rose on a sudden, too, and confronted him curiously. The young man heard the rain; then he bowed down his face with an awed air, not visible, but audible, in the still darkness. "It has come!" he said, with superstitious terror. "It has come at last! my lord has brought it!"

After that, Felix lay awake for some hours, hearing the

rain on the roof, and puzzled in his own head by a half-uncertain memory. What was it in his school reading that that ceremony with the water indefinitely reminded him of? Wasn't there some Greek or Roman superstition about shaking your head when water was poured upon it? What could that superstition be, and what light might it cast on that mysterious ceremony? He wished he could remember; but it was so long since he'd read it, and he never cared much at school for Greek or Roman antiquities.

Suddenly, in a lull of the rain, the whole context at once came back with a rush to him. He remembered now he had read it, some time or other, in some classical dictionary. It was a custom connected with Greek sacrifices. The officiating priest poured water or wine on the head of the sheep, bullock, or other victim. If the victim shook its head and knocked off the drops, that was a sign that it was fit for the sacrifice, and that the god accepted it. If the victim trembled visibly, that was a most favorable omen. If it stood quite still and didn't move its neck, then the god rejected it as unfit for his purpose. Couldn't *that* be the meaning of the ceremony performed on Muriel and himself in "Heaven" that morning? Were they merely intended as human sacrifices? Were they to be kept meanwhile and, as it were, fed up for the slaughter? It was too horrible to believe; yet it almost looked like it.

He wished he knew the meaning of that strange word, "Korong." Clearly, it contained the true key to the mystery.

Anyhow, he had always his trusty knife. If the worst came to the worst—those wretches should never harm his spotless Muriel.

For he loved her to-night; he would watch over and protect her. He would save her at least from the deadliest of insults.

CHAPTER VII.

INTERCHANGE OF CIVILITIES.

All night long, without intermission, the heavy tropical rain descended in torrents; at sunrise it ceased, and a bright blue vault of sky stood in a spotless dome over the island of Boupari.

As soon as the sun was well risen, and the rain had ceased, one shy native girl after another came straggling up timidly to the white line that marked the taboo round Felix and Muriel's huts. They came with more baskets of fruit and eggs. Humbly saluting three times as they drew near, they laid down their gifts modestly just outside the line, with many loud ejaculations of praise and gratitude to the gods in their own language.

"What do they say?" Muriel asked, in a dazed and frightened way, looking out of the hut door, and turning in wonder to Mali.

"They say, 'Thank you, Queenie, for rain and fruits,'" Mali answered, unconcerned, bustling about in the hut. "Missy want to wash him face and hands this morning? Lady always wash every day over yonder in Queensland."

Muriel nodded assent. It was all so strange to her. But Mali went to the door and beckoned carelessly to one of the native girls just outside, who drew near the line at the summons, with a somewhat frightened air, putting one finger to her mouth in coyly uncertain savage fashion.

"Fetch me water from the spring!" Mali said, authoritatively, in Polynesian. Without a moment's delay the girl darted off at the top of her speed, and soon returned with a large calabash full of fresh cool water, which she lay down respectfully by the taboo line, not daring to cross it.

"Why didn't you get it yourself?" Muriel asked of

her Shadow, rather relieved than otherwise that Mali
hadn't left her. It was something in these dire straits to
have somebody always near who could at least speak a
little English.

Mali started back in surprise. "Oh, that would never
do," she answered, catching a colloquial phrase she had
often heard long before in Queensland. "Me missy's
Shadow. That great Taboo. If me go away out of
missy's sight, very big sin—very big danger. Man-a-Bou-
pari catch me and kill me like Jani, for no me stop and
wait all the time on missy."

It was clear that human life was held very cheap on the
island of Boupari.

Muriel made her scanty toilet in the hut as well as she
was able, with the calabash and water, aided by a rough
shell comb which Mali had provided for her. Then she
breakfasted, not ill, off eggs and fruit, which Mali cooked
with some rude native skill over the open-air fire without
in the precincts.

After breakfast, Felix came in to inquire how she had
passed the night in her new quarters. Already Muriel
felt how odd was the contrast between the quiet politeness
of his manner as an English gentleman and the strange
savage surroundings in which they both now found themselves. Civilization is an attribute of communities ; we
necessarily leave it behind when we find ourselves isolated
among barbarians or savages. But culture is a purely
personal and individual possession ; we carry it with us
wherever we go ; and no circumstances of life can ever
deprive us of it.

As they sat there talking, with a deep and abiding sense
of awe at the change (Muriel more conscious than ever
now of how deep was her interest in Felix Thurstan, who
represented for her all that was dearest and best in England), a curious noise, as of a discordant drum or tom-tom,
beaten in a sort of recurrent tune, was heard toward the
hills ; and at its very first sound both the Shadows, fling-

ing themselves upon their faces with every sign of terror, endeavored to hide themselves under the native mats with which the bare little hut was roughly carpeted.

"What's the matter?" Felix cried, in English, to Mali; for Muriel had already explained to him how the girl had picked up some knowledge of our tongue in Queensland.

Mali trembled in every limb, so that she could hardly speak. "Tu-Kila-Kila come," she answered, all breathless. "No blackfellow look at him. Burn blackfellow up. You and Missy Korong. All right for you. Go out to meet him!"

"Tu-Kila-Kila is coming," the young man-Shadow said, in Polynesian, almost in the same breath, and no less tremulously. "We dare not look upon his face lest he burn us to ashes. He is a very great Taboo. His face is fire. But you two are gods. Step forth to receive him."

Felix took Muriel's hand in his, somewhat trembling himself, and led her forth on to the open space in front of the huts to meet the man-god. She followed him like a child. She was woman enough for that. She had implicit trust in him.

As they emerged, a strange procession met their eyes unawares, coming down the zig-zag path that led from the hills to the shore of the lagoon, where their huts were situated. At its head marched two men—tall, straight, and supple—wearing huge feather masks over their faces, and beating tom-toms, decorated with long strings of shiny cowries. After them, in order, came a sort of hollow square of chiefs or warriors, surrounding with fan-palms a central object all shrouded from the view with the utmost precaution. This central object was covered with a huge regal umbrella, from whose edge hung rows of small nautilus and other shells, so as to form a kind of screen, like the Japanese portières now so common in English doorways. Two supporters held it up, one on either side, in long cloaks of feathers. Under the umbrella, a man seemed to move; and as he approached, the natives, to

right and left, fled precipitately to their huts, snatching up
their naked little ones from the ground as they went, and
crying aloud, "Taboo, Taboo! He comes! he comes.
Tu-Kila-Kila! Tu-Kila-Kila!"

. The procession wound slowly on, unheeding these common creatures, till it reached the huts. Then the chiefs
who formed the hollow square fell back one by one, and
the man under the umbrella, with his two supporters,
came forward boldly. Felix noticed that they crossed
without scruple the thick white line of sand which all the
other natives so carefully respected. The man within the
umbrella drew aside the curtain of hanging nautilus shells.
His face was covered with a thin mask of paper mulberry
bark ; but Felix knew he was the self-same person whom
they had seen the day before in the central temple.

Tu-Kila-Kila's air was more insolent and arrogant than
even before. He was clearly in high spirits. "You have
done well, O King of the Rain," he said, turning gayly to
Felix ; "and you too, O Queen of the Clouds ; you have
done right bravely. We have all acquitted ourselves as
our people would wish. We have made our showers to
descend abundantly from heaven ; we have caused the crops
to grow ; we have wetted the plantain bushes. See ; Tu-
Kila-Kila, who is so great a god, has come from his own
home on the hills to greet you."

"It has certainly rained in the night," Felix answered,
dryly.

But Tu-Kila-Kila was not to be put off thus. Adjusting
his thin mask or veil of bark, so as to hide his face more
thoroughly from the inferior god, he turned round once
more to the chiefs, who even so hardly dared to look openly
upon him. Then he struck an attitude. The man was
clearly bursting with spiritual pride. He knew himself to
be a god, and was filled with the insolence of his supernatural power. "See, my people," he cried, holding up
his hands, palm outward, in his accustomed god-like way ;
"I am indeed a great deity—Lord of Heaven, Lord of

Earth, Life of the World, Master of Time, Measurer of the Sun's Course, Spirit of Growth, Creator of the Harvest, Master of Mortals, Bestower of Breath upon Men, Chief Pillar of Heaven ! "

The warriors bowed down before their bloated master with unquestioning assent. " Giver of Life to all the host of the gods," they cried, " you are indeed a mighty one. Weigher of the equipoise of Heaven and Earth, we acknowledge your might ; we give you thanks eternally."

Tu-Kila-Kila swelled with visible importance. " Did I not tell you, my meat," he exclaimed, " I would bring you new gods, great spirits from the sun, fetchers of fire from my bright home in the heavens ? And have they not come ? Are they not here to-day ? Have they not brought the precious gift of fresh fire with them ? "

" Tu-Kila-Kila speaks true," the chiefs echoed, submissively, with bent heads.

" Did I not make one of them King of the Rain ? " Tu-Kila-Kila asked once more, stretching one hand toward the sky with theatrical magnificence. " Did I not declare the other Queen of the Clouds in Heaven ? And have I not caused them to bring down showers this night upon our crops ? Has not the dry earth drunk ? Am I not the great god, the Saviour of Boupari ? "

" Tu-Kila-Kila says well," the chiefs responded, once more, in unanimous chorus.

Tu-Kila-Kila struck another attitude with childish self-satisfaction. " I go into the hut to speak with my ministers," he said, grandiloquently. " Fire and Water, wait you here outside while I enter and speak with my friends from the sun, whom I have brought for the salvation of the crops to Boupari."

The King of Fire and the King of Water, supporting the umbrella, bowed assent to his words. Tu-Kila-Kila motioned Felix and Muriel into the nearest hut. It was the one where the two Shadows lay crouching in terror among the native mats. As the god tried to enter, the two cowering wretches set up a loud shout, "Taboo! Taboo! Mercy! Mercy! Mercy!" Tu-Kila-Kila retreated with a contemptuous smile. "I want to see you alone," he said, in Polynesian, to Felix. "Is the other hut empty? If not, go in and cut their throats who sit there, and make the place a solitude for Tu-Kila-Kila."

"There is no one in the hut," Felix answered, with a nod, concealing his disgust at the command as far as he was able.

"That is well," Tu-Kila-Kila answered, and walked into it carelessly. Felix followed him close and deemed it best to make Muriel enter also.

As soon as they were alone, Tu-Kila-Kila's manner altered greatly. "Come, now," he said, quite genially, yet with a curious under-current of hate in his steely gray eye; "we three are all gods. We who are in heaven need have no secrets from one another. Tell me the truth; did you really come to us direct from the sun, or are you sailing gods, dropped from a great canoe belonging to the warriors who seek laborers for the white men in the distant country?"

Felix told him briefly, in as few words as possible, the story of their arrival.

Tu-Kila-Kila listened with lively interest, then he said, very decisively, with great bravado, "It was *I* who made the big wave wash your sister overboard. I sent it to your ship. I wanted a Korong just now in Boupari. It was *I* who brought you."

"You are mistaken," Felix said, simply, not thinking it worth while to contradict him further. "It was a purely natural accident."

"Well, tell me," the savage god went on once more, eying him close and sharp, "they say you have brought fresh fire from the sun with you, and that you know how to make it burst out like lightning at will. My people have seen it. They tell me the wonder. I wish to see it too. We are all gods here; we need have no secrets.

Only, I didn't want to let those common people outside see
I asked you to show me. Make fire leap forth. I desire
to behold it."

Felix took out the match-box from his pocket, and struck
a vesta carefully. Tu-Kila Kila looked on with profound
interest. " It is wonderful," he said, taking the vesta in
his own hand as it burned, and examining it closely. " I
have heard of this before, but I have never seen it. You
are indeed gods, you white men, you sailors of the sea."
He glanced at Muriel. " And the woman, too," he said,
with a horrible leer, " the woman is pretty."

Felix took the measure of his man at once. He opened
his knife, and held it up threateningly. " See here, fellow," he said, in a low, slow tone, but with great decision,
" if you dare to speak or look like that at that lady—god
or no god, I'll drive this knife straight up to the handle in
your heart, though your people kill me for it afterward ten
thousand times over. I am not afraid of you. These savages may be afraid, and may think you are a god ; but if
you are, then I am a god ten thousand times stronger than
you. One more word—one more look like that, I say—and
I plunge this knife remorselessly into you."   .

Tu-Kila-Kila drew back, and smiled benignly. Stalwart
ruffian as he was, and absolute master of his own people's
lives, he was yet afraid in a way of the strange new-comer.
Vague stories of the men with white faces—the " sailing
gods "—had reached him from time to time ; and though
only twice within his memory had European boats landed
on his island, he yet knew enough of the race to know that
they were at least very powerful deities—more powerful
with their weapons than even he was. Besides, a man who
could draw down fire from heaven with a piece of wax and
a little metal box might surely wither him to ashes, if he
would, as he stood before him. The very fact that Felix
bearded him thus openly to his face astonished and somewhat terrified the superstitious savage. Everybody else on
the island was afraid of him ; then certainly a man who

was not afraid must be the possessor of some most effica-
cious and magical medicine. His one fear now was lest his
followers should hear and discover his discomfiture. He
peered about him cautiously, with that careful gleam shining bright in his eye ; then he said with a leer, in a very
low voice, " We two need not quarrel. We are both of us
gods. Neither of us is the stronger. We are equal, that's
all. Let us live like brothers, not like enemies, on the
island."

"I don't want to be your brother," Felix answered, unable to conceal his loathing any more. " I hate and detest
you."

"What does he say ? " Muriel asked, in an agony of fear
at the savage's black looks. " Is he going to kill us ? "

" No," Felix answered, boldly. " I think he's afraid of
us. He's going to do nothing. You needn't fear him."

" Can she not speak ? " the savage asked, pointing with
his finger somewhat rudely toward Muriel. " Has she no
voice but this, the chatter of birds ? Does she not know
the human language ? "

"She can speak," Felix replied, placing himself like a
shield between Muriel and the astonished savage. " She
can speak the language of the people of our distant country—a beautiful language which is as far superior to the
speech of the brown men of Polynesia as the sun in the
heavens is superior to the light of a candlenut. But she
can't speak the wretched tongue of you Boupari cannibals.
I thank Heaven she can't, for it saves her from understanding the hateful things your people would say of her. Now
go ! I have seen already enough of you. I am not afraid.
Remember, I am as powerful a god as you. I need not
fear. You cannot hurt me."

A baleful light gleamed in the cannibal's eye. But he
thought it best to temporize. Powerful as he was on his
island, there was one thing yet more powerful by far than
he ; and that was Taboo—the custom and superstition
handed down from his ancestors. These strangers were

Korong ; he dare not touch them, except in the way and manner and time appointed by custom. If he did, god as he was, his people themselves would turn and rend him. He was a god, but he was bound on every side by the strictest taboos. He dare not himself offer violence to Felix.

So he turned with a smile and bided his time. He knew it would come. He could afford to laugh. Then, going to the door, he said, with his grand affable manner to his chiefs around, " I have spoken with the gods, my ministers, within. They have kissed my hands. My rain has fallen. All is well in the land. Arise, let us go away hence to my temple."

The savages put themselves in marching order at once. " It is the voice of a god," they said, reverently. " Let us take back Tu-Kila-Kila to his temple home. Let us escort the lord of the divine umbrella. Wherever he is, there trees and plants put forth green leaves and flourish. At his bidding flowers bloom and springs of water rise up in fountains. His presence diffuses heavenly blessings."

" I think," Felix said, turning to poor, terrified Muriel, " I've sent the wretch away with a bee in his bonnet."

CHAPTER VIII.

THE CUSTOMS OF BOUPARI.

Human nature cannot always keep on the full stretch of excitement. It was wonderful to both Felix and Muriel how soon they settled down into a quiet routine of life on the island of Boupari. A week passed away—two weeks —three weeks—and the chances of release seemed to grow slenderer and slenderer. All they could do now was to wait for the stray accident of a passing ship, and then try, if possible, to signal it, or to put out to it in a canoe, if the natives would allow them.

Meanwhile, their lives for the moment seemed fairly safe. Though for the first few days they lived in constant alarm, this feeling, after a time, gave way to one of comparative security. The strange institution of Taboo protected them more efficiently in their wattled huts than the whole police force of London could have done in a Belgravian mansion. There thieves break through and steal, in spite of bolts and bars and metropolitan constables; but at Boupari no native, however daring or however wicked, would ever venture to transgress the narrow line of white coral sand which protected the castaways like an intangible wall from all outer interference. Within this impalpable ring-fence they were absolutely safe from all rude intrusion, save that of the two Shadows, who waited upon them, day and night, with unfailing willingness.

In other respects, considering the circumstances, their life was an easy one. The natives brought them freely of their simple store—yam, taro, bread-fruit, and cocoanut, with plenty of fish, crabs, and lobsters, as well as eggs by the basketful, and even sometimes chickens. They required no pay beyond a nod and a smile, and went away happy at those slender recognitions. Felix discovered, in fact, that they had got into a region where the arid generalizations of political economy do not apply; where Adam Smith is unread, and Mill neglected; where the medium of exchange is an unknown quantity, and where supply and demand readjust themselves continuously by simpler and more generous principles than the familiar European one of "the higgling of the market."

The people, too, though utter savages, were not in their own way altogether unpleasing. It was their customs and superstitions, rather than themselves, that were so cruel and horrible. Personally, they seemed for the most part simple-minded and good-natured creatures. At first, indeed, Muriel was afraid to venture for a step beyond the precincts of their own huts; and it was long before she could make up her mind to go alone through the jungle

paths with Mali, unaccompanied by Felix. But by degrees she learned that she could walk by herself (of
course, with the inevitable Shadow ever by her side) over
the whole island, and meet everywhere with nothing from
men, women, and children but the utmost respect and
gracious courtesy. The young lads, as she passed, would
stand aside from the path, with downcast eyes, and let her
go by with all the politeness of chivalrous English gentlemen. The old men would raise their eyes, but cross their
hands on their breasts, and stand motionless for a few
minutes till she got almost out of sight. The women
would bring their pretty brown babies for the fair English lady to admire or to pat on the head; and when Muriel now and again stooped down to caress some fat little
naked child, lolling in the dust outside the hut, with true
tropical laziness, the mothers would run up at the sight
with delight and joy, and throw themselves down in ec-
stacies of gratitude for the notice she had taken of their
favored little ones. "The gods of Heaven," they would
say, with every sign of pleasure, "have looked graciously
upon our Unaloa."

At first Felix and Muriel were mainly struck with the
politeness and deference which the natives displayed
toward them. But after a time Felix at least began to
observe, behind it all, that a certain amount of affection,
and even of something like commiseration as well, seemed
to be mingled with the respect and reverence showered
upon them by their hosts. The women, especially, were
often evidently touched by Muriel's innocence and beauty.
As she walked past their huts with her light, girlish tread,
they would come forth shyly, bowing many times as they
approached, and offer her a long spray of the flower-
ing hibiscus, or a pretty garland of crimson ti-leaves,
saying at the same time, many times over, in their own
tongue, "Receive it, Korong; receive it, Queen of the
Clouds! You are good. You are kind. You are a daughter of the Sun. We are glad you have come to us."

A young girl soon makes herself at home anywhere; and Muriel, protected alike by her native innocence and by the invisible cloak of Polynesian taboo, quickly learned to understand and to sympathize with these poor dusky mothers. One morning, some weeks after their arrival, she passed down the main street of the village, accompanied by Felix and their two attendants, and reached the *marae*—the open forum or place of public assembly—which stood in its midst; a circular platform, surrounded by bread-fruit trees, under whose broad, cool shade the people were sitting in little groups and talking together. They were dressed in the regular old-time festive costume of Polynesia; for Bouparia, being a small and remote island, too insignificant to be visited by European ships, retained still all its aboriginal heathen manners and customs. The sight was, indeed, a curious and picturesque one. The girls, large-limbed, soft-skinned, and with delicately rounded figures, sat on the ground, laughing and talking, with their knees crossed under them; their wrists were encinctured with girdles of dark-red dracœna leaves, their swelling bosoms half concealed, half accentuated by hanging necklets of flowers. Their beautiful brown arms and shoulders were bare throughout; their long, black hair was gracefully twined and knotted with bright scarlet flowers. The men, strong and stalwart, sat behind on short stools or lounged on the buttressed roots of the bread-fruit trees, clad like the women in narrow waist-belts of the long red dracœna leaves, with necklets of sharks' teeth, pendent chain of pearly shells, a warrior's cap on their well-shaped heads, and an armlet of native beans, arranged below the shoulder, around their powerful arms. Altogether, it was a striking and beautiful picture. Muriel, now almost released from her early sense of fear, stood still to look at it.

The men and girls were laughing and chatting merrily together. Most of them were engaged in holding up before them fine mats; and a row of mulberry cloth, spread along on the ground, led to a hut near one side of the *marae*. Toward this the eyes of the spectators were turned. "What is it, Mali?" Muriel whispered, her woman's instinct leading her at once to expect that something special was going on in the way of local festivities.

And Mali answered at once, with many nods and smiles, "All right, Missy Queenie. Him a wedding, a marriage."

The words had hardly escaped her lips when a very pretty young girl, half smothered in flowers, and decked out in beads and fancy shells, emerged slowly from the hut, and took her way with stately tread along the path carpeted with native cloth. She was girt round the waist with rich-colored mats, which formed a long train, like a court dress, trailing on the ground five or six feet behind her.

"That's the bride, I suppose," Muriel whispered, now really interested—for what woman on earth, wherever she may be, can resist the seductive delights of a wedding?

"Yes, her a bride," Mali answered; "and ladies what follow, them her bridesmaids."

At the word, six other girls, similarly dressed, though without the train, and demure as nuns, emerged from the hut in slow order, two and two, behind her.

Muriel and Felix moved forward with natural curiosity toward the scene. The natives, now ranged in a row along the path, with mats turned inward, made way for them gladly. All seem pleased that Heaven should thus auspiciously honor the occasion ; and the bride herself, as well as the bridegroom, who, decked in shells and teeth, advanced from the opposite side along the path to meet her, looked up with grateful smiles at the two Europeans. Muriel, in return, smiled her most gracious and girlish recognition. As the bride drew near, she couldn't refrain from bending forward a little to look at the girl's really graceful costume. As she did so, the skirt of her own European dress brushed for a second against the bride's train, trailed carelessly many yards on the ground behind her.

Almost before they could know what had happened, a wild commotion arose, as if by magic, in the crowd around them. Loud cries of "Taboo! Taboo!" mixed with inarticulate screams, burst on every side from the assembled natives. In the twinkling of an eye they were surrounded by an angry, threatening throng, who didn't dare to draw near, but, standing a yard or two off, drew stone knives freely and shook their fists, scowling, in the strangers' faces. The change was appalling in its electric suddenness. Muriel drew back horrified, in an agony of alarm. "Oh, what have I done!" she cried, piteously, clinging to Felix for support. "Why on earth are they angry with us?"

"I don't know," Felix answered, taken aback himself. "I can't say exactly in what you've transgressed. But you must, unconsciously, in some way have offended their prejudices. I hope it's not much. At any rate they're clearly afraid to touch us."

"Missy Queenie break taboo," Mali explained at once, with Polynesian frankness. "That make people angry. So him want to kill you. Missy Queenie touch bride with end of her dress. Korong may smile on bride—that very good luck ; but Korong taboo ; no must touch him."

The crowd gathered around them, still very threatening in attitude, yet clearly afraid to approach within arm's-length of the strangers. Muriel was much frightened at their noise and at their frantic gestures. "Come away," she cried, catching Felix by the arm once more. "Oh, what are they going to do to us? Will they kill us for this? I'm so horribly afraid! Oh, why did I ever do it!"

The poor little bride, meanwhile, left alone on the carpet, and unnoticed by everybody, sank suddenly down on the mats where she stood, buried her face in her hands, and began to sob as if her heart would break. Evidently, something very untoward of some sort had happened to the dusky lady on her wedding morning.

The final touch was too much for poor Muriel's overwrought nerves. She, too, gave way in a tempest of sobs, and, subsiding on one of the native stools hard by, burst into tears herself with half-hysterical violence.

Instantly, as she did so, the whole assembly seemed to change its mind again as if by contagious magic. A loud shout of "She cries; the Queen of the Clouds cries!" went up from all the assembled mob to heaven. "It is a good omen," Toko, the Shadow, whispered in Polynesian to Felix, seeing his puzzled look. "We shall have plenty of rain now; the clouds will break; our crops will flourish." Almost before she understood it, Muriel was surrounded by an eager and friendly crowd, still afraid to draw near, but evidently anxious to see and to comfort and console her. Many of the women eagerly held forward their native mats, which Mali took from them, and, pressing them for a second against Muriel's eyes, handed them back with just a suspicion of wet tears left glistening in the corner. The happy recipients leaped and shouted with joy. "No more drought!" they cried merrily, with loud shouts and gesticulations. "The Queen of the Clouds is good: she will weep well from heaven upon my yam and taro plots!"

Muriel looked up, all dazed, and saw, to her intense surprise, the crowd was now nothing but affection and sympathy. Slowly they gathered in closer and closer, till they almost touched the hem of her robe; then the men stood by respectfully, laying their fingers on whatever she had wetted with her tears, while the women and girls took her hand in theirs and pressed it sympathetically. Mali explained their meaning with ready interpretation. "No cry too much, them say," she observed, nodding her head sagely. "Not good for Missy Queenie to cry too much. Them say, kind lady, be comforted."

There was genuine good-nature in the way they consoled her; and Felix was touched by the tenderness of those savage hearts; but the additional explanation, given him in Polynesian by his own Shadow, tended somewhat to detract from the disinterestedness of their sympathy. "They say, 'It is good for the Queen of the Clouds to weep,'" Toko said, with frank bluntness; "'but not too much— for fear the rain should wash away all our yam and taro plants.'"

By this time the little bride had roused herself from her stupor, and, smiling away as if nothing had happened, said a few words in a very low voice to Felix's Shadow. The Shadow turned most respectfully to his master, and, touching his sleeve-link, which was of bright gold, said, in a very doubtful voice, "She asks you, oh king, will you allow her, just for to-day, to wear this ornament?"

Felix unbuttoned the shining bauble at once, and was about to hand it to the bride with polite gallantry. "She may wear it forever, for the matter of that, if she likes," he said, good-humoredly. "I make her a present of it."

But the bride drew back as before in speechless terror, as he held out his hand, and seemed just on the point of bursting out into tears again at this untoward incident. The Shadow intervened with fortunate perception of the cause of the misunderstanding. "Korong must not touch or give anything to a bride," he said, quietly; "not with his own hand. He must not lay his finger on her; that would be unlucky. But he may hand it by his Shadow." Then he turned to his fellow-tribesmen. These gods," he said, in an explanatory voice, like one bespeaking forgiveness, "though they are divine, and Korong, and very powerful—see, they have come from the sun, and they are but strangers in Boupari—they do not yet know the ways of our island. They have not eaten of human flesh. They do not understand Taboo. But they will soon be wiser. They mean very well, but they do not know. Behold, he gives her this divine shining ornament from the sun as a present!" And, taking it in his hand, he held it up for a moment to public admiration. Then he passed on the trinket ostentatiously to the bride, who, smiling and delighted, hung it low on her breast among her other decorations.

The whole party seemed so surprised and gratified at this proof of condescension on the part of the divine stranger that they crowded round Felix once more, praising and thanking him volubly. Muriel, anxious to remove the bad impression she had created by touching the bride's dress, hastily withdrew her own little brooch and offered it in turn to the Shadow as an additional present. But Toko, shaking his head vigorously, pointed with his fore· finger many times to Mali. "Toko say him no can take it," Mali explained hastily, in her broken English. "Him no 'your Shadow ; me your Shadow ; me do everything for you ; me give it to the lady." And, taking the brooch in her hand, she passed it over in turn amid loud cries of delight and shouts of approval.

Thereupon, the ceremony began all over again. They seemed by their intervention to have interrupted some set formula. At its close the women crowded around Muriel and took her hand in theirs, kissing it many times over, with tears in their eyes, and betraying an immense amount of genuine feeling. One phrase in Polynesian they repeated again and again ; a phrase that made Felix's cheek turn white, as he leaned over the poor English girl with a profound emotion.

"What does it mean that they say ?" Muriel asked at last, perceiving it was all one phrase, many times repeated.

Felix was about to give some evasive explanation, when Mali interposed with her simple, unthinking translation. "Them say, Missy Queenie very good and kind. Make them sad to think. Make them cry to see her. Make them cry to see Missy Queenie Korong. Too good. Too pretty."

"Why so ?" Muriel exclaimed, drawing back with some faint presentiment of unspeakable horror.

Felix tried to stop her ; but the girl would not be

stopped. "Because, when Korong time up," she answered, blurting it out, " Korong must——"

Felix clapped his hand to her mouth in wild haste, and silenced her. He knew the worst now. He had divined the truth. But Muriel, at least, must be spared that knowledge.

CHAPTER IX.

SOWING THE WIND.

Vaguely and indefinitely one terrible truth had been forced by slow degrees upon Felix's mind ; whatever else Korong meant, it implied at least some fearful doom in store, sooner or later, for the persons who bore it. How awful that doom might be, he could hardly imagine ; but he must devote himself henceforth to the task of discovering what its nature was, and, if possible, of averting it.

Yet how to reconcile this impending terror with the other obvious facts of the situation ? the fact that they were considered divine beings and treated like gods ; and the fact that the whole population seemed really to regard them with a devotion and kindliness closely bordering on religious reverence ? If Korongs were gods, why should the people want to kill them ? If they meant to kill them, why pay them meanwhile such respect and affection ?

One point at least was now, however, quite clear to Felix. While the natives, especially the women, displayed toward both of them in their personal aspect a sort of regretful sympathy, he could not help noticing at the same time that the men, at any rate, regarded them also largely in an impersonal light, as a sort of generalized abstraction of the powers of nature—an embodied form of the rain and the weather. The islanders were anxious to keep their white guests well supplied, well fed, and in perfect health, not so much for the strangers' sakes as for their own advantage ; they evidently considered that if

anything went wrong with either of their two new gods,
corresponding misfortunes might happen to their crops
and the produce of their bread-fruit groves. Some mysterious sympathy was held to subsist between the persons
of the castaways and the state of the weather. The natives effusively thanked them after welcome rain, and
looked askance at them, scowling, after long dry spells.
It was for this, no doubt, that they took such pains to provide them with attentive Shadows, and to gird round their
movements with taboos of excessive stringency. Nothing that the new-comers said or did was indifferent, it
seemed, to the welfare of the community ; plenty and
prosperity depended upon the passing state of Muriel's
health, and famine or drought might be brought about
at any moment by the slightest imprudence in Felix's
diet.

How stringent these taboos really were Felix learned
by slow degrees alone to realize. From the very beginning he had observed, to be sure, that they might only
eat and drink the food provided for them ; that they were
supplied with a clean and fresh-built hut, as well as with
brand-new cocoanut cups, spoons, and platters ; that no
litter of any sort was allowed to accumulate near their
enclosure ; and that their Shadows never left them, or
went out of their sight, by day or by night, for a single
moment. Now, however, he began to perceive also that
the Shadows were there for that very purpose, to watch
over them, as it were, like guards, on behalf of the community ; to see that they ate or drank no tabooed object ; to
keep them from heedlessly transgressing any unwritten law
of the creed of Boupari ; and to be answerable for their
good behavior generally. They were partly servants, it
was true, and partly sureties ; but they were partly also
keepers, and keepers who kept a close and constant watch
upon the persons of their prisoners. Once or twice
Felix, growing tired for the moment of this continual sur-
veillance, had tried to give Toko the slip, and to stroll

away from his hut, unattended, for a walk through the
island, in the early morning, before his Shadow had
waked ; but on each such occasion he found to his surprise that, as he opened the hut door, the Shadow rose at
once and confronted him angrily, with an inquiring eye ;
and in time he perceived that a thin string was fastened
to the bottom of the door, the other end of which was
tied to the Shadow's ankle ; and this string could not be
cut without letting fall a sort of latch or bar which closed
the door outside, only to be raised again by some external
person.

Clearly, it was intended that the Korong should have no
chance of escape without the knowledge of the Shadow,
who, as Felix afterward learned, would have paid with his
own body by a cruel death for the Korong's disappearance.

He might as well have tried to escape his own shadow
as to escape the one the islanders had tacked on to him.

All Felix's energies were now devoted to the arduous
task of discovering what Korong really meant, and what
possibility he might have of saving Muriel from the mysterious fate that seemed to be held in store for them.

One evening, about six weeks after their arrival in the
island, the young Englishman was strolling by himself
(after the sun sank low in heaven) along a pretty tangled
hill-side path, overhung with lianas and rope-like tropical
creepers, while his faithful Shadow lingered a step or two
behind, keeping a sharp lookout meanwhile on all his
movements.

Near the top of a little crag of volcanic rock, in the centre of the hills, he came suddenly upon a hut with a
cleared space around it, somewhat neater in appearance
than any of the native cottages he had yet seen, and surrounded by a broad white belt of coral sand, exactly like
that which ringed round and protected their own enclosure. But what specially attracted Felix's attention was
the fact that the space outside this circle had been cleared

into a regular flower-garden, quite European in the defin-
iteness and orderliness of its quaint arrangement.

"Why, who lives here?" Felix asked in Polynesian,
turning round in surprise to his respectful Shadow.

The Shadow waved his hand vaguely in an expansive
way toward the sky, as he answered, with a certain air of
awe, often observable in his speech when taboos were in
question, "The King of Birds. A very great god. He
speaks the bird language."

"Who is he?" Felix inquired, taken aback, wondering
vaguely to himself whether here, perchance, he might have
lighted upon some stray and shipwrecked compatriot.

"He comes from the sun like yourselves," the Shadow
answered, all deference, but with obvious reserve. "He
is a very great god. I may not speak much of him. But
he is not Korong. He is greater than that, and less. He
is Tula, the same as Tu-Kila-Kila."

"Is he as powerful as Tu-Kila-Kila?" Felix asked, with
intense interest.

"Oh, no, he's not nearly so powerful as that," the Shadow answered, half terrified at the bare suggestion. "No
god in heaven or earth is like Tu-Kila-Kila. This one is
only king of the birds, which is a little province, while
Tu-Kila-Kila is king of heaven and earth, of plants and
animals, of gods and men, of all things created. At his
nod the sky shakes and the rocks tremble. But still, this
god is Tula, like Tu-Kila-Kila. He is not for a year. He
goes on forever, till some other supplants him."

"You say he comes from the sun," Felix put in, de-
voured with curiosity. "And he speaks the bird language?
What do you mean by that? Does he speak like the
Queen of the Clouds and myself when we talk together?"

"Oh, dear, no," the Shadow answered, in a very confident tone. "He doesn't speak the least bit in the world
like that. He speaks shriller and higher, and still more
bird-like. It is chatter, chatter, chatter, like the parrots
in a tree; tirra, tirra, tirra; tarra, tarra, tarra; la, la, la;

lo, lo, lo ; lu, lu, lu ; li la. And he sings to himself all the time. He sings this way——"

And then the Shadow, with that wonderful power of accurate mimicry which is so strong in all natural human beings, began to trill out at once, with a very good Parisian accent, a few lines from a well-known song in "La Fille de Madame Angot : "

> " Quand on conspi-re,
>   Quand sans frayeur
> On peut se di-re
>   Conspirateur,
> Pour tout le mon-de
>   Il faut avoir
> Perruque blon-de
>   Et collet noir—
> Perruque blon-de
>   Et collet noir."

"That's how the King of the Birds sings," the Shadow said, as he finished, throwing back his head, and laughing with all his might at his own imitation. " So funny, isn't it ? It's exactly like the song of the pink-crested parrot."

"Why, Toko, it's French," Felix exclaimed, using the Fijian word for a Frenchman, which the Shadow, of course, on his remote island, had never before heard. " How on earth did he come here ? "

" I can't tell you," Toko answered, waving his arms seaward. " He came from the sun, like yourselves. But not in a sun-boat. It had no fire. He came in a canoe, all by himself. And Mali says "—here the Shadow lowered his voice to a most mysterious whisper—" he's a man-a-oui-oui."

Felix quivered with excitement. " Man-a-oui-oui " is the universal name over semi-civilized Polynesia for a Frenchman. Felix seized upon it with avidity. " A man-a-oui-oui ! " he cried, delighted. " How strange ! How wonderful ! I must go in at once to his hut and see him ! "

He had lifted his foot and was just going to cross the

white line of coral-sand, when his Shadow, catching him suddenly and stoutly round the waist, pulled him back from the enclosure with every sign of horror, alarm, and astonishment. "No, you can't go," he cried, grappling with him with all his force, yet using him very tenderly for all that, as becomes a god. "Taboo! Taboo there!"

"But I am a god myself," Felix cried, insisting upon his privileges. If you have to submit to the disadvantages of taboo, you may as well claim its advantages as well. "The King of Fire and the King of Water crossed my taboo line. Why shouldn't I cross equally the King of the Birds', then?"

"So you might—as a rule," the Shadow answered with promptitude. "You are both gods. Your taboos do not cross. You may visit each other. You may transgress one another's lines without danger of falling dead on the ground as common men would do if they broke taboo-lines. But this is the Month of Birds. The king is in retreat. No man may see him except his own Shadow, the Little Cockatoo who brings him his food and drink. Do you see that hawk's head, stuck upon the post by the door at the side. That is his Special Taboo. He keeps it for this month. Even gods must respect that sign, for a reason which it would be very bad medicine to mention. While the Month of Birds lasts, no man may look upon the king or hear him. If they did, they would die, and the carrion birds would eat them. Come away. This is dangerous."

Scarcely were the words well out of his mouth when from the recesses of the hut a rollicking French voice was heard, trilling out merrily :

> " Quand on con-spi-re,
>   Quand, sans frayeur ——"

Without waiting for more, the Shadow seized Felix's arm in an agony of terror. "Come away!" he cried, hurriedly, "come away! What will become of us? This is horrible, horrible! We have broken taboo. We have heard the

god's voice. The sky will fall on us. If his Shadow were
to find it out and tell my people, my people would tear us
limb from limb. Quick, quick ! Hide away ! Let us
run fast through the forest before any man discover it."

The Shadow's voice rang deep with alarm. Felix felt
he dare not trifle with this superstition. Profound as was
his curiosity about the mysterious Frenchman, he was compelled to bottle up his eagerness and anxiety for the moment, and patiently wait till the Month of Birds had run
its course, and taken its inconvenient taboo along with it.
These limitations were terrible. Yet he counted much
upon the information the Frenchman could give him. The
man had been some time on the island, it was clear, and
doubtless he understood its ways thoroughly ; he might
cast some light at last upon the Korong mystery.

So he went back through the woods with a heart somewhat lighter.

Not far from their own huts he met Muriel and Mali.

As they walked home together, Felix told his companion
in a very few words the strange discovery about the Frenchman, and the impenetrable taboo by which he was at present surrounded. Muriel drew a deep sigh. " Oh, Felix,"
she said—for they were naturally by this time very much
at home with one another, " did you ever know anything so
dreadful as the mystery of these taboos ? It seems as if we
should never get really to the bottom of them. Mali's
always springing some new one upon me. I don't believe
we shall ever be able to leave the island—we're so hedged
round with taboos. Even if we were to see a ship to-day,
I don't believe they'd allow us to signal it."

There was a red sunset ; a lurid, tropical, red-and-green
sunset. It boded mischief.

They were passing by some huts at the moment, and
over the stockade of one of them a tree was hanging with
small yellow fruits, which Felix knew well in Fiji as whole-
some and agreeable. He broke off a small branch as he
passed, and offered a couple thoughtlessly to Muriel. She

took them in her fingers, and tasted them gingerly. "They're not so bad," she said, taking another from the bough. "They're very much like gooseberries."

At the same moment, Felix popped one into his own mouth, and swallowed it without thinking.

Almost before they knew what had happened, with the same extraordinary rapidity as in the case of the wedding, the people in the cottages ran out, with every sign of fear and apprehension, and, seizing the branch from Felix's hands, began upbraiding the two Shadows for their want of attention.

"We couldn't help it," Toko exclaimed, with every appearance of guilt and horror on his face. "They were much too sharp for us. Their hearts are black. How could we two interfere? These gods are so quick! They had picked and eaten them before we ever saw them."

One of the men raised his hand with a threatening air— but against the Shadow, not against the sacred person of Felix. "He will be ill," he said, angrily, pointing toward the white man ; "and she will, too. Their hearts are indeed black. They have sown the seed of the wind. They have both of them eaten of it. They will both be ill. You deserve to die! And what will come now to our trees and plantations ? "

The crowd gathered round them, cursing low and horribly. The two terrified Europeans slunk off to their huts, unaware of their exact crime, and closely followed by a scowling but despondent mob of natives. As they crossed their sacred boundary, Muriel cried, with a sudden outburst of tears, "Oh, Felix, what on earth shall we ever do to get rid of this terrible, unendurable godship ! "

The natives without set up a great shout of horror. "See, see ! she cries !" they exclaimed, in indescribable panic. "She has eaten the storm-fruit, and already she cries ! Oh, clouds, restrain yourselves ! Oh, great queen, mercy ! Whatever will become of us and our poor huts and gardens ! "

And for hours they crouched around, beating their breasts and shrieking.

That evening, Muriel sat up late in Felix's hut, with Mali by her side, too frightened to go back into her own alone before those angry people. And all the time, just beyond the barrier line, they could hear, above the whistle of the wind around the hut, the droning voices of dozens of natives, cowering low on the ground ; they seemed to be going through some litany or chant, as if to deprecate the result of this imprudent action.

"What are they doing outside?" Felix asked of his Shadow at last, after a peculiarly long wail of misery.

And the Shadow made answer, in very solemn tones, " They are trying to propitiate your mightiness, and to avert the omen, lest the rain should fall, and the wind should blow, and the storm-cloud should burst over the island to destroy them."

Then Felix remembered suddenly of himself that the season when this storm-fruit, or storm-apple, as they called it, was ripe in Fiji, was also the season when the great Pacific cyclones most often swept over the land in full fury —storms unexampled on any other sea, like that famous one which wrecked so many European men-of-war a few years since in the harbor of Samoa.

And without, the wail came louder and clearer still ! "If you sow the bread-fruit seed, you will reap the bread-fruit. If you sow the wind, you will reap the whirlwind. They have **eaten the storm-fruit. Oh, great king, save us !** "

CHAPTER X.

REAPING THE WHIRLWIND.

Toward midnight Muriel began to doze lightly from pure fatigue.

" Put a pillow under her head, and let her sleep," Felix said in a whisper. " Poor child, it would be cruel to send her alone to-night into her own quarters."

And Mali slipped a pillow of mulberry paper under her mistress's head, and laid it on her own lap, and bent down to watch her.

But outside, beyond the line, the natives murmured loud their discontent. " The Queen of the Clouds stays in the King of the Rain's hut to-night," they muttered, angrily. "She will not listen to us. Before morning, be sure, the Tempest will be born of their meeting to destroy us."

About two o'clock there came a lull in the wind, which had been rising steadily ever since that lurid sunset. Felix looked out of the hut door. The moon was full. It was almost as clear as day with the bright tropical moonlight, silvery in the open, pale green in the shadow. The people were still squatting in great rings round the hut, just outside the taboo line, and beating gongs and sticks and human bones, to keep time to the lilt of their lugubrious litany.

The air felt unusually heavy and oppressive. Felix raised his eyes to the sky, and saw whisps of light cloud drifting in rapid flight over the scudding moon. Below, an ominous fog bank gathered steadily westward. Then one clap of thunder rent the sky. After it came a deadly silence. The moon was veiled. All was dark as pitch. The natives themselves fell on their faces and prayed with mute lips. Three minutes later, the cyclone had burst upon them in all its frenzy.

Such a hurricane Felix had never before experienced.

Its energy was awful. Round the palm-trees the wind played a frantic and capricious devil's dance. It pirouetted about the atoll in the mad glee of unconsciousness. Here and there it cleared lanes, hundreds of yards in length, among the forest-trees and the cocoanut plantations. The noise of snapping and falling trunks rang thick on the air. At times the cyclone would swoop down from above upon the swaying stem of some tall and stately palm that bent like grass before the wind, break it off short with a roar at the bottom, and lay it low at once upon the ground, with a crash like thunder. In other places, little playful whirlwinds seemed to descend from the sky in the very midst of the dense brushwood, where they cleared circular patches, strewn thick under foot with trunks and branches in their titanic sport, and yet left unhurt all about the surrounding forest. Then again a special cyclone of gigantic proportions would advance, as it were, in a single column against one stem of a clump, whirl round it spirally like a lightning flash, and, deserting it for another, leave it still standing, but turned and twisted like a screw by the irresistible force of its invisible fingers. The storm-god, said Toko, was dancing with the palm-trees. The sight was awful. Such destructive energy Felix had never even imagined before. No wonder the savages all round beheld in it the personal wrath of some mighty spirit.

For in spite of the black clouds they could *see* it all—both the Europeans and the islanders. The intense darkness of the night was lighted up for them every minute by an almost incessant blaze of sheet and forked lightning. The roar of the thunder mingled with the roar of the tempest, each in turn overtopping and drowning the other. The hut where Felix and Muriel sheltered themselves shook before the storm ; the very ground of the island trembled and quivered—like the timbers of a great ship before a mighty sea—at each onset of the breakers upon the surrounding fringe-reef. And side by side with it all, to crown their misery, wild torrents of rain, descending in waterspouts, as it seemed, or dashed in great sheets against the roof of their frail tenement, poured fitfully on with fierce tropical energy.

In the midst of the hut Muriel crouched and prayed with bloodless lips to Heaven. This was too, too terrible. It seemed incredible to her that on top of all they had been called upon to suffer of fear and suspense at the hands of the savages, the very dumb forces of nature themselves should thus be stirred up to open war against them. Her faith in Providence was sorely tried. Dumb forces, indeed! Why, they roared with more terrible voices than any wild beast on earth could possibly compass. The thunder and the wind were howling each other down in emulous din, and the very hiss of the lightning could be distinctly heard, like some huge snake, at times above the creaking and snapping of the trees before the gale in the surrounding forest.

Muriel crouched there long, in the mute misery of utter despair. At her feet Mali crouched too, as frightened as herself, but muttering aloud from time to time, in a reproachful voice, "I tell Missy Queenie what going to happen. I warn her not. I tell her she must not eat that very bad storm-apple. But Missy Queenie no listen. Her take her own way, then storm come down upon us."

And Felix's Shadow, in his own tongue, exclaimed more than once in the self-same tone, half terror, half expostulation, "See now what comes from breaking taboo? You eat the storm-fruit. The storm-fruit suits ill with the King of the Rain and the Queen of the Clouds. The heavens have broken loose. The sea has boiled. See what wind and what flood you are bringing upon us."

By and by, above even the fierce roar of the mingled thunder and cyclone, a wild orgy of noise burst upon them all from without the hut. It was a sound as of numberless drums and tom-toms, all beaten in unison with the mad energy of fear; a hideous sound, suggestive of some hateful heathen devil-worship. Muriel clapped her hands to her ears in horror. "Oh, what's that?" she cried to Felix, at this new addition to their endless alarms. "Are the savages out there rising in a body? Have they come to murder us?"

"Perhaps," Felix said, smoothing her hair with his hand, as a mother might soothe her terrified child, "perhaps they're angry with us for having caused this storm, as they think, by our foolish action. I believe they all set it down to our having unluckily eaten that unfortunate fruit. I'll go out to the door myself and speak to them."

Muriel clung to his arm with a passionate clinging.

"Oh, Felix," she cried, "no! Don't leave me here alone. My darling, I love you. You're all the world there is left to me now, Felix. Don't go out to those wretches and leave me here alone. They'll murder you! they'll murder you! Don't go out, I implore you. If they mean to kill us, let them kill us both together, in one another's arms. Oh, Felix, I am yours, and you are mine, my darling!"

It was the first time either of them had acknowledged the fact; but there, before the face of that awful convulsion of nature, all the little deceptions and veils of life seemed rent asunder forever as by a flash of lightning. They stood face to face with each other's souls, and forgot all else in the agony of the moment. Felix clasped the trembling girl in his arms like a lover. The two Shadows looked on and shook with silent terror. If the King of the Rain thus embraced the Queen of the Clouds before their very eyes, amid so awful a storm, what unspeakable effects might not follow at once from it! But they had too much respect for those supernatural creatures to attempt to interfere with their action at such a moment. They accepted their masters almost as passively as they accepted the wind and the thunder, which they believed to arise from them.

Felix laid his poor Muriel tenderly down on the mud floor again. "I *must* go out, my child," he said. "For

6

the very love of *you*, I must play the man, and find out
what these savages mean by their drumming."

He crept to the door of the hut (for no man could walk
upright before that awful storm), and peered out into the
darkness once more, awaiting one of the frequent flashes
of lightning. He had not long to wait. In a moment
the sky was all ablaze again from end to end, and continued so for many seconds consecutively. By the light
of the continuous zigzags of fire, Felix could see for himself that hundreds and hundreds of natives—men, women,
and children, naked, or nearly so, with their hair loose
and wet about their cheeks—lay flat on their faces, many
courses deep, just outside the taboo line. The wind swept
over them with extraordinary force, and the tropical rain
descended in great floods upon their bare backs and
shoulders. But the savages, as if entranced, seemed to
take no heed of all these earthly things. They lay grovelling in the mud before some unseen power ; and beating
their tom-toms in unison, with barbaric concord, they
cried aloud once more as Felix appeared, in a weird litany
that overtopped the tumultuous noise of the tempest,
"Oh, Storm-God, hear us ! Oh, great spirit, deliver us !
King of the Rain and Queen of the Clouds, befriend us !
Be angry no more ! Hide your wrath from your people !
Take away your hurricane, and we will bring you many
gifts. Eat no longer of the storm-apple—the seed of the
wind—and we will feed you with yam and turtle, and much
choice bread-fruit. Great king, we are yours ; you shall
choose which you will of our children for your meat and
drink ; you shall sup on our blood. But take your storm
away ; do not utterly drown and submerge our island !"

As they spoke they crawled nearer and nearer, with
gliding serpentine motion, till their heads almost touched
the white line of coral. But not a man of them all went
one inch beyond it. They stopped there and gazed at
him. Felix signed to them with his hand, and pointed
vaguely to the sky, as much as to say *he* was not responsi-

ble. At the gesture the whole assembly burst into one loud shout of gratitude. "He has heard us, he has heard us!" they exclaimed, with a perfect wail of joy. "He will not utterly destroy us. He will take away his storm. He will bring the sun and the moon back to us."

Felix returned into the hut, somewhat reassured so far as the attitude of the savages went. "Don't be afraid of them, Muriel," he cried, taking her passionately once more in a tender embrace. "They daren't cross the taboo. They won't come near; they're too frightened themselves to dream of hurting us."

CHAPTER XI.

AFTER THE STORM.

Next morning the day broke bright and calm, as if the tempest had been but an evil dream of the night, now past forever. The birds sang loud; the lizards came forth from their holes in the wall, and basked, green and gold, in the warm, dry sunshine. But though the sky overhead was blue and the air clear, as usually happen after these alarming tropical cyclones and rainstorms, the memorials of the great wind that had raged all night long among the forests of the island were neither few nor far between. Everywhere the ground was strewn with leaves and branches and huge stems of cocoa-palms. All nature was draggled. Many of the trees were stripped clean of their foliage, as completely as oaks in an English winter; on others, big strands of twisted fibres marked the scars and joints where mighty boughs had been torn away by main force; while, elsewhere, bare stumps alone remained to mark the former presence of some noble dracæna or some gigantic banyan. Bread-fruits and cocoanuts lay tossed in the wildest confusion on the ground; the banana and plantain-patches were beaten level with the soil or buried deep in the mud; many of the huts had given way entirely; abundant wreckage strewed every corner of the island. It was an awful sight. Muriel shuddered to herself to see how much the two that night had passed through.

What the outer fringing reef had suffered from the storm they hardly knew as yet; but from the door of the hut Felix could see for himself how even the calm waters of the inner lagoon had been lashed into wild fury by the fierce swoop of the tempest. Round the entire atoll the solid conglomerate coral floor was scooped under, broken up, chewed fine by the waves, or thrown in vast fragments on the beach of the island. By the eastern shore, in particular, just opposite their hut, Felix observed a regular wall of many feet in height, piled up by the waves like the familiar Chesil Beach near his old home in Dorsetshire. It was the shelter of that temporary barrier alone, no doubt, that had preserved their huts last night from the full fury of the gale, and that had allowed the natives to congregate in such numbers prone on their faces in the mud and rain, upon the unconsecrated ground outside their taboo-line.

But now not an islander was to be seen within ear-shot. All had gone away to look after their ruined huts or their beaten-down plantain-patches, leaving the cruel gods, who, as they thought, had wrought all the mischief out of pure wantonness, to repent at leisure the harm done during the night to their obedient votaries.

Felix was just about to cross the taboo-line and walk down to the shore to examine the barrier, when Toko, his Shadow, laying his hand on his shoulder with more genuine interest and affection than he had ever yet shown, exclaimed, with some horror, "Oh, no! Not that! Don't dare to go outside! It would be very dangerous for you. If my people were to catch you on profane soil just now, there's no saying what harm they might do to you."

"Why so?" Felix exclaimed, in surprise. "Last night,

surely, they were all prayers and promises and vows and entreaties."

The young man nodded his head in acquiescence. "Ah, yes; last night," he answered. "That was very well then. Vows were sore needed. The storm was raging, and you were within your taboo. How could they dare to touch you, a mighty god of the tempest, at the very moment when you were rending their banyan-trees and snapping their cocoanut stems with your mighty arms like so many little chicken-bones? Even Tu-Kila-Kila himself, I expect, the very high god, lay frightened in his temple, cowering by his tree, annoyed at your wrath; he sent Fire and Water among the worshippers, no doubt, to offer up vows and to appease your anger."

Then Felix remembered, as his Shadow spoke, that, as a matter of fact, he had observed the men who usually wore the red and white feather cloaks among the motley crowd of grovelling natives who lay flat on their faces in the mud of the cleared space the night before, and prayed hard for mercy. Only they were not wearing their robes of office at the moment, in accordance with a well-known savage custom; they had come naked and in disgrace, as befits all suppliants. They had left behind them the insignia of their rank in their own shaken huts, and bowed down their bare backs to the rain and the lightning.

"Yes, I saw them among the other islanders," Felix answered, half-smiling, but prudently remaining within the taboo-line, as his Shadow advised him.

Toko kept his hand still on his master's shoulder. "Oh, king," he said, beseechingly, and with great solemnity, "I am doing wrong to warn you; I am breaking a very great Taboo. I don't know what harm may come to me for telling you. Perhaps Tu-Kila-Kila will burn me to ashes with one glance of his eyes. He may know this minute what I'm saying here alone to you."

It is hard for a white man to meet scruples like this; but Felix was bold enough to answer outright: "Tu-Kila-

Kila knows nothing of the sort, and can never find out. Take my word for it, Toko, nothing that you say to me will ever reach Tu-Kila-Kila."

The Shadow looked at him doubtfully, and trembled as he spoke. " I like you, Korong," he said, with a genuinely truthful ring in his voice. " You seem to me so kind and good—so different from other gods, who are very cruel. You never beat me. Nobody I ever served treated me as well or as kindly as you have done. And for *your* sake I will even dare to break taboo—if you're quite, quite sure Tu-Kila-Kila will never discover it."

" I'm quite sure," Felix answered, with perfect confidence. " I know it for certain. I swear a great oath to it."

" You swear by Tu-Kila-Kila himself ? " the young savage asked, anxiously.

" I swear by Tu-Kila-Kila himself," Felix replied at once. "I swear, without doubt. He can never know it."

" That is a great Taboo," the Shadow went on, meditatively, stroking Felix's arm. " A very great Taboo indeed. A terrible medicine. And you are a god ; I can trust you. Well, then, you see, the secret is this : you are Korong, but you are a stranger, and you don't understand the ways of Boupari. If for three days after the end of this storm, which Tu-Kila-Kila has sent Fire and Water to pray and vow against, you or the Queen of the Clouds show yourselves outside your own taboo-line—why, then, the people are clear of sin ; whoever takes you may rend you alive ; they will tear you limb from limb and cut you into pieces."

" Why so ? " Felix asked, aghast at this discovery. They seemed to live on a perpetual volcano in this wonderful island ; and a volcano ever breaking out in fresh places. They could never get to the bottom of its horrible superstitions.

" Because you ate the storm-apple," the Shadow answered, confidently. " That was very wrong. You brought the tempest upon us yourselves by your own trespass ; therefore, by the custom of Boupari, which we learn in the mysteries, you become full Korong for the sacrifice at once. That makes the term for you. The people will give you all your dues ; then they will say, 'We are free ; we have bought you with a price ; we have brought your cocoanuts. No sin attaches to us ; we are righteous ; we are righteous.' And then they will kill you, and Fire and Water will roast you and boil you."

"But only if we go outside the taboo-line?" Felix asked, anxiously.

"Only if you go outside the taboo-line," the Shadow replied, nodding a hasty assent. "Inside it, till your term comes, even Tu-Kila-Kila himself, the very high god, whose meat we all are, dare never hurt you."

"Till our term comes?" Felix inquired, once more astonished and perplexed. "What do you mean by that, my Shadow?"

But the Shadow was either bound by some superstitious fear, or else incapable of putting himself into Felix's point of view. "Why, till you are full Korong," he answered, like one who speaks of some familiar fact, as who should say, till you are forty years old, or, till your beard grows white. "Of course, by and by, you will be full Korong. I cannot help you then ; but, till that time comes, I would like to do my best by you. You have been very kind to me. I tell you much. More than this, it would not be lawful for me to mention."

And that was the most that, by dexterous questioning, Felix could ever manage to get out of his mysterious Shadow.

"At the end of three days we will be safe, though?" he inquired at last, after all other questions failed to produce an answer.

"Oh, yes, at the end of three days the storm will have blown over," the young man answered, easily. "All will then be well. You may venture out once more. The rain will have dried over all the island. Fire and Water will have no more power over you."

Felix went back to the hut to inform Muriel of this new peril thus suddenly sprung upon them. Poor Muriel, now almost worn out with endless terrors, received it calmly. "I'm growing accustomed to it all, Felix," she answered, resignedly. "If only I know that you will keep your promise, and never let me fall alive into these wretches' hands, I shall feel quite safe. Oh, Felix, do you know when you took me in your arms like that last night, in spite of everything, I felt positively happy."

About ten o'clock they were suddenly roused by a sound of many natives, coming in quick succession, single file, to the huts, and shouting aloud, "Oh, King of the Rain, oh, Queen of the Clouds, come forth for our vows ! Receive your presents! "

Felix went forth to the door to look. With a warning look in his eyes, his Shadow followed him. The natives were now coming up by dozens at a time, bringing with them, in great arm-loads, fallen cocoanuts and bread-fruits, and branches of bananas, and large draggled clusters of half-ripe plantains.

"Why, what are all these?" Felix exclaimed in surprise.

His Shadow looked up at him, as if amused at the absurd simplicity of the question. "These are yours, of course," he said ; "yours and the Queen's ; they are the windfalls you made. Did you not knock them all off the trees for yourselves when you were coming down in such sheets from the sky last evening ?"

Felix wrung his hands in positive despair. It was clear, indeed, that to the minds of the natives there was no distinguishing personally between himself and Muriel, and the rain or the cyclone.

"Will they bring them all in ?" he asked, gazing in alarm at the huge pile of fruits the natives were making outside the huts,

"Yes, all," the Shadow answered; "they are vows; they are godsends; but if you like, you can give some of them back. If you give much back, of course it will make my people less angry with you."

Felix advanced near the line, holding his hand up before him to command silence. As he did so, he was absolutely appalled himself at the perfect storm of execration and abuse which his appearance excited. The foremost natives, brandishing their clubs and stone-tipped spears, or shaking their fists by the line, poured forth upon his devoted head at once all the most frightful curses of the Polynesian vocabulary. "Oh, evil god," they cried aloud with angry faces, "oh, wicked spirit! you have a bad heart. See what a wrong you have purposely done us. If your heart were not bad, would you treat us like this? If you are indeed a god, come out across the line, and let us try issues together. Don't skulk like a coward in your hut and within your taboo, but come out and fight us. *We* are not afraid, who are only men. Why are *you* afraid of us?"

Felix tried to speak once more, but the din drowned his voice. As he paused, the people set up their loud shouts again. "Oh, you wicked god! You eat the storm-apple! You have wrought us much harm. You have spoiled our harvest. How you came down in great sheets last night! It was pitiful, pitiful! We would like to kill you. You might have taken our bread-fruits and our bananas, if you would; we give you them freely; they are yours; here, take them. We feed you well; we make you many offerings. But why did you wish to have our huts also? Why did you beat down our young plantations and break our canoes against the beach of the island? That shows a bad heart! You are an evil god! You dare not defend yourself. Come out and meet us."

CHAPTER XII.

A POINT OF THEOLOGY.

At last, with great difficulty, Felix managed to secure a certain momentary lull of silence. The natives, clustering round the line till they almost touched it, listened with scowling brows, and brandished threatening spears, tipped with points of stone or shark's teeth or turtle-bone, while he made his speech to them. From time to time, one or another interrupted him, coaxing and wheedling him, as it were, to cross the line; but Felix never heeded them. He was beginning to understand now how to treat this strange people. He took no notice of their threats or their entreaties either.

By and by, partly by words and partly by gestures, he made them understand that they might take back and keep for themselves all the cocoanuts and bread-fruits they had brought as windfalls. At this the people seemed a little appeased. "His heart is not quite so bad as we thought," they murmured among themselves; "but if he didn't want them, what did he mean? Why did he beat down our huts and our plantations?"

Then Felix tried to explain to them—a somewhat dangerous task—that neither he nor Muriel were really responsible for last night's storm; but at that the people, with one accord, raised a great loud shout of unmixed derision. "He is a god," they cried, "and yet he is ashamed of his own acts and deeds, afraid of what we, mere men, will do to him! Ha! ha! Take care! These are lies that he tells. Listen to him! Hear him!"

Meanwhile, more and more natives kept coming up with windfalls of fruit, or with objects they had vowed in their terror to dedicate during the night; and Felix all the time kept explaining at the top of his voice, to all as they came, that he wanted nothing, and that they could take all back again. This curiously inconsistent action seemed to puzzle the wondering natives strangely. Had he made the storm, then, they asked, and eaten the storm-apple, for no use to himself, but out of pure perverseness? If he didn't even want the windfalls and the objects vowed to him, why had he beaten down their crops and broken their houses? They looked at him meaningly; but they dared not cross that great line of taboo. It was their own superstition alone, in that moment of danger, that kept their hands off those defenceless white people.

At last a happy idea seemed to strike the crowd. "What he wants is a child?" they cried, effusively. "He thirsts for blood! Let us kill and roast him a proper victim!"

Felix's horror at this appalling proposition knew no bounds. "If you do," he cried, turning their own superstition against them in this last hour of need, "I will raise up a storm worse even than last night's! You do it at your peril! I want no victim. The people of my country eat not of human flesh. It is a thing detestable, horrible, hateful to God and man. With us, all human life alike is sacred. We spill no blood. If you dare to do as you say, I will raise such a storm over your heads to-night as will submerge and drown the whole of your island."

The natives listened to him with profound interest. "We must spill no blood!" they repeated, looking aghast at one another. "Hear what the King says! We must not cut the victim's throat. We must bind a child with cords and roast it alive for him!"

Felix hardly knew what to do or say at this atrocious proposal. "If you roast it alive," he cried, "you deserve to be all scorched up with lightning. Take care what you do! Spare the child's life! I will have no victim. Beware how you anger me!"

But the savage no sooner says than he does. With him deliberation is unknown, and impulse everything. In a moment the natives had gathered in a circle a little way off, and began drawing lots. Several children, seized

hurriedly up among the crowd, were huddled like so many
sheep in the centre. Felix looked on from his enclosure,
half petrified with horror. The lot fell upon a pretty little
girl of five years old. Without one word of warning, without one sign of remorse, before Felix's very eyes, they
began to bind the struggling and terrified child just outside the circle.

The white man could stand this horrid barbarity no
longer. At the risk of his life—at the risk of Muriel's—
he must rush out to prevent them. They should never
dare to kill that helpless child before his very eyes. Come
what might—though even Muriel should suffer for it—he
felt he *must* rescue that trembling little creature. Drawing his trusty knife, and opening the big blade ostentatiously before their eyes, he made a sudden dart like a
wild beast across the line, and pounced down upon the
party that guarded the victim.

Was it a ruse to make him cross the line, alone, or did
they really mean it? He hardly knew; but he had no
time to debate the abstract question. Bursting into their
midst, he seized the child with a rush in his circling arms,
and tried to hurry back with it within the protecting taboo-
line.

Quick as lightning he was surrounded and almost cut
down by a furious and frantic mob of half-naked savages.
"Kill him! Tear him to pieces!" they cried in their
rage. "He has a bad heart! He destroyed our huts!
He broke down our plantations! Kill him, kill him, kill
him!"

As they closed in upon him, with spears and tomahawks
and clubs, Felix saw he had nothing left for it now but a
hard fight for life to return to the taboo-line. Holding
the child in one arm, and striking wildly out with his
knife with the other, he tried to hack his way back by
main force to the shelter of the taboo-line in frantic lunges.
The distance was but a few feet, but the savages pressed
round him, half frightened still, yet gnashing their teeth

and distorting their faces with anger. "He has broken the Taboo," they cried in vehement tones. "He has crossed the line willingly. Kill him! Kill him! We are free from sin. We have bought him with a price—with many cocoanuts!"

At the sound of the struggle going on so close outside, Muriel rushed in frantic haste and terror from the hut. Her face was pale, but her demeanor was resolute. Before Mali could stop her, she, too, had crossed the sacred line of the coral mark, and had flung herself madly upon Felix's assailants, to cover his retreat with her own frail body.

"Hold off!" she cried, in her horror, in English, but in accents even those savages could read. "You shall not touch him!"

With a fierce effort Felix tore his way back, through the spears and clubs, toward the place of safety. The savages wounded him on the way more than once with their jagged stone spear-tips, and blood flowed from his breast and arms in profusion. But they didn't dare even so to touch Muriel. The sight of that pure white woman, rushing out in her weakness to protect her lover's life from attack, seemed to strike them with some fresh access of superstitious awe. One or two of themselves were wounded by Felix's knife, for they were unaccustomed to steel, though they had a few blades made out of old European barrel-hoops. For a minute or two the conflict was sharp and hotly contested. Then at last Felix managed to fling the child across the line, to push Muriel with one hand at arm's-length before him, and to rush himself within the sacred circle.

No sooner had he crossed it than the savages drew up around, undecided as yet, but in a threatening body. Rank behind rank, their loose hair in their eyes, they stood like wild beasts balked of their prey, and yelled at him. Some of them brandished their spears and their stone hatchets angrily in their victims' faces. Others contented themselves with howling aloud as before, and piling curses afresh on the heads of the unpopular storm-gods. " Look at her," they cried, in their wrath, pointing their skinny brown fingers angrily at Muriel. " See, she weeps even now. She would flood us with her rain. She isn't satisfied with all the harm she has poured down upon Boupari already. She wants to drown us."

And then a little knot drew up close to the line of taboo itself, and began to discuss in loud and serious tones a pressing question of savage theology and religious practice.

" They have crossed the line within the three days," some of the foremost warriors exclaimed, in excited voices. " They are no longer taboo. We can do as we please with them. We may cross the line now ourselves if we will, and tear them to pieces. Come on! Who follows? Korong! Korong! Let us rend them! Let us eat them!"

But though they spoke so bravely they hung back themselves, fearful of passing that mysterious barrier. Others of the crowd answered them back, warmly: "No, no; not so. Be careful what you do. Anger not the gods. Don't ruin Boupari. If the Taboo is not indeed broken, then how dare we break it? They are gods. Fear their vengeance. They are, indeed, terrible. See what happened to us when they merely ate of the storm-apple! What might not happen if we were to break taboo without due cause and kill them? "

One old, gray-bearded warrior, in particular, held his countrymen back. " Mind how you trifle with gods," the old chief said, in a tone of solemn warning. " Mind how you provoke them. They are very mighty. When I was young, our people killed three sailing gods who came ashore in a small canoe, built of thin split logs ; and within a month an awful earthquake devastated Boupari, and fire burst forth from a mouth in the ground, and the people knew that the spirits of the sailing gods were very angry.

Wait, therefore, till Tu-Kila-Kila himself comes, and then
ask of him, and of Fire and Water. As Tu-Kila-Kila bids
you, that do you do. Is he not our great god, the king of
us all, and the guardian of the customs of the island of
Boupari?"

"Is Tu-Kila-Kila coming?" some of the warriors asked,
with bated breath.

"How should he not come?" the old chief asked, drawing himself up very erect. "Know you not the mysteries?
The rain has put out all the fires in Boupari. The King of
Fire himself, even his hearth is cold. He tried his best in
the storm to keep his sacred embers still smouldering; but
the King of the Rain was stronger than he was, and put it
out at last in spite of his endeavors. Be careful, therefore,
how you deal with the King of the Rain, who comes down
among lightnings, and is so very powerful."

"And Tu-Kila-Kila comes to fetch fresh fire?" one of
the nearest savages asked, with profound awe.

"He comes to fetch fresh fire, new fire from the sun,"
the old man answered, with awe in his voice. "These for-
eign gods, are they not strangers from the sun? They
have brought the divine seeds of fire, growing in a shining
box that reflects the sunlight. They need no rubbing-
sticks and no drill to kindle fresh flame. They touch the
seed on the box, and, lo, like a miracle, fire bursts forth
from the wood spontaneous. Tu-Kila-Kila comes, to behold this miracle."

The warriors hung back with doubtful eyes for a moment. Then they spoke with one accord, "Tu-Kila-Kila
shall decide. Tu-Kila-Kila! Tu-Kila-Kila! If the great
god says the Taboo holds good, we will not hurt or offend
the strangers. But if the great god says the Taboo is
broken, and we are all without sin—then, Korong! Korong!
we will kill them! We will eat them!"

As the two parties thus stood glaring at one another,
across that narrow imaginary wall, another cry went up to
heaven at the distant sound of a peculiar tom-tom. "Tu-

Kila-Kila comes!" they shouted. "Our great god ap-
proaches! Women, begone! Men, hide your eyes! Fly,
fly from the brightness of his face, which is as the sun in
glory! Tu-Kila-Kila comes! Fly far, all profane ones!"

And in a moment the women had disappeared into space,
and the men lay flat on the moist ground with low groans
of surprise, and hid their faces in their hands in abject terror.

CHAPTER XIII.

AS BETWEEN GODS.

Tu-Kila-Kila came up in his grandest panoply. The
great umbrella, with the hanging cords, rose high over his
head; the King of Fire and the King of Water, in their
robes of state, marched slowly by his side; a whole group
of slaves and temple attendants, clapping hands in unison,
followed obedient at his sacred heels. But as soon as he
reached the open space in front of the huts and began to
speak, Felix could easily see, in spite of his own agitation
and the excitement of the moment, that the implacable
god himself was profoundly frightened. Last night's storm
had, indeed, been terrible; but Tu-Kila-Kila mentally
coupled it with Felix's attitude toward himself at their last
interview, and really believed in his own heart he had met,
after all, with a stronger god, more powerful than himself,
who could make the clouds burst forth in fire and the
earth tremble. The savage swaggered a good deal, to be
sure, as is often the fashion with savages when frightened;
but Felix could see between the lines, that he swaggered
only on the familiar principle of whistling to keep your
courage up, and that in his heart of hearts he was most
unspeakably terrified.

"You did not do well, O King of the Rain, last night,"
he said, after an interchange of civilities, as becomes
great gods. "You have put out even the sacred flame on

the holy hearth of the King of Fire. You have a bad heart. Why do you use us so?"

"Why do you let your people offer human sacrifices?" Felix answered, boldly, taking advantage of his position. "They are hateful in our sight, these cannibal ways. While we remain on the island, no human life shall be unjustly taken. Do you understand me?"

Tu-Kila-Kila drew back, and gazed around him suspiciously. In all his experience no one had ever dared to address him like that. Assuredly, the stranger from the sun must be a very great god—how great, he hardly dared to himself to realize. He shrugged his shoulders. "When we mighty deities of the first order speak together, face to face," he said, with an uneasy air, "it is not well that the mere common herd of men should overhear our profound deliberations. Let us go inside your hut. Let us confer in private."

They entered the hut alone, Muriel still clinging to Felix's arm, in speechless terror. Then Felix at once began to explain the situation. As he spoke, a baleful light gleamed in Tu-Kila-Kila's eye. The great god removed his mulberry-paper mask. He was evidently delighted at the turn things had taken. If only he dared—but there; he dared not. "Fire and Water would never allow it," he murmured softly to himself. "They know the taboos as well as I do." It was clear to Felix that the savage would gladly have sacrificed him if he dared, and that he made no bones about letting him know it; but the custom of the islanders bound him as tightly as it bound themselves, and he was afraid to transgress it.

"Now listen," Felix said, at last, after a long palaver, looking in the savage's face with a resolute air: "Tu-Kila-Kila, we are not afraid of you. We are not afraid of all your people. I went out alone just now to rescue that child, and, as you see, I succeeded in rescuing it. Your people have wounded me—look at the blood on my arms and chest—but I don't mind for wounds. I mean you to

7

do as I say, and to make your people do so, too. Understand, the nation to which I belong is very powerful. You
have heard of the sailing gods who go over the sea in canoes of fire, as swift as the wind, and whose weapons are
hollow tubes, that belch forth great bolts of lightning and
thunder ? Very well, I am one of them. If ever you harm
a hair of our heads, those sailing gods will before long send
one of their mighty fire-canoes, and bring to bear upon
your island their thunder and lightning, and destroy your
huts, and punish you for the wrong you have ventured to
do us. So now you know. Remember that you act exactly as I tell you."

Tu-Kila-Kila was evidently overawed by the white man's
resolute voice and manner. He had heard before of the
sailing gods (as the Polynesians of the old school still call
the Europeans) ; and though but one or two stray individ-
uals among them had ever reached his remote island
(mostly as castaways), he was quite well enough acquainted with their might and power to be deeply im-
pressed by Felix's exhortation. So he tried to temporize.
"Very well," he made answer, with his jauntiest air, as-
suming a tone of friendly good-fellowship toward his
brother-god. " I will bear it in mind. I will try to humor you. While your time lasts, no man shall hurt you.
But if I promise you that, you must do a good turn for
me instead. You must come out before the people and
give me a new fire from the sun, that you carry in a shining box about with you. The King of Fire has allowed
his sacred flame to go out in deference to your flood ; for
last night, you know, you came down heavily. Never in
my life have I known you come down heavier. The King
of Fire acknowledges himself beaten. So give us light
now before the people, that they may know we are gods,
and may fear to disobey us."

"Only on one condition," Felix answered, sternly ; for
he felt he had Tu-Kila-Kila more or less in his power now,
and that he could drive a bargain with him. Why, he

wasn't sure ; but he saw Tu-Kila-Kila attached a profound importance to having the sacred fire relighted, as he thought, direct from heaven.

"What condition is that ?" Tu-Kila-Kila asked, glancing about him suspiciously.

"Why, that you give up in future human sacrifices."

Tu-Kila-Kila gave a start. Then he reflected for a moment. Evidently, the condition seemed to him a very hard one. "Do you want all the victims for yourself and her, then ?" he asked, with a casual nod aside toward Muriel.

Felix drew back, with horror depicted on every line of his face. "Heaven forbid !" he answered, fervently. "We want no bloodshed, no human victims. We ask you to give up these horrid practices, because they shock and revolt us. If you would have your fire lighted, you must promise us to put down cannibalism altogether henceforth in your island."

Tu-Kila-Kila hesitated. After all, it was only for a very short time that these strangers could thus beard him. Their day would come soon. They were but Korongs. Meanwhile, it was best, no doubt, to effect a compromise. "Agreed," he answered, slowly. "I will put down human sacrifices—so long as you live among us. And I will tell the people your taboo is not broken. All shall be done as you will in this matter. Now, come out before the crowd and light the fire from Heaven."

"Remember," Felix repeated, "if you break your word, my people will come down upon you, sooner or later, in their mighty fire-canoes, and will take vengeance for your crime, and destroy you utterly."

Tu-Kila-Kila smiled a cunning smile. "I know all that," he answered. "I am a god myself, not a fool, don't you see ? You are a very great god, too ; but I am the greater. No more of words between us two. It is as between gods. The fire ! the fire !"

Tu-Kila-Kila replaced his mask. They proceeded from

the hut to the open space within the taboo-line. The people still lay all flat on their faces. " Fire and Water," Tu-Kila-Kila said, in a commanding tone, "come forward and screen me ! "

The King of Fire and the King of Water unrolled a large square of native cloth, which they held up as a screen on two poles in front of their superior deity. Tu-Kila-Kila sat down on the ground, hugging his knees, in the common squatting savage fashion, behind the veil thus readily formed for him. "Taboo is removed," he said, in loud, clear tones. "My people may rise. The light will not burn them. They may look toward the place where Tu-Kila-Kila's face is hidden from them."

The people all rose with one accord, and gazed straight before them.

" The King of Fire will bring dry sticks," Tu-Kila-Kila said, in his accustomed regal manner.

The King of Fire, sticking one pole of the screen into the ground securely, brought forward a bundle of sun-dried sticks and leaves from a basket beside him.

"The King of the Rain, who has put out all our hearths with his flood last night, will relight them again with new fire, fresh flame from the sun, rays of our disk, divine, mystic, wonderful," Tu-Kila-Kila proclaimed, in his droning monotone.

Felix advanced as he spoke to the pile, and struck a match before the eyes of all the islanders. As they saw it light, and then set fire to the wood, a loud cry went up once more, " Tu-Kila-Kila is great ! His words are true ! He has brought fire from the sun ! His ways are wonderful ! "

Tu-Kila-Kila, from his point of vantage behind the curtain, strove to improve the occasion with a theological lesson. " That is the way we have learned from our divine ancestors," he said, slowly ; "the rule of the gods in our island of Boupari. Each god, as he grows old, reincarnates himself visibly. Before he can grow feeble and die he immolates himself willingly on his own altar ; and a younger and a stronger than he receives his spirit. Thus the gods are always young and always with you. Behold myself, Tu-Kila-Kila! Am I not from old times? Am I not very ancient? Have I not passed through many bodies? Do I not spring ever fresh from my own ashes? Do I not eat perpetually the flesh of new victims? Even so with fire. The flames of our island were becoming impure. The King of Fire saw his cinders flickering. So I gave my word. The King of the Rain descended in floods upon them. He put them all out. And now he re-kindles them. They burn up brighter and fresher than ever. They burn to cook my meat, the limbs of my victims. Take heed that you do the King of the Rain no harm as long as he remains within his sacred circle. He is a very great god. He is fierce ; he is cruel. His taboo is not broken. Beware ! Beware ! Disobey at your peril. I, Tu-Kila-Kila, have spoken."

As he spoke, it seemed to Felix that these strange mystic words about each god springing fresh from his own ashes must contain the solution of that dread problem they were trying in vain to read. That, perhaps, was the secret of Korong. If only they could ever manage to understand it !

Tu-Kila-Kila beat his tom-tom twice. In a second all the people fell flat on their faces again. Tu-Kila-Kila rose ; the kings of Fire and Water held the umbrella over him. The attendants on either side clapped hands in time to the sacred tom-tom. With proud, slow tread, the god retraced his steps to his own palace-temple ; and Muriel and Felix were left alone at last in their dusty enclosure.

"Tu-Kila-Kila hates me," Felix said, later in the day, to his attentive Shadow.

"Of course," the young man answered, with a tone of natural assent. "To be sure he hates you. How could he do otherwise? You are Korong. You may any day be his enemy."

"But he's afraid of me, too," Felix went on. "He would have liked to let the people tear me in pieces. Yet he dared not risk it. He seems to dread offending me."

"Of course," the Shadow replied, as readily as before. "He is very much afraid of you. You are Korong. You may any day supplant him. He would like to get rid of you, if he could see his way. But till your time comes he dare not touch you."

"When will my time come?" Felix asked, with that dim apprehension of some horrible end coming over him yet again in all its vague weirdness.

The Shadow shook his head. "That," he answered, "it is not lawful for me so much as to mention. I tell you too far. You will know soon enough. Wait, and be patient."

CHAPTER XIV.

"MR. THURSTAN, I PRESUME."

Naturally enough, it was some time before Felix and Muriel could recover from the shock of their deadly peril. Yet, strange to say, the natives at the end of three days seemed positively to have forgotten all about it. Their loves and their hates were as shortlived as children's. As soon as the period of seclusion was over, their attentions to the two strangers redoubled in intensity. They were evidently most anxious, after this brief disagreement, to reassure the new gods, who came from the sun, of their gratitude and devotion. The men who had wounded Felix, in particular, now came daily in the morning with exceptional gifts of fish, fruit, and flowers; they would bring a crab from the sea, or a joint of turtle-meat. "Forgive us, O king," they cried, prostrating themselves humbly. "We did not mean to hurt you; we thought your time had really come. You are a Korong. We would not offend you. Do not refuse us your showers because of our sin.

We are very penitent. We will do what you ask of us. Your look is poison. See, here is wood ; here are leaves and fire ; we are but your meat ; choose and cook which you will of us ! "

It was useless Felix's trying to explain to them that he wanted no victims, and no propitiation. The more he protested, the more they brought gifts. "He is a very great god," they exclaimed. "He wants nothing from us. What can we give him that will be an acceptable gift ? Shall we offer him ourselves, our wives, our children ? "

As for the women, when they saw how thoroughly frightened of them Muriel now was, they couldn't find means to express their regret and devotion. Mothers brought their little children, whom she had patted on the head, and offered them, just outside the line, as presents for her acceptance. They explained to her Shadow that they never meant to hurt her, and that, if only she would venture without the line, as of old, all should be well, and they would love and adore her. Mali translated to her mistress these speeches and prayers. "Them say, 'You come back, Queenie,' " she explained in her broken Queensland English. " ' Boupari women love you very much. Boupari women glad you come. You kind ; you beautiful ! All Boupari men and women very much pleased with you and the gentleman, because you give back him cocoanut and fruit that you pick in the storm, and because you bring down fresh fire from heaven.' "

Gradually, after several days, Felix's confidence was so far restored that he ventured to stroll beyond the line again ; and he found himself, indeed, most popular among the people. In various ways he picked up gradually the idea that the islanders generally disliked Tu-Kila-Kila, and liked himself ; and that they somehow regarded him as Tu-Kila-Kila's natural enemy. What it could all mean he did not yet understand, though some inklings of an explanation occasionally occurred to him. Oh, how he longed now for the Month of Birds to end, in order that he might pay his

long-deferred visit to the mysterious Frenchman, from
whose voice his Shadow had fled on that fateful evening
with such sudden precipitancy.   The Frenchman, he
judged, must have been long on the island, and could
probably give him some satisfactory solution of this ab-
struse problem.

So he was glad, indeed, when one evening, some weeks
later, his Shadow, observing the sky narrowly, remarked
to him in a low voice, " New moon to-morrow ! The Month
of Birds will then be up.   In the morning you can go and
see your brother god at the Abode of Birds without breaking taboo.   The Month of Turtles begins at sunrise.   My
family god is a turtle, so I know the day for it."

So great was Felix's impatience to settle this question,
that almost before the sun was up next day he had set
forth from his hut, accompanied as usual by his faithful
Shadow.   Their way lay past Tu-Kila-Kila's temple.   As
they went by the entrance with the bamboo posts, Felix
happened to glance aside through the gate to the sacred
enclosure.   Early as it was, Tu-Kila-Kila was afoot already ;
and, to Felix's great surprise, was pacing up and down,
with that stealthy, wary look upon his cunning face that
Muriel had so particularly noted on the day of their first
arrival.   His spear stood in his hand, and his tomahawk
hung by his left side ; he peered about him suspiciously,
with a cautious glance, as he walked round and round the
sacred tree he guarded so continually.   There was something weird and awful in the sight of that savage god, thus
condemned by his own superstition and the custom of his
people to tramp ceaselessly up and down before the sacred
banyan.

At sight of Felix, however, a sudden burst of frenzy
seemed to possess at once all Tu-Kila-Kila's limbs.   He
brandished his spear violently, and set himself spasmodic-
ally in a posture of defence.   His brow grew black, and
his eyes darted out eternal hate and suspicion.   It was
evident he expected an instant attack, and was prepared

with all his might and main to resist aggression. Yet he never offered to desert his post by the tree or to assume the offensive. Clearly, he was guarding the sacred grove itself with jealous care, and was as eager for its safety as for his own life and honor.

Felix passed on, wondering what it all could mean, and turned with an inquiring glance to his trembling Shadow. As for Toko, he had held his face averted meanwhile, lest he should behold the great god, and be scorched to a cinder; but in answer to Felix's mute inquiry he murmured low : "Was Tu-Kila-Kila there? Were all things right? Was he on guard at his post by the tree already?"

"Yes," Felix replied, with that weird sense of mystery creeping over him now more profoundly than ever. "He was on guard by the tree and he looked at me angrily."

"Ah," the Shadow remarked, with a sigh of regret, "he keeps watch well. It will be hard work to assail him. No god in Boupari ever held his place so tight. Who wishes to take Tu-Kila-Kila's divinity must get up early."

They went on in silence to the little volcanic knoll near the centre of the island. There, in the neat garden plot they had observed before, a man, in the last relics of a very tattered European costume, much covered with a short cape of native cloth, was tending his flowers and singing to himself merrily. His back was turned to them as they came up. Felix paused a moment, unseen, and caught the words the stranger was singing :

> " Très jolie,
> Peu polie,
>   Possédant un gros magot ;
> Fort en gueule,
> Pas bégueule ;
> Telle était—"

The stranger looked up, and paused in the midst of his lines, open-mouthed. For a moment he stood and stared

astonished. Then, raising his native cap with a graceful
air, and bowing low, as he would have bowed to a lady on
the Boulevard, he advanced to greet a brother European
with the familiar words, in good educated French, " Monsieur, I salute you ! "

To Felix, the sound of a civilized voice in the midst of
so much strange and primitive barbarism, was like a sudden return to some forgotten world, so deeply and profoundly did it move and impress him. He grasped the
sunburnt Frenchman's rugged hand in his. " Who are
you ? " he cried, in the very best Parisian he could muster
up on the spur of the moment. " And how did you come
here ? "

" Monsieur," the Frenchman answered, no less profoundly moved than himself, " this is, indeed, wonderful !
Do I hear once more that beautiful language spoken ? Do
I find myself once more in the presence of a civilized person ? What fortune ! What happiness ! Ah, it is glorious, glorious."

For some seconds they stood and looked at one another
in silence, grasping their hands hard again and again with
intense emotion ; then Felix repeated his question a second time : " Who are you, monsieur ? and where do you
come from ? "

" Your name, surname, age, occupation ? " the Frenchman repeated, bursting forth at last into national levity.
" Ah, monsieur, what a joy to hear those well-known in-
quiries in my ear once more. I hasten to gratify your
legitimate curiosity. Name : Peyron ; Christian name :
Jules ; age : forty-one ; occupation : convict, escaped
from New Caledonia."

Under any other circumstances that last qualification
might possibly have been held an undesirable one in a
new acquaintance. But on the island of Boupari, among
so many heathen cannibals, prejudices pale before community of blood ; even a New Caledonian convict is at
least a Christian European. Felix received the strange

announcement without the faintest shock of surprise or disgust. He would gladly have shaken hands then and there with M. Jules Peyron, indeed, had he introduced himself in even less equivocal language as a forger, a pickpocket, or an escaped house-breaker.

"And you, monsieur?" the ex-convict inquired, politely.

Felix told him in a few words the history of their accident and their arrival on the island.

"*Comment?*" the Frenchman exclaimed, with surprise and delight. "A lady as well; a charming English lady! What an acquisition to the society of Boupari! *Quelle chance! Quel bonheur!* Monsieur, you are welcome, and mademoiselle too! And in what quality do you live here? You are a god, I see; otherwise you would not have dared to transgress my taboo, nor would this young man —your Shadow, I suppose—have permitted you to do so. But which sort of god, pray? Korong—or Tula?"

"They call me Korong," Felix answered, all tremulous, feeling himself now on the very verge of solving this profound mystery.

"And mademoiselle as well?" the Frenchman exclaimed, in a tone of dismay.

"And mademoiselle as well," Felix replied. "At least, so I make out. We are both Korong. I have many times heard the natives call us so."

His new acquaintance seized his hand with every appearance of genuine alarm and regret. "My poor friend," he exclaimed, with a horrified face, "this is terrible, terrible! Tu-Kila-Kila is a very hard man. What can we do to save your life and mademoiselle's! We are powerless! Powerless! I have only that much to say. I condole with you! I commiserate you!"

"Why, what does Korong mean?" Felix asked, with blanched lips. "Is it then something so very terrible?"

"Terrible! Ah, terrible!" the Frenchman answered, holding up his hands in horror and alarm. "I hardly

know how we can avert your fate. Step within my poor
hut, or under the shade of my Tree of Liberty here, and
I will tell you all the little I know about it."

CHAPTER XV.

THE SECRET OF KORONG.

' "You have lived here long?" Felix asked, with tremulous interest, as he took a seat on the bench under the big
tree, toward which his new host politely motioned him.
"You know the people well, and all their superstitions?"

" *Hélas,* yes, monsieur," the Frenchman answered, with
a sigh of regret. "Eighteen years have I spent altogether in this beast of a Pacific; nine as a convict in New
Caledonia, and nine more as a god here ; and, believe me,
I hardly know which is the harder post. Yours is the first
white face I have ever seen since my arrival in this cursed
island."

"And how did you come here?" Felix asked, half
breathless, for the very magnitude of the stake at issue—
no less a stake than Muriel's life—made him hesitate to
put point-blank the question he had most at heart for the
moment.

"Monsieur," the Frenchman answered, trying to cover
his rags with his native cape, "that explains itself easily.
I was a medical student in Paris in the days of the Com-
mune. Ah! that beloved Paris—how far away it seems
now from Boupari! Like all other students I was advanced—Republican, Socialist—what you will—a political enthusiast. When the events took place—the events
of '70—I espoused with all my heart the cause of the people. You know the rest. The bourgeoisie conquered: I
was taken red-handed, as the Versaillais said—my pistol in
my grasp—an open revolutionist. They tried me by court-
martial—br'r'r—no delay—guilty, M. le Président—hard

labor to perpetuity. They sent me with that brave Louise Michel and so many other good comrades of the cause to New Caledonia. There, nine years of convict life was more than enough for me. One day I found a canoe on the shore—a little Kanaka canoe—you know the type—a mere shapeless dug-out. Hastily I loaded it with food— yam, taro, bread-fruit—I pushed it off into the sea—I em- barked alone—I intrusted myself and all my fortunes to the Bon Dieu and the wide Pacific. The Bon Dieu did not wholly justify my confidence. It is a way he has— that inscrutable one. Six weeks I floated hither and thither before varying winds. At last one evening I reached this island. I floated ashore. And, *enfin, me voilà !* "

"Then you were a political prisoner only ? " Felix said, politely.

M. Jules Peyron drew himself up with much dignity in his tattered costume. "Do I look like a card-sharper, monsieur ? " he asked simply, with offended honor.

Felix hastened to reassure him of his perfect confi- dence. "On the contrary, monsieur," he said, "the mo- ment I heard you were a convict from New Caledonia, I felt certain in my heart you could be nothing less than one of those unfortunate and ill-treated Communards."

"Monsieur," the Frenchman said, seizing his hand a second time, "I perceive that I have to do with a man of honor and a man of feeling. Well, I landed on this isl- and, and they made me a god. From that day to this I have been anxious only to shuffle off my unwelcome divin- ity, and return as a mere man to the shores of Europe. Better be a valet in Paris, say I, than a deity of the best in Polynesia. It is a monotonous existence here—no so- ciety, no life—and the *cuisine*—bah, execrable ! But till the other day, when your steamer passed, I have scarcely even sighted a European ship. A boat came here once, worse luck, to put off two girls (who didn't belong to Boupari), returned indentured laborers from Queensland ;

but, unhappily, it was during my taboo—the Month of
Birds, as my jailers call it—and though I tried to go down
to it or to make signals of distress, the natives stood round
my hut with their spears in line, and prevented me by
main force from signalling to them or communicating
with them.   Even the other day, I never heard of your arrival till a fortnight had elapsed, for I had been sick with
fever, the fever of the country, and as soon as my Shadow
told me of your advent it was my taboo again, and I was
obliged to defer for myself the honor of calling upon my
new acquaintances.   I am a god, of course, and can do
what I like ; but while my taboo is on, *ma foi*, monsieur,
I can hardly call my life my own, I assure you."

"But your taboo is up to-day," Felix said, "so my
Shadow tells me."

"Your Shadow is a well-informed young man," M.
Peyron answered, with easy French sprightliness.   As for
my donkey of a valet, he never by any chance knows or
tells me anything.   I had just sent him out—the pig—to
learn, if possible, your nationality and name, and what
hours you preferred, as I proposed later in the day to pay
my respects to mademoiselle, your friend, if she would
deign to receive me."

"Miss Ellis would be charmed, I'm sure," Felix replied,
smiling in spite of himself at so much Parisian courtliness
under so ragged an exterior.   "It is a great pleasure to
us to find we are not really alone on this barbarous island.
But you were going to explain to me, I believe, the exact
nature of this peril in which we both stand—the precise
distinction between Korong and Tula ? "

"Alas, monsieur," the Frenchman replied, drawing cir-
cles in the dust with his stick with much discomposure,
"I can only tell you I have been trying to make out the
secret of this distinction myself ever since the first day I
came to the island ; but so reticent are all the natives
about it, and so deep is the taboo by which the mystery is
guarded, that even now I, who am myself Tula, can tell you

but very little with certainty on the subject. All I can say for sure is this—that gods called Tula retain their godship in permanency for a very long time, although at the end some violent fate, which I do not clearly understand, is destined to befall them. That is my condition as King of the Birds—for no doubt they have told you that I, Jules Peyron—Republican, Socialist, Communist—have been elevated against my will to the honors of royalty. That is my condition, and it matters but little to me, for I know not when the end may come ; and we can but die once ; how or where, what matters ? Meanwhile, I have my distractions, my little *agréments*—my gardens, my music, my birds, my native friends, my coquetteries, my aviary. As King of the Birds, I keep a small collection of my subjects in the living form, not unworthy of a scientific eye. Monsieur is no ornithologist ? Ah, no, I thought not. Well, for me, it matters little ; my time is long. But for you and Mademoiselle, who are both Korong—" He paused significantly.

"What happens, then, to those who are Korong ?" Felix asked, with a lump in his throat—not for himself, but for Muriel.

The Frenchman looked at him with a doubtful look. "Monsieur," he said, after a pause, " I hardly know how to break the truth to you properly. You are new to the island, and do not yet understand these savages. It is so terrible a fate. So deadly. So certain. Compose your mind to hear the worst. And remember that the worst is very terrible."

Felix's blood froze within him ; but he answered bravely all the same, " I think I have guessed it myself already. The Korong are offered as human sacrifices to Tu-Kila-Kila."

" That is nearly so," his new friend replied, with a solemn nod of his head. "Every Korong is bound to die when his time comes. Your time will depend on the particular date when you were admitted to Heaven."

Felix reflected a moment. "It was on the 26th of last month," he answered, shortly.

"Very well," M. Peyron replied, after a brief calculation. "You have just six months in all to live from that date. They will offer you up by Tu-Kila-Kila's hut the day the sun reaches the summer solstice."

"But why did they make us gods then?" Felix interposed, with tremulous lips. "Why treat us with such honors meanwhile, if they mean in the end to kill us?"

He received his sentence of death with greater calmness than the Frenchman had expected. "Monsieur," the older arrival answered, with a reflective air, "there comes in the mystery. If we could solve that, we could find out also the way of escape for you. For there *is* a way of escape for every Korong : I know it well ; I gather it from all the natives say ; it is a part of their mysteries ; but what it may be, I have hitherto, in spite of all my efforts, failed to discover. All I *do* know is this : Tu-Kila-Kila hates and dreads in his heart every Korong that is elevated to Heaven, and would do anything, if he dared, to get rid of him quietly. But he doesn't dare, because he is bound hand and foot himself, too, by taboos innumerable. Taboo is the real god and king of Boupari. All the island alike bows down to it and worships it."

"Have you ever known Korongs killed?" Felix asked once more, trembling.

"Yes, monsieur. Many of them, alas ! And this is what happens. When the Korong's time is come, as these creatures say, either on the summer or winter solstice, he is bound with native ropes, and carried up so pinioned to Tu-Kila-Kila's temple. In the time before this man was Tu-Kila-Kila, I remember——"

"Stop," Felix cried. "I don't understand. Has there then been more than one Tu-Kila-Kila?"

"Why, yes," the Frenchman answered. "Certainly, many. And there the mystery comes in again. We have always among us one Tu-Kila-Kila or another. He is a

sort of pope, or grand lama, *voyez-vous ?* No sooner is the
last god dead than another god succeeds him and takes his
name, or rather his title. This young man who now holds
the place was known originally as Lavita, the son of Sami.
But what is more curious still, the islanders always treat
the new god as if he were precisely the self-same person
as the old one. So far as I have been able to understand
their theology, they believe in a sort of transmigration of
souls. The soul of the Tu-Kila-Kila who is just dead passes
into and animates the body of the Tu-Kila-Kila who succeeds to the office. Thus they speak as though Tu-Kila-
Kila were a continuous existence ; and the god of the
moment, himself, will even often refer to events which
occurred to him, as he says, a hundred years ago or more,
but which he really knows, of course, only by the persistent tradition of the islanders. They are a very curious
people, these Bouparese. But what would you have ?
Among savages, one expects things to be as among savages."

Felix drew a quiet sigh. It was certain that on the island
of Boupari that expectation, at least, was never doomed to
disappointment. "And when a Korong is taken to Tu-
Kila-Kila's temple," he asked, continuing the subject of
most immediate interest, " what happens next to him ? "

" Monsieur," the Frenchman answered, " I hardly know
whether I do right or not to say the truth to you. Each
Korong is a god for one season only ; when the year
renews itself, as the savages believe, by a change of season,
then a new Korong must be chosen by Heaven to fill the
place of the old ones who are to be sacrificed. This they
do in order that the seasons may be ever fresh and vigorous. Especially is that the case with the two meteorolo-
gical gods, so to speak, the King of the Rain and the Queen
of the Clouds. Those, I understand, are the posts in their
pantheon which you and the lady who accompanies you
occupy."

" You are right," Felix answered, with profoundly pain-

8

ful interest. "And what, then, becomes of the king and queen who are sacrificed ? "

"I will tell you," M. Peyron answered, dropping his voice still lower into a sympathetic key. " But steel your mind for the worst beforehand. It is sufficiently terrible. On the day of your arrival, this, I learn from my Shadow, is just what happened. That night, Tu-Kila-Kila made his great feast, and offered up the two chief human sacrifices of the year, the free-will offering and the scapegoat of trespass. They keep then a festival, which answers to our own New-Year's day in Europe. Next morning, in accordance with custom, the King of the Rain and the Queen of the Clouds were to be publicly slain, in order that a new and more vigorous king and queen should be chosen in their place, who might make the crops grow better and the sky more clement. In the midst of this horrid ceremony, you and mademoiselle, by pure chance, arrived. You were immediately selected by Tu-Kila-Kila, for some reason of his own, which I do not sufficiently understand, but which is, nevertheless, obvious to all the initiated, as the next representatives of the rain-giving gods. You were presented to Heaven on their little platform raised about the ground, and Heaven accepted you. Then you were envisaged with the attributes of divinity ; the care of the rain and the clouds was made over to you ; and immediately after, as soon as you were gone, the old king and queen were laid on an altar near Tu-Kila-Kila's home, and slain with tomahawks. Their flesh was next hacked from their bodies with knives, cooked, and eaten ; their bones were thrown into the sea, the mother of all waters, as the natives call it. And that is the fate, I fear the inevitable fate, that will befall you and mademoiselle at these wretches' hands about the commencement of a fresh season."

Felix knew the worst now, and bent his head in silence. His worst fears were confirmed ; but, after all, even this knowledge was better than so much uncertainty.

And now that he knew when "his time was up," as the natives phrased it, he would know when to redeem his promise to Muriel.

CHAPTER XVI.

A VERY FAINT CLUE.

"But you hinted at some hope, some chance of escape," Felix cried at last, looking up from the ground and mastering his emotion. "What now is that hope? Conceal nothing from me."

"Monsieur," the Frenchman answered, shrugging his shoulders with an expression of utter impotence, "I have as good reasons for wishing to find out all that as even you can have. *Your* secret is *my* secret; but with all my pains and astuteness I have been unable to discover it. The natives are reticent, very reticent indeed, about all these matters. They fear taboo; and they fear Tu-Kila-Kila. The women, to be sure, in a moment of expansion, might possibly tell one; but, then, the women, unfortunately, are not admitted to the mysteries. They know no more of all these things than we do. The most I have been able to gather for certain is this—that on the discovery of the secret depend Tu-Kila-Kila's life and power. Every Boupari man knows this Great Taboo; it is communicated to him in the assembly of adults when he gets tattooed and reaches manhood. But no Boupari man ever communicates it to strangers; and for that reason, perhaps, as I believe, Tu·Kila-Kila often chooses for Korong, as far as possible, those persons who are cast by chance upon the island. It has always been the custom, so far as I can make out, to treat castaways or prisoners taken in war as gods, and then at the end of their term to kill them ruthlessly. This plan is popular with the people at large, because it saves themselves from the dangerous honors of deification ; but it also serves Tu-Kila-Kila's purpose, because it usually elevates to Heaven those innocent persons who are unacquainted with that fatal secret which is, as the natives say, Tu-Kila-Kila's death—his word of dismissal."

"Then if only we could find out this secret—" Felix cried.

His new friend interrupted him. "What hope is there of your finding it out, monsieur," he exclaimed, "you, who have only a few months to live—when I, who have spent nine long years of exile on the island, and seen two Tu-Kila-Kilas rise and fall, have been unable, with my utmost pains, to discover it ? *Tenez;* you have no idea yet of the superstitions of these people, or the difficulties that lie in the way of fathoming them. Come this way to my aviary ; I will show you something that will help you to realize the complexities of the situation."

He rose and led the way to another cleared space at the back of the hut, where several birds of gaudy plumage were fastened to perches on sticks by leathery lashes of dried shark's skin, tied just above their talons. "I am the King of the Birds, monsieur, you must remember," the Frenchman said, fondling one of his screaming *protégés.* "These are a few of my subjects. But I do not keep them for mere curiosity. Each of them is the Soul of the tribe to which it belongs. This, for example—my Cluseret—is the Soul of all the gray parrots ; that that you see yonder—Badinguet, I call him—is the Soul of the hawks ; this, my Mimi, is the Soul of the little yellow-crested kingfisher. My task as King of the Birds is to keep a representative of each of these always on hand ; in which endeavor I am faithfully aided by the whole population of the island, who bring me eggs and nests and young birds in abundance. If the Soul of the little yellow kingfisher now were to die, without a successor being found ready at once to receive and embody it, then the whole race of little yellow kingfishers would vanish altogether ; and if I myself, the

King of the Birds, who am, as it were, the Soul and life of all of them, were to die without a successor being at hand to receive my spirit, then all the race of birds, with one accord, would become extinct forthwith and forever."

He moved among his pets easily, like a king among his subjects. Most of them seemed to know him and love his presence. Presently, he came to one very old parrot, quite different from any Felix had ever seen on any trees in the island ; it was a parrot with a black crest and a red mark on its throat, half blind with age, and tottering on its pedestal. This solemn old bird sat apart from all the others, nodding its head oracularly in the sunlight, and blinking now and again with its white eyelids in a curious senile fashion.

The Frenchman turned to Felix with an air of profound mystery. " This bird," he said, solemnly stroking its head with his hand, while the parrot turned round to him and bit at his finger with half-doddering affection—" this bird is the oldest of all my birds—is it not so, Methuselah ?— and illustrates well in one of its aspects the superstition of these people. Yes, my friend, you are the last of a kind now otherwise extinct, are you not, *mon vieux?* No, no, there—gently ! Once upon a time, the natives tell me, dozens of these parrots existed in the island ; they flocked among the trees, and were held very sacred ; but they were hard to catch and difficult to keep, and the Kings of the Birds, my predecessors, failed to secure an heir and coadjutor to this one. So as the Soul of the species, which you see here before you, grew old and feeble, the whole of the race to which it belonged grew old and feeble with it. One by one they withered away and died, till at last this solitary specimen alone remained to vouch for the former existence of the race in the island. Now, the islanders say, nothing but the Soul itself is left ; and when the Soul dies, the red-throated parrots will be gone forever. One of my predecessors paid with his life in awful tortures for his remissness in not providing for the succession to the

soulship. I tell you these things in order that you may
see whether they cast any light for you upon your own
position ; and also because the oldest and wisest natives
say that this parrot alone, among beasts or birds or unini-
tiated things, knows the secret on which depends the life
of the Tu-Kila-Kila for the time being."

"Can the parrot speak ?" Felix asked, with profound
emotion.

"Monsieur, he can speak, and he speaks frequently.
But not one word of all he says is comprehensible either
to me or to any other living being. His tongue is that of
a forgotten nation. The islanders understand him no
more than I do. He has a very long sermon or poem,
which he knows by heart, in some unknown language, and
he repeats it often at full length from time to time, especially when he has eaten well and feels full and happy. The
oldest natives tell a romantic legend about this strange
recitation of the good Methuselah—I call him Methuselah
because of his great age—but I do not really know whether
their tale is true or purely fanciful. You never can trust
these Polynesian traditions."

"What is the legend ?" Felix asked, with intense interest. " In an island where we find ourselves so girt round
by mystery within mystery, and taboo within taboo, as this,
every key is worth trying. It is well for us at least to
learn everything we can about the ideas of the natives.
Who knows what clue may supply us at last with the
missing link, which will enable us to break through this
intolerable servitude ? "

"Well, the story they tell us is this," the Frenchman
replied, "though I have gathered it only a hint at a time,
from very old men, who declared at the same moment
that some religious fear—of which they have many—prevented them from telling me any further about it. It
seems that a long time ago—how many years ago nobody
knows, only that it was in the time of the thirty-ninth Tu-
Kila-Kila, before the reign of Lavita, the son of Sami—a

strange Korong was cast up upon this island by the waves
of the sea, much as you and I have been in the present generation. By accident, says the story, or else, as others aver,
through the indiscretion of a native woman who fell in love
with him, and who worried the taboo out of her husband,
the stranger became acquainted with the secret of Tu-Kila-
Kila. As the natives themselves put it, he learned the
Death of the High God, and where in the world his Soul
was hidden. Thereupon, in some mysterious way or
other, he became Tu-Kila-Kila himself, and ruled as High
God for ten years or more here on this island. Now, up
to that time, the legend goes on, none but the men of the
island knew the secret; they learned it as soon as they
were initiated in the great mysteries, which occur before
a boy is given a spear and admitted to the rank of com-
plete manhood. But sometimes a woman was told the
secret wrongfully by her husband or her lover; and one
such woman, apparently, told the strange Korong, and so
enabled him to become Tu-Kila-Kila."

"But where does the parrot come in?" Felix asked,
with still profounder excitement than ever. Something
within him seemed to tell him instinctively he was now
within touch of the special key that must sooner or later
unlock the mystery.

"Well," the Frenchman went on, still stroking the parrot affectionately with his hand, and smoothing down the
feathers on its ruffled back, "the strange Tu-Kila-Kila,
who thus ruled in the island, though he learned to speak
Polynesian well, had a language of his own, a language
of the birds, which no man on earth could ever talk with
him. So, to beguile his time and to have someone who
could converse with him in his native dialect, he taught
this parrot to speak his own tongue, and spent most of his
days in talking with it and fondling it. At last, after he
had instructed it by slow degrees how to repeat this long
sermon or poem—which I have often heard it recite in a
sing-song voice from beginning to end—his time came, as

they say, and he had to give way to another Tu-Kila-Kila ;
for the Bouparese have a proverb like our own about the
king, 'The High God is dead ; may the High God live
forever !'   But before he gave up his Soul to his successor, and was eaten or buried, whichever is the custom,
he handed over his pet to the King of the Birds, strictly
charging all future bearers of that divine office to care for
the parrot as they would care for a son or a daughter.
And so the natives make much of the parrot to the present day, saying he is greater than any, save a Korong or
a god, for he is the Soul of a dead race, summing it up in
himself, and he knows the secret of the Death of Tu-Kila-
Kila."

"But you can't tell me what language he' speaks ? "
Felix asked with a despairing gesture.   It was terrible
to stand thus within measurable distance of the secret
which might, perhaps, save Muriel's life, and yet be perpetually balked by wheel within wheel of more than
Egyptian mystery.

"Who can say ? " the Frenchman answered, shrugging
his shoulders helplessly.   "It isn't Polynesian ; that I
know well, for I speak Bouparese now like a native of
Boupari ; and it isn't the only other language spoken at
the present day in the South Seas—the Melanesian of
New Caledonia—for that I learned well from the Kanakas
while I was serving my time as a convict among them.
All we can say for certain is that it may, perhaps, be
some very ancient tongue.   For parrots, we know, are im-
mensely long-lived.   Some of them, it is said, exceed
their century.   Is it not so, eh, my friend Methuselah ? "

CHAPTER XVII.

FACING THE WORST.

Muriel, meanwhile, sat alone in her hut, frightened at Felix's unexpected disappearance so early in the morning, and anxiously awaiting her lover's return, for she made no pretences now to herself that she did not really love Felix. Though the two might never return to Europe to be husband and wife, she did not doubt that before the eye of Heaven they were already betrothed to one another as truly as though they had plighted their troth in solemn fashion. Felix had risked his life for her, and had brought all this misery upon himself in the attempt to save her. Felix was now all the world that was left her. With Felix, she was happy, even on this horrible island ; without him, she was miserable and terrified, no matter what happened.

"Mali," she cried to her faithful attendant, as soon as she found Felix was missing from his tent, "what's become of Mr. Thurstan ? Where can he be gone, I wonder, this morning ? "

"You no fear, Missy Queenie," Mali answered, with the childish confidence of the native Polynesian. "Mistah Thurstan, him gone to see man-a-oui-oui, the King of the Birds. Month of Birds finish last night ; man-a-oui-oui no taboo any longer. King of the Birds keep very old parrot, Boupari folk tell me ; and old parrot very wise, know how to make Tu-Kila-Kila. Mistah Thurstan, him gone to find man-a-oui-oui. Parrot tell him plenty wise thing. Parrot wiser than Boupari people ; know very good medicine ; wise like Queensland lady and gentleman." And Mali set herself vigorously to work to wash the wooden platter on which she served up her mistress's yam for breakfast.

It was curious to Muriel to see how readily Mali had

slipped from savagery to civilization in Queensland, and how easily she had slipped back again from civilization to savagery in Boupari. In waiting on her mistress she was just the ordinary trained native Australian servant ; in every other respect she was the simple unadulterated heathen Polynesian. She recognized in Muriel a white lady of the English sort, and treated her within the hut as white ladies were invariably treated in Queensland ; but she considered that at Boupari one must do as Boupari does, and it never for a moment occurred to her simple mind to doubt the omnipotence of Tu-Kila-Kila in his island realm any more than she had doubted the omnipotence of the white man and his local religion in their proper place (as she thought it) in Queensland.

An hour or two passed before Felix returned. At last he arrived, very white and pale, and Muriel saw at once by the mere look on his face that he had learned some terrible news at the Frenchman's.

"Well, you found him ?" she cried, taking his hand in hers, but hardly daring to ask the fatal question at once.

And Felix, sitting down, as pale as a ghost, answered faintly, " Yes, Muriel, I found him !"

"And he told you everything ? "

"Everything he knew, my poor child. Oh, Muriel, Muriel, don't ask me what it is. It's too terrible to tell you."

Muriel clasped her white hands together, held bloodless downward, and looked at him fixedly. "Mali, you can go," she said. And the Shadow, rising up with childish confidence, glided from the hut, and left them, for the first time since their arrival on the central island, alone together.

Muriel looked at him once more with the same deadly fixed look. "With you, Felix," she said, slowly, " I can bear or dare anything. I feel as if the bitterness of death were past long ago. I know it must come. I only want

to be quite sure when. . . . And besides, you must
remember, I have your promise."

Felix clasped his own hands despondently in return,
and gazed across at her from his seat a few feet off in unspeakable misery.

"Muriel," he cried, "I couldn't. I haven't the heart.
I daren't."

Muriel rose and laid her hand solemnly on his arm.
"You will!" she answered, boldly. "You can! You
must! I know I can trust your promise for that. This
moment, if you like. I would not shrink. But you will
never let me fall alive into the hands of those wretches.
Felix, from *your* hand I could stand anything. I'm not
afraid to die. I love you too dearly."

Felix held her white little wrist in his grasp and sobbed
like a child. Her very bravery and confidence seemed to
unman him, utterly.

She looked at him once more. "When?" she asked,
quietly, but with lips as pale as death.

"In about four months from now," Felix answered,
endeavoring to be calm.

"And they will kill us both?"

"Yes, both. I think so."

"Together?"

"Together."

Muriel drew a deep sigh.

"Will you know the day beforehand?" she asked.

"Yes. The Frenchman told me it. He has known
others killed in the self-same fashion."

"Then, Felix—the night before it comes, you will
promise me, will you?"

"Muriel, Muriel, I could never dare to kill you."

She laid her hand soothingly on his. She stroked him
gently. "You are a man," she said, looking up into his
eyes with confidence. "I trust you. I believe in you.
I know you will never let these savages hurt me. . . .
Felix, in spite of everything, I've been happier since we

came to this island together than ever I have been in my
life before. I've had my wish. I didn't want to miss in
life the one thing that life has best worth giving. I haven't
missed it now. I know I haven't ; for I love you, and you
love me. After that, I can die, and die gladly. If I die
with *you*, that's all I ask. These seven or eight terrible
weeks have made me feel somehow unnaturally calm.
When I came here first I lived all the time in an agony of
terror. I've got over the agony of terror now. I'm quite
resigned and happy. All I ask is to be saved—by you—
from the cruel hands of these hateful cannibals."

Felix raised her white hand just once to his lips. It
was the first time he had ever ventured to kiss her. He
kissed it fervently. She let it drop as if dead by her side.

"Now tell me all that happened," she said. "I'm strong
enough to bear it. I feel such a woman now—so wise and
calm. These few weeks have made me grow from a girl
into a woman all at once. There's nothing I daren't hear,
if you'll tell me it, Felix."

Felix took up her hand again and held it in his, as he
narrated the whole story of his visit to the Frenchman.
When Muriel had heard it, she said once more, slowly, "I
don't think there's any hope in all these wild plans of playing off superstition against superstition. To my mind
there are only two chances left for us now. One is to
concoct with the Frenchman some means of getting away
by canoe from the island—I'd rather trust the sea than the
tender mercy of these dreadful people ; the other is to
keep a closer lookout than ever for the merest chance of
a passing steamer."

Felix drew a deep sigh. "I'm afraid neither's much
use," he said. "If we tried to get away, dogged as we
are, day and night, by our Shadows, the natives would
follow us with their war-canoes in battle array and hack
us to pieces ; for Peyron says that, regarding us as gods,
they think the rain would vanish from their island forever
if once they allowed us to get away alive and carry the

luck with us. And as to the steamers, we haven't seen a trace of one since we left the Australasian. Probably it was only by the purest accident that even she ever came so close in to Boupari."

"At any rate," Muriel cried, still clasping his hand tight, and letting the tears now trickle slowly down her pale white cheeks, "we can talk it all over some day with M. Peyron."

"We can talk it over to-day," Felix answered, "if it comes to that ; for Peyron means to step round, he says, a little later in the afternoon, to pay his respects to the first white lady he has ever seen since he left New Caledonia."

CHAPTER XVIII.

TU-KILA-KILA PLAYS A CARD.

Before the Frenchman could carry out his plan, however, he was himself the recipient of the high honor of a visit from his superior god and chief, Tu-Kila-Kila.

Every day and all day long, save on a few rare occasions when special duties absolved him, the custom and religion of the islanders prescribed that their supreme incarnate deity should keep watch and ward without cessation over the great spreading banyan-tree that overshadowed with its dark boughs his temple-palace. High god as he was held to be, and all-powerful within the limits of his own strict taboos, Tu-Kila-Kila was yet as rigidly bound within those iron laws of custom and religious usage as the meanest and poorest of his subject worshippers. From sunrise to sunset, and far on into the night, the Pillar of Heaven was compelled to prowl up and down, with spear in hand and tomahawk at side, as Felix had so often seen him, before the sacred trunk, of which he appeared to be in some mysterious way the appointed guardian. His very power, it seemed, was intimately bound up with the performance

of that ceaseless and irksome duty ; he was a god in whose
hands the lives of his people were but as dust in the balance ; but he remained so only on the onerous condition
of pacing to and fro, like a sentry, forever before the still
more holy and venerable object he was chosen to protect
from attack or injury. Had he failed in his task, had he
slumbered at his post, all god though he might be, his
people themselves would have risen in a body and torn
him limb from limb before their ancestral fetich as a sacrilegious pretender.

   At certain times and seasons, however, as for example
at all high feasts and festivals, Tu-Kila-Kila had respite for
a while from this constant treadmill of mechanical divinity. Whenever the moon was at the half-quarter, or the
planets were in lucky conjunctions, or a red glow lit up
the sky by night, or the sacred sacrificial fires of human
flesh were lighted, then Tu·Kila·Kila could lay aside his
tomahawk and spear, and become for a while as the islanders, his fellows, were. At other times, too, when he
went out in state to visit the lesser deities of his court, the
King of Fire and the King of Water made a solemn taboo
before he left his home, which protected the sacred tree
from aggression during its guardian's absence. Then Tu-
Kila·Kila, shaded by his divine umbrella, and preceded by
the noise of the holy tom-toms, could go like a monarch
over all parts of his realm, giving such orders as he
pleased (within the limits of custom) to his inferior officers.
It was in this way that he now paid his visit to M. Jules
Peyron, King of the Birds. And he did so for what to
him were amply sufficient reasons.

   It had not escaped Tu-Kila-Kila's keen eye, as he paced
among the skeletons in his yard that morning, that Felix
Thurstan, the King of the Rain, had taken his way openly
toward the Frenchman's quarters. He felt pretty sure,
therefore, that Felix had by this time learned another white
man was living on the island ; and he thought it an ominous fact that the new-comer should make his way toward

his fellow-European's hut on the very first morning when
the law of taboo rendered such a visit possible. The savage is always by nature suspicious ; and Tu-Kila-Kila had
grounds enough of his own for suspicion in this particular
instance. The two white men were surely brewing mischief together for the Lord of Heaven and Earth, the Il-
luminer of the Glowing Light of the Sun ; he must make
haste and see what plan they were concocting against the
sacred tree and the person of its representative, the King
of Plants and of the Host of Heaven.

But it isn't so easy to make haste when all your movements are impeded and hampered by endless taboos and
a minutely annoying ritual. Before Tu-Kila-Kila could
get himself under way, sacred umbrella, tom-toms, and all,
it was necessary for the King of Fire and the King of
Water to make taboo on an elaborate scale with their re-
spective elements ; and so by the time the high god had
reached M. Jules Peyron's garden, Felix Thurstan had already some time since returned to Muriel's hut and his
own quarters.

Tu-Kila-Kila approached the King of the Birds, amid
loud clapping of hands, with considerable haughtiness.
To say the truth, there was no love lost between the cannibal god and his European subordinate. The savage,
puffed up as he was in his own conceit, had nevertheless
always an uncomfortable sense that, in his heart of hearts,
the impassive Frenchman had but a low opinion of him.
So he invariably tried to make up by the solemnity of his
manner and the loudness of his assertions for any trifling
scepticism that might possibly exist in the mind of his
follower.

On this particular occasion, as he reached the Frenchman's plot, Tu-Kila-Kila stepped forward across the white
taboo-line with a suspicious and peering eye. "The King
of the Rain has been here," he said, in a pompous tone, as
the Frenchman rose and saluted him ceremoniously. "Tu-
Kila-Kila's eyes are sharp. They never sleep. The sun

is his sight. He beholds all things. You cannot hide aught in heaven or earth from the knowledge of him that dwells in heaven. I look down upon land and sea, and spy out all that takes place or is planned in them. I am very holy and very cruel. I see all earth and I drink the blood of all men. The King of the Rain has come this morning to visit the King of the Birds. Where is he now? What has your divinity done with him?"

He spoke from under the sheltering cover of his veiled umbrella. The Frenchman looked back at him with as little love as Tu-Kila-Kila himself would have displayed had his face been visible. "Yes, you are a very great god," he answered, in the conventional tone of Polynesian adulation, with just a faint under-current of irony running through his accent as he spoke. "You say the truth. You do, indeed, know all things. What need for me, then, to tell you, whose eye is the sun, that my brother, the King of the Rain, has been here and gone again? You know it yourself. Your eye has looked upon it. My brother was indeed with me. He consulted me as to the showers I should need from his clouds for the birds, my subjects."

"And where is he gone now?" Tu-Kila-Kila asked, without attempting to conceal the displeasure in his tone, for he more than half suspected the Frenchman of a sacrilegious and monstrous design of chaffing him.

The King of the Birds bowed low once more. "Tu-Kila-Kila's glance is keener than my hawk's," he answered, with the accustomed Polynesian imagery. "He sees over the land with a glance, like my parrots, and over the sea with sharp sight, like my albatrosses. He knows where my brother, the King of the Rain, has gone. For me, who am the least among all the gods, I sit here on my perch and blink like a crow. I do not know these things. They are too high and too deep for me."

Tu-Kila-Kila did not like the turn the conversation was taking. Before his own attendants such hints, indeed, were almost dangerous. Once let the savage begin to doubt, and the Moral Order goes with a crash immediately. Besides, he must know what these white men had been talking about. "Fire and Water," he said in a loud voice, turning round to his two chief satellites, "go far down the path, and beat the tom-toms. Fence off with flood and flame the airy height where the King of the Birds lives; fence it off from all profane intrusion. I wish to confer in secret with this god, my brother. When we gods talk together, it is not well that others should hear our converse. Make a great Taboo. I, Tu-Kila-Kila, myself have said it."

Fire and Water, bowing low, backed down the path, beating tom-toms as they went, and left the savage and the Frenchman alone together.

As soon as they were gone, Tu-Kila-Kila laid aside his umbrella with a positive sigh of relief. Now his fellow-countrymen were well out of the way, his manner altered in a trice, as if by magic. Barbarian as he was, he was quite astute enough to guess that Europeans cared nothing in their hearts for all his mumbo-jumbo. He believed in it himself, but they did not, and their very unbelief made him respect and fear them.

"Now that we two are alone," he said, glancing carelessly around him, "we two who are gods, and know the world well—we two who see everything in heaven or earth—there is no need for concealment—we may talk as plainly as we will with one another. Come, tell me the truth! The new white man has seen you?"

"He has seen me, yes, certainly," the Frenchman admitted, taking a keen look deep into the savage's cunning eyes.

"Does he speak your language—the language of birds?" Tu-Kila-Kila asked once more, with insinuating cunning. "I have heard that the sailing gods are of many languages. Are you and he of one speech or two? Aliens, or countrymen?"

"He speaks my language as he speaks Polynesian," the

9   (

Frenchman replied, keeping his eye firmly fixed on his doubtful guest, "but it is not his own. He has a tongue apart—the tongue of an island not far from my country, which we call England."

Tu-Kila-Kila drew nearer, and dropped his voice to a confidential whisper. "Has he seen the Soul of all dead parrots?" he asked, with keen interest in his voice. "The parrot that knows Tu-Kila-Kila's secret? That one over there—the old, the very sacred one?"

M. Peyron gazed round his aviary carelessly. "Oh, that one," he answered, with a casual glance at Methu-selah, as though one parrot or another were much the same to him. "Yes, I think he saw it. I pointed it out to him, in fact, as the oldest and strangest of all my sub-jects."

Tu-Kila-Kila's countenance fell. "Did he hear it speak?" he asked, in evident alarm. "Did it tell him the story of Tu-Kila-Kila's secret?"

"No, it didn't speak," the Frenchman answered. "It seldom does now. It is very old. And if it did, I don't suppose the King of the Rain would have understood one word of it. Look here, great god, allay your fears. You're a terrible coward. I expect the real fact about the parrot is this : it is the last of its own race ; it speaks the language of some tribe of men who once inhabited these islands, but are now extinct. No human being at present alive, most probably, knows one word of that for-gotten language."

"You think not?" Tu-Kila-Kila asked, a little re-lieved.

"I am the King of the Birds, and I know the voices of my subjects by heart ; I assure you it is as I say," M. Peyron answered, drawing himself up solemnly.

Tu-Kila-Kila looked askance, with something very closely approaching a wink in his left eye. "We two are both gods," he said, with a tinge of irony in his tone. "We know what that means. . . . *I* do not feel so certain."

He stood close by the parrot with itching fingers. "It is very, very old," he went on to himself, musingly. "It can't live long. And then—none but Boupari men will know the secret."

As he spoke he darted a strange glance of hatred toward the unconscious bird, the innocent repository, as he firmly believed, of the secret that doomed him. The Frenchman had turned his back for a moment now, to fetch out a stool. Tu-Kila-Kila, casting a quick, suspicious eye to the right and left, took a step nearer. The parrot sat mumbling on its perch, inarticulately, putting its head on one side, and blinking its half-blinded eyes in the bright tropical sunshine. Tu-Kila-Kila paused irresolute before its face for a second. If he only dared—one wring of the neck—one pinch of his finger and thumb almost!—and all would be over. But he dared not! he dared not! Your savage is overawed by the blind terrors of taboo. His predecessor, some elder Tu-Kila-Kila of forgotten days, had laid a great charm upon that parrot's life. Whoever hurt it was to die an awful death of unspeakable torment. The King of the Birds had special charge to guard it. If even the Cannibal God himself wrought it harm, who could tell what judgment might fall upon him forthwith, what terrible vengeance the dead Tu-Kila-Kila might wreak upon him in his ghostly anger? And that dead Tu-Kila-Kila was his own Soul! His own Soul might flare up within him in some mystic way and burn him to ashes.

And yet—suppose this hateful new-comer, the King of the Rain, whom he had himself made Korong on purpose to get rid of him the more easily, and so had elevated into his own worst potential enemy—suppose this new-comer, the King of the Rain, were by chance to speak that other dialect of the bird-language, which the King of the Birds himself knew not, but which the parrot had learned from his old master, the ancient Tu-Kila-Kila of other days, and in which the bird still recited the secret of the sacred tree and the Death of the Great God—ah, then he might still have to fight hard for his divinity. He gazed angrily at the bird. Methuselah blinked, and put his head on one side, and looked craftily askance at him. Tu-Kila-Kila hated it, that insolent creature. Was he not a god, and should he be thus bearded in his own island by a mere Soul of dead birds, a poor, wretched parrot ? But the curse ! What might not that portend ? Ah, well, he would risk it. Glancing around him once more to the right and left, to make sure that nobody was looking, the cunning savage put forth his hand stealthily, and tried with a friendly caress to seize the parrot.

In a moment, before he had time to know what was happening, Methuselah—sleepy old dotard as he seemed —had woke up at once to a sense of danger. Turning suddenly round upon the sleek, caressing hand, he darted his beak with a vicious peck at his assailant, and bit the divine finger of the Pillar of Heaven as carelessly as he would have bitten any child on Boupari. Tu-Kila-Kila, thunder-struck, drew back his arm with a start of surprise and a loud cry of pain. The bird had wounded him. He shook his hand and stamped. Blood was dropping on the ground from the man-god's finger. He hardly knew what strange evil this omen of harm might portend for the world. The Soul of all dead parrots had carried out the curse, and had drawn red drops from the sacred veins of Tu-Kila-Kila.

One must be a savage one's self, and superstitious at that, fully to understand the awful significance of this deadly occurrence. To draw blood from a god, and, above all, to let that blood fall upon the dust of the ground, is the very worst luck—too awful for the human mind to contemplate.

At the same moment, the parrot, awakened by the un-expected attack, threw back its head on its perch, and, laughing loud and long to itself in its own harsh way, be-gan to pour forth a whole volley of oaths in a guttural language, of which neither Tu-Kila-Kila nor the Frenchman understood one syllable. And at the same moment, too, M. Peyron himself, recalled from the door of his hut by Tu-Kila-Kila's sharp cry of pain and by his liege subject's voluble flow of loud speech and laughter, ran up all agog to know what was the matter.

Tu-Kila-Kila, with an effort, tried to hide in his robe his wounded finger. But the Frenchman caught at the meaning of the whole scene at once, and interposed himself hastily between the parrot and its assailant. "*Hé!* my Methuselah," he cried, in French, stroking the exultant bird with his hand, and smoothing its ruffled feathers, "did he try to choke you, then? Did he try to get over you? That was a brave bird! You did well, *mon ami,* to bite him! . . . No, no, Life of the World, and Measurer of the Sun's Course," he went on, in Polynesian, "you shall not go near him. Keep your distance, I beg of you. You may be a high god—though you were a scurvy wretch enough, don't you recollect, when you were only Lavita, the son of Sami—but I know your tricks. Hands off from my birds, say I. A curse is on the head of the Soul of dead parrots. You tried to hurt him, and see how the curse has worked itself out! The blood of the great god, the Pillar of Heaven, has stained the gray dust of the island of Boupari."

Tu-Kila-Kila stood sucking his finger, and looking the very picture of the most savage sheepishness.

CHAPTER XIX.

DOMESTIC BLISS.

Tu-Kila-Kila went home that day in a very bad humor. The portent of the bitten finger had seriously disturbed him. For, strange as it sounds to us, he really believed himself in his own divinity; and the bare thought that the holy soil of earth should be dabbled and wet with the

blood of a god gave him no little uneasiness in his own
mind on his way homeward. Besides, what would his people
think of it if they found it out? At all hazards almost, he
must strive to conceal this episode of the bite from the
men of Boupari. A god who gets wounded, and, worse
still, gets wounded in the very act of trying to break a
great taboo laid on by himself in a previous incarnation—
such a god undoubtedly lays himself open to the gravest
misapprehensions on the part of his worshippers. Indeed,
it was not even certain whether his people, if they knew,
would any longer regard him as a god at all. The devotion
of savages is profound, but it is far from personal. When
deities pass so readily from one body to another, you must
always keep a sharp lookout lest the great spirit should at
any minute have deserted his earthly tabernacle, and have
taken up his abode in a fresh representative. Honor the
gods by all means ; but make sure at the same time what
particular house they are just then inhabiting.

It was the hour of siesta in Tu-Kila-Kila's tent. For a
short space in the middle of the day, during the heat of
the sun, while Fire and Water, with their embers and their
calabash, sat on guard in a porch by the bamboo gate, Tu-
Kila-Kila, Pillar of Heaven and Threshold of Earth, had
respite for a while from his daily task of guarding the
sacred banyan, and could take his ease after his meal in his
own quarters. While that precious hour of taboo lasted,
no wandering dragon or spirit of the air could hurt the
holy tree, and no human assailant dare touch or approach
it. Even the disease-making gods, who walk in the pesti-
lence, could not blight or wither it. At all other times Tu-
Kila-Kila mounted guard over his tree with a jealousy
that fairly astonished Felix Thurstan's soul ; for Felix
Thurstan only dimly understood as yet how implicitly Tu-
Kila-Kila's own life and office were bound up with the inviolability of the banyan he protected.

Within the hut, during that playtime of siesta, while the
lizards (who are also gods) ran up and down the wall, and

puffed their orange throats, Tu-Kila-Kila lounged at his ease that afternoon, with one of his many wives—a tall and beautiful Polynesian woman, lithe and supple, as is the wont of her race, and as exquisitely formed in every limb and feature as a sculptured Greek goddess. A graceful wreath of crimson hibiscus adorned her shapely head, round which her long and glossy black hair was coiled in great rings with artistic profusion. A festoon of blue flowers and dark-red dracæna leaves hung like a chaplet over her olive-brown neck and swelling bust. One breadth of native cloth did duty for an apron or girdle round her waist and hips. All else was naked. Her plump brown arms were set off by the green and crimson of the flowers that decked her. Tu-Kila-Kila glanced at his slave with approving eyes. He always liked Ula ; she pleased him the best of all his women. And she knew his ways, too : she never contradicted him.

Among savages, guile is woman's best protection. The wife who knows when to give way with hypocritical obedience, and when to coax or wheedle her yielding lord, runs the best chance in the end for her life. Her model is not the oak, but the willow. She must be able to watch for the rising signs of ill-humor in her master's mind, and guard against them carefully. If she is wise, she keeps out of her husband's way when his anger is aroused, but soothes and flatters him to the top of his bent when his temper is just slightly or momentarily ruffled.

"The Lord of Heaven and Earth is ill at ease," Ula murmured, insinuatingly, as Tu-Kila-Kila winced once with the pain of his swollen finger. "What has happened to-day to the Increaser of Bread-Fruit ? My lord is sad. His eye is downcast. Who has crossed my master's will ? Who has dared to anger him ? "

Tu-Kila-Kila kept the wounded hand wrapped up in a soft leaf, like a woolly mullein. All the way home he had been obliged to conceal it, and disguise the pain he felt, lest Fire and Water should discover his secret. For he dared not let his people know that the Soul of all dead parrots had bitten his finger, and drawn blood from the sacred veins of the man-god. But he almost hesitated now whether or not he should confide in Ula. A god may surely trust his own wedded wives. And yet—such need to be careful—women are so treacherous! He suspected Ula sometimes of being a great deal too fond of that young man Toko, who used to be one of the temple attendants, and whom he had given as Shadow accordingly to the King of the Rain, so as to get rid of him altogether from among the crowd of his followers. So he kept his own counsel for the moment, and disguised his misfortune. "I· have been to see the King of the Birds this morning," he said, in a grumbling voice ; "and I do not like him. That God is too insolent. For my part I hate these strangers, one and all. They have no respect for Tu-Kila-Kila like the men of Boupari. They are as bad as atheists. They fear not the gods, and the customs of our fathers are not in them."

Ula crept nearer, with one lithe round arm laid caressingly close to her master's neck. "Then why do you make them Korong?" she asked, with feminine curiosity, like some wife who seeks to worm out of her husband the secret of freemasonry. "Why do you not cook them and eat them at once, as soon as they arrive ? They are very good food—so white and fine. That last new-comer, now—the Queen of the Clouds—why not eat her? She is plump and tender."

"I like her," Tu Kila-Kila responded, in a gloating tone. "I like her every way. I would have brought her here to my temple and admitted her at once to be one of Tu-Kila-Kila's wives—only that Fire and Water would not have permitted me. They have too many taboos, those awkward gods. I do not love them. But I make my strangers Korong for a very wise reason. You women are fools; you understand nothing ; you do not know the mysteries. These things are a great deal too high and too deep for you.

monsieur was gone, I retired to my hut, I sat down on
the floor, I gave myself over to tears, tears of joy and
gratitude, to think I should once more catch a glimpse
of civilization! This afternoon, I ask myself, can I venture to go out and pay my respects, thus attired, in
these rags, to a European lady? For a long time I doubt,
I wonder, I hesitate. In my quality of Frenchman, I
would have wished to call in civilized costume upon a
civilized household. But what would you have? Necessity knows no law. I am compelled to envelope myself
in my savage robe of office as a Polynesian god—a robe
of office which, for the rest, is not without an interest of
its own for the scientific ethnologist. It belongs to me
especially as King of the Birds, and in it, in effect, is
represented at least one feather of each kind or color
from every part of the body of every species of bird
that inhabits Boupari. I thus sum up, *pour ainsi dire*,
in my official costume all the birds of the island, as Tu-
Kila-Kila, the very high god, sums up, in his quaint and
curious dress, the land and the sea, the trees and the
stones, earth and air, and fire and water."

Familiarity with danger begets at last a certain callous
indifference. Muriel was surprised in her own mind to
discover how easily they could chat with M. Peyron on
such indifferent subjects, with that awful doom of an approaching death hanging over them so shortly. But the
fact was, terrors of every kind had so encompassed them
round since their arrival on the island that the mere additional certainty of a date and mode of execution was
rather a relief to their minds than otherwise. It partook
of the nature of a reprieve, not of a sentence. Besides, this
meeting with another speaker of a European tongue
seemed to them so full of promise and hope that they
almost forgot the terrors of their threatened end in their
discussion of possible schemes for escape to freedom.
Even M. Peyron himself, who had spent nine long years
of exile in the island, felt that the arrival of two new

You could not comprehend them. But men know well why. They are wise; they have been initiated. Much more, then, do I, who am the very high god—who eat human flesh and drink blood like water—who cause the sun to shine and the fruits to grow—without whom the day in heaven would fade and die out, and the foundations of the earth would be shaken like a plantain leaf."

Ula laid her soft brown hand soothingly on the great god's arm just above the elbow. "Tell me," she said, leaning forward toward him, and looking deep into his eyes with those great speaking gray orbs of hers; "tell me, O Sustainer of the Equipoise of Heaven; I know you are great; I know you are mighty; I know you are holy and wise and cruel; but why must you let these sailing gods who come from unknown lands beyond the place where the sun rises or sets—why must you let them so trouble and annoy you? Why do you not at once eat them up and be done with them? Is not their flesh sweet? Is not their blood red? Are they not a dainty well fit for the banquet of Tu-Kila-Kila?"

The savage looked at her for a moment and hesitated. A very beautiful woman this Ula, certainly. Not one of all his wives had larger brown limbs, or whiter teeth, or a deeper respect for his divine nature. He had almost a mind—it was only Ula? Why not break the silence enjoined upon gods toward women, and explain this matter to her? Not the great secret itself, of course—the secret on which hung the Death and Transmigration of Tu-Kila-Kila—oh, no; not that one. The savage was far too cunning in his generation to intrust that final terrible Taboo to the ears of a woman. But the reason why he made all strangers Korong. A woman might surely be trusted with that—especially Ula. She was so very handsome. And she was always so respectful to him.

"Well, the fact of it is," he answered, laying his hand on her neck, that plump brown neck of hers, under the garland of dracæna leaves, and stroking it voluptuously,

"the sailing gods who happen upon this island from time
to time are made Korong—but hush! it is taboo." He
gazed around the hut suspiciously. "Are all the others
away?" he asked, in a frightened tone. "Fire and Water
would denounce me to all my people if once they found I
had told a taboo to a woman. And as for you, they would
take you, because you knew it, and would pull your flesh
from your bones with hot stone pincers!"

Ula rose and looked about her at the door of the tent.
She nodded thrice; then she glided back, serpentine, and
threw herself gracefully, in a statuesque pose, on the native mat beside him. "Here, drink some more kava," she
cried, holding a bowl to his lips, and wheedling him with
her eyes. "Kava is good; it is fit for gods. It makes
them royally drunk, as becomes great deities. The spirits
of our ancestors dwell in the bowl; when you drink of the
kava they mount by degrees into your heart and head.
They inspire brave words. They give you thoughts of
heaven. Drink, my master, drink. The Ruler of the Sun
in Heaven is thirsty."

She lay propped on one elbow, with her face close to
his; and offered him, with one brown, irresistible hand,
the intoxicating liquor. Tu-Kila-Kila took the bowl, and
drank a second time, for he had drunk of it once with his
dinner already. It was seldom he allowed himself the lux-
ury of a second draught of that very stupefying native in-
toxicant, for he knew too well the danger of insecurely
guarding his sacred tree; but on this particular occasion,
as on so many others in the collective life of humanity,
"the woman tempted him," and he acted as she told him.
He drank it off deep. "Ha, ha! that is good!" he cried,
smacking his lips. "That is a drink fit for a god. No
woman can make kava like you, Ula." He toyed with her
arms and neck lazily once more. "You are the queen of
my wives," he went on, in a dreamy voice. "I like you
so well, that, plump as you are, I really believe, Ula, I
could never make up my mind to eat you."

"My lord is very gracious," Ula made answer, in a soft, low tone, pretending to caress him. And for some minutes more she continued to make much of him in the fulsome strain of Polynesian flattery.

At last the kava had clearly got into Tu Kila-Kila's head. Then Ula bent forward once more and again attacked him. "Now I know you will tell me," she said, coaxingly, "why you make them Korong. As long as I live, I will never speak or hint of it to anybody anywhere. And if I do— why, the remedy is near. I am your meat—take me and eat me."

Even cannibals are human ; and at the touch of her soft hand, Tu-Kila-Kila gave way slowly. "I made them Korong," he answered, in rather thick accents, "because it is less dangerous for me to make them so than to choose for the post from among our own islanders. Sooner or later, my day must come ; but I can put it off best by making my enemies out of strangers who arrive upon our island, and not out of those of my own household. All Boupari men who have been initiated know the terrible secret— they know where lies the Death of Tu-Kila-Kila. The strangers who come to us from the sun or the sea do not know it ; and therefore my life is safest with them. So I make them Korong whenever I can, to prolong my own days, and to guard my secret."

"And the Death of Tu-Kila-Kila ?" the woman whispered, very low, still soothing his arm with her hand and patting his cheek softly from time to time with a gentle, caressing motion. "Tell me where does that live ? Who holds it in charge ? Where is Tu-Kila-Kila's great spirit laid by in safety ? I know it is in the tree ; but where and in what part of it ? "

Tu-Kila-Kila drew back with a little cry of surprise. "You know it is in the tree !" he cried. "You know my soul is kept there ! Why, Ula, who told you that ? and you a woman ! Bad medicine indeed ! Some man has been blabbing what he learned in the mysteries. If this

should reach the ears of the King of the Rain—" he paused
mysteriously.

"What? What?" Ula cried, seizing his hand in hers,
and pressing it hard to her bosom in her anxiety and
eagerness. "Tell me the secret! Tell me!"

With a sudden sharp howl of darting pain, Tu-Kila-Kila
withdrew his hand. She had squeezed the finger the parrot had bitten, and blood began once more to flow from it
freely.

A wild impulse of revenge came over the savage. He
caught her by the neck with his other hand, pressed her
throat hard, till she was black in the face, kicked her
several times with ferocious rage, and then flung her away
from him to the other side of the hut with a fierce and un-
translatable native imprecation.

Ula, shaken and hurt, darted away toward the door,
with a face of abject terror. For every reason on earth
she was intensely alarmed. Were it merely as a matter of
purely earthly fear, she had ground enough for fright in
having so roused the hasty anger of that powerful and
implacable creature. He would kill her and eat her with
far less compunction than an English farmer would kill
and eat one of his own barnyard chickens. But besides
that, it terrified her not a little in more mysterious ways to
see the blood of a god falling upon the earth so freely.
She knew not what awful results to herself and her race
might follow from so terrible a desecration.

But, to her utter astonishment, the great god himself,
mad with rage as he was, seemed none the less almost as
profoundly frightened and surprised as she herself was.
"What did you do that for?" he cried, now sufficiently
recovered for thought and speech, wringing his hand with
pain, and then popping his finger hastily into his mouth
to ease it. "You are a clumsy thing. And you want to
destroy me, too, with your foolish clumsiness."

He looked at her and scowled. He was very angry.
But the savage woman is nothing if not quick-witted and

politic. In a flash of intuition, Ula saw at once he was more frightened than hurt ; he was afraid of the effect of this strange revelation upon his own reputation for supreme godship. With every mark and gesture of deprecatory servility the woman sidled back to his side like a whipped dog. For a second she looked down on the floor at the drops of blood ; then, without one word of warning or one instant's hesitation, she bit her own finger hard till blood flowed from it freely. " I will show this to Fire and Water," she said, holding it up before his eyes, all red and bleeding. " I will say you were angry with me and bit me for a punishment, as you often do. They will never find out it was the blood of a god. Have no fear for their eyes. Let me look at your finger."

Tu-Kila-Kila, half appeased by her clever quickness, held his hand out sulkily, like a disobedient child. Ula examined it close. "A bite," she said, shortly. "A bite from a bird ! a peck from a parrot."

Tu-Kila-Kila jerked out a surly assent. " Yes, the Soul of all dead parrots," he answered, with an angry glare. "It bit me this morning at the King of the Birds'. A vicious brute. But no one else saw it."

Ula put the finger up to her own mouth, and sucked the wound gently. Her medicine stanched it. Then she took a thin leaf of the paper mulberry, soft, cool, and soothing, and bound it round the place with a strip of the lace-like inner bark, as deftly as any hospital nurse in London would have done it. These savage women are capital hands in sickness. Tu-Kila-Kila sat and sulked meanwhile, like a disappointed child. When Ula had finished, she nodded her head and glided softly away. She knew her chance of learning the secret was gone for the moment, and she had too much of the guile of the savage woman to spoil her chances by loitering about unnecessarily while her lord was in his present ungracious humor.

As she stole from the hut, Tu-Kila-Kila, looking ruefully at his wounded hand, and then at that light and supple retreating figure, muttered sulkily to himself, with a very bad grace, "the woman knows too much. She nearly wormed my secret out of me. She knows that Tu-Kila-Kila's life and soul are bound up in the tree. She knows that I bled, and that the parrot bit me. If she blabs, as women will do, mischief may come of it. I am a great god, a very great god—keen, bloodthirsty, cruel. And I like that woman. But it would be wiser and safer, perhaps, after all, to forego my affection and to make a great feast of her."

And Ula, looking back with a smile and a nod, and holding up her own bitten and bleeding hand with a farewell shake, as if to remind her divine husband of her promise to show it to Fire and Water, murmured low to herself as she went, " He is a very great god ; a very great god, no doubt ; but I hate him, I hate him ! He would eat me to-morrow if I didn't coax him and wheedle him and keep him in a good temper. You want to be sharp, indeed, to be the wife of a god. I got off to-day with the skin of my teeth. He might have turned and killed me. If only I could find out the Great Taboo, I would tell it to the stranger, the King of the Rain ; and then, perhaps, Tu-Kila-Kila would die. And the stranger would become Tu-Kila-Kila in turn, and I would be one of his wives ; and Toko, who is his Shadow, would return again to the service of Tu-Kila-Kila's temple."

But Fire, as she passed, was saying to Water, "We are getting tired in Boupari of Lavita, the son of Sami. If the luck of the island is not to change, it is high time, I think, we should have a new Tu-Kila-Kila."

CHAPTER XX.

COUNCIL OF WAR.

That same afternoon Muriel had a visitor. M. Jules Peyron, formerly of the Collége de France, no longer a mere Polynesian god, but a French gentleman of the Boulevards in voice and manner, came to pay his respects, as in duty bound, to Mademoiselle Ellis. M. Peyron had performed his toilet under trying circumstances, to the best of his ability. The remnants of his European clothes, much patched and overhung with squares of native tappa cloth, were hidden as much as possible by a wide feather cloak, very savage in effect, but more seemly, at any rate, than the tattered garments in which Felix had first found him in his own garden parterre. M. Peyron, however, was fully aware of the defects of his costume, and profoundly apologetic. " It is with ten thousand regrets, mademoiselle," he said, many times over, bowing low and simpering, "that I venture to appear in a lady's *salon*— for, after all, wherever a European lady goes, there her *salon* follows her—in such a *tenue* as that in which I am now compelled to present myself. *Mais que voulez-vous? Nous ne sommes pas à Paris!*" For to M. Peyron, as innocent in his way as Mali herself, the whole world divided itself into Paris and the Provinces.

Nevertheless, it was touching to both the new-comers to see the Frenchman's delight at meeting once more with civilized beings. "Figure to yourself, mademoiselle," he said, with true French effusion—"figure to yourself the joy and surprise with which I, this morning, receive monsieur, your friend, at my humble cottage ! For the first time after nine years on this hateful island, I see again a European face ; I hear again the sound, the beautiful sound of that charming French language. My emotion, believe me, was too profound for words. When monsieur was gone, I retired to my hut, I sat down on the floor, I gave myself over to tears, tears of joy and gratitude, to think I should once more catch a glimpse of civilization! This afternoon, I ask myself, can I venture to go out and pay my respects, thus attired, in these rags, to a European lady? For a long time I doubt, I wonder, I hesitate. In my quality of Frenchman, I would have wished to call in civilized costume upon a civilized household. But what would you have? Necessity knows no law. I am compelled to envelope myself in my savage robe of office as a Polynesian god—a robe of office which, for the rest, is not without an interest of its own for the scientific ethnologist. It belongs to me especially as King of the Birds, and in it, in effect, is represented at least one feather of each kind or color from every part of the body of every species of bird that inhabits Boupari. I thus sum up, *pour ainsi dire,* in my official costume all the birds of the island, as Tu-Kila-Kila, the very high god, sums up, in his quaint and curious dress, the land and the sea, the trees and the stones, earth and air, and fire and water."

Familiarity with danger begets at last a certain callous indifference. Muriel was surprised in her own mind to discover how easily they could chat with M. Peyron on such indifferent subjects, with that awful doom of an approaching death hanging over them so shortly. But the fact was, terrors of every kind had so encompassed them round since their arrival on the island that the mere additional certainty of a date and mode of execution was rather a relief to their minds than otherwise. It partook of the nature of a reprieve, not of a sentence. Besides, this meeting with another speaker of a European tongue seemed to them so full of promise and hope that they almost forgot the terrors of their threatened end in their discussion of possible schemes for escape to freedom. Even M. Peyron himself, who had spent nine long years of exile in the island, felt that the arrival of two new

Europeans gave him some hope of effecting at last his own retreat from this unendurable position. His talk was all of passing steamers. If the Australasian had come near enough once to sight the island, he argued, then the homeward-bound vessel, *en route* for Honolulu, must have begun to take a new course considerably to the eastward of the old navigable channel. If this were so, their obvious plan was to keep a watch, day and night, for another passing Australian liner, and whenever one hove in sight, to steal away to the shore, seize a stray canoe, overpower, if possible, their Shadows, or give them the slip, and make one bold stroke for freedom on the open ocean.

None of them could conceal from their own minds, to be sure, the extreme difficulty of carrying out this programme. In the first place, it was a toss-up whether they ever sighted another steamer at all ; for during the weeks they had already passed on the island, not a sign of one had appeared from any quarter. Then, again, even supposing a steamer ever hove in sight, what likelihood that they could make out for her in an open canoe in time to attract attention before she had passed the island? Tu-Kila-Kila would never willingly let them go ; their Shadows would watch them with unceasing care ; the whole body of natives would combine together to prevent their departure. If they ran away at all, they must run for their lives ; as soon as the islanders discovered they were gone, every war-canoe in the place would be manned at once with bloodthirsty savages, who would follow on their track with relentless persistence.

As for Muriel, less prepared for such dangerous adventures than the two men, she was rather inclined to attach a certain romantic importance (as a girl might do) to the story of the parrot and the possible disclosures which it could make if it could only communicate with them. The mysterious element in the history of that unique bird attracted her fancy. "The only one of its race now left alive," she said, with slow reflectiveness. "Like Dolly

10

Pentreath, the last old woman who could speak Cornish!
I wonder how long parrots ever live? Do you know at all,
monsieur ? You are the King of the Birds—you ought to
be an authority on their habits and manners."

The Frenchman smiled a gallant smile. "Unhappily,
mademoiselle," he said, " though, as a medical student, I
took up to a certain extent biological science in general at
the Collége de France, I never paid any special or peculiar
attention in Paris to birds in particular. But it is the
universal opinion of the natives (if that counts for much)
that parrots live to a very great age ; and this one old parrot of mine, whom I call Methuselah on account of his
advanced years, is considered by them all to be a perfect
patriarch. In effect, when the oldest men now living on
the island were little boys, they tell me that Methuselah
was already a venerable and much-venerated parrot. He
must certainly have outlived all the rest of his race by at
least the best part of three-quarters of a century. For the
islanders themselves not infrequently live, by unanimous
consent, to be over a hundred."

"I remember to have read somewhere," Felix said,
turning it over in his mind, "that when Humboldt was
travelling in the wilds of South America he found one very
old parrot in an Indian village, which, the Indians assured
him, spoke the language of an extinct tribe, incomprehensible then by any living person. If I recollect aright,
Humboldt believed that particular bird must have lived to
be nearly a hundred and fifty."

"That is so, monsieur," the Frenchman answered. " I
remember the case well, and have often recalled it. I recollect our professor mentioning it one day in the course
of his lectures. And I have always mentally coupled that
parrot of Humboldt's with my own old friend and subject,
Methuselah. However, that only impresses upon one
more fully the folly of hoping that we can learn anything
worth knowing from him. I have heard him recite his
story many times over, though now he repeats it less fre-

quently than he used formerly to do ; and I feel convinced
it is couched in some unknown and, no doubt, forgotten
language. It is a much more guttural and unpleasant
tongue than any of the soft dialects now spoken in Polynesia. It belonged, I am convinced, to that yet earlier
and more savage race which the Polynesians must have
displaced ; and as such it is now, I feel certain, practically
irrecoverable."

"If they were more savage than the Polynesians," Muriel
said, with a profound sigh, "I'm sorry for anybody who
fell into their clutches."

"But what would not many philologists at home in England give," Felix murmured, philosophically, "for a tran-
script of the words that parrot can speak—perhaps a last
relic of the very earliest and most primitive form of human
language!"

At the very moment when these things were passing
under the wattled roof of Muriel's hut, it happened that
on the taboo-space outside, Toko, the Shadow, stood talking for a moment with Ula, the fourteenth wife of the
great Tu-Kila-Kila.

"I never see you now, Toko," the beautiful Polynesian
said, leaning almost across the white line of coral-sand
which she dared not transgress. "Times are dull at the
temple since you came to be Shadow to the white-faced
stranger."

"It was for that that Tu-Kila-Kila sent me here," the
Shadow answered, with profound conviction. "He is jealous, the great god. He is bad. He is cruel. He wanted
to get rid of me. So he sent me away to the King of the
Rain that I might not see you."

Ula pouted, and held up her wounded finger before his
eyes coquettishly. "See what he did to me," she said,
with a mute appeal for sympathy—though in that particular matter the truth was not in her. "Your god was angry
with me to-day because I hurt his hand, and he clutched

me by the throat, and almost choked me. He has a bad heart. See how he bit me and drew blood. Some of these days, I believe, he will kill me and eat me."

The Shadow glanced around him suspiciously with an uneasy air. Then he whispered low, in a voice half grudge, half terror, "If he does, he is a great god—he can search all the world—I fear him much, but Toko's heart is warm. Let Tu-Kila-Kila look out for vengeance."

The woman glanced across at him open-eyed, with her enticing look. "If the King of the Rain, who is Korong, knew all the secret," she murmured, slowly, "he would soon be Tu-Kila-Kila himself; and you and I could then meet together freely."

The Shadow started. It was a terrible suggestion. "You mean to say—" he cried; then fear overcame him, and, crouching down where he sat, he gazed around him, terrified. Who could say that the wind would not report his words to Tu-Kila-Kila?

Ula laughed at his fears. "Pooh," she answered, smiling. "You are a man; and yet you are afraid of a little taboo. I am a woman; and yet if I knew the secret as you do, I would break taboo as easily as I would break an egg-shell. I would tell the white-faced stranger all—if only it would bring you and me together for-ever."

"It is a great risk, a very great risk," the Shadow an-swered, trembling. "Tu-Kila-Kila is a mighty god. He may be listening this moment, and may pinch us to death by his spirits for our words, or burn us to ashes with a flash of his anger."

The woman smiled an incredulous smile. "If you had lived as near Tu-Kila-Kila as I have," she answered, boldly, "you would think as little, perhaps, of his divinity as I do."

For even in Polynesia, superstitious as it is, no hero is a god to his wives or his valets.

CHAPTER XXI.

METHUSELAH GIVES SIGN.

All the hopes of the three Europeans were concentrated now on the bare off-chance of a passing steamer. M. Peyron in particular was fully convinced that, if the Australasian had found the inner channel practicable, other ships in future would follow her example. With this idea firmly fixed in his head, he arranged with Felix that one or other of them should keep watch alternately by night as far as possible ; and he also undertook that a canoe should constantly be in readiness to carry them away to the supposititious ship, if occasion arose for it. Muriel took counsel with Mali on the question of rousing the Frenchman if a steamer appeared, and they were the first to sight it ; and Mali, in whom renewed intercourse with white people had restored to some extent the civilized Queensland attitude of mind, readily enough promised to assist in their scheme, provided she was herself taken with them, and so relieved from the terrible vengeance which would otherwise overtake her. "If Boupari man catch me," she said, in her simple, graphic, Polynesian way, " Boupari man kill me, and lay me in leaves, and cook me very nice, and make great feast of me, like him do with Jani." From that untimely end both Felix and Muriel promised faithfully, as far as in them lay, to protect her.

To communicate with M. Peyron by daytime, without arousing the ever-wakeful suspicion of the natives, Felix hit upon an excellent plan. He burnished his metal match-box to the very highest polish it was capable of taking, and then heliographed by means of sun-flashes on the Morse code. He had learned the code in Fiji in the course of his official duties ; and he taught the Frenchman now readily enough how to read and reply with the other half of the box, torn off for the purpose.

It was three or four days, however, before the two English wanderers ventured to return M. Peyron's visit. They
didn't wish to attract too greatly the attention of the
islanders. Gradually, as their stay on the island went on,
they learned the truth that Tu-Kila-Kila's eyes, as he himself had boasted, were literally everywhere. For he had
spies of his own, told off in every direction, who dogged
the steps of his victims unseen. Sometimes, as Felix and
Muriel walked unsuspecting through the jungle paths,
closely followed by their Shadows, a stealthy brown figure,
crouched low to the ground, would cross the road for a
moment behind them, and disappear again noiselessly into
the dense mass of underbrush. Then Mali or Toko, turning round, all hushed, with a terrified look, would murmur
low to themselves, or to one another, "There goes one of
the Eyes of Tu-Kila-Kila!" It was only by slow degrees
that this system of espionage grew clear to the strangers;
but as soon as they had learned its reality and ubiquity,
they felt at once how undesirable it would be for them to
excite the terrible man-god's jealousy and suspicion by
being observed too often in close personal intercourse
with their fellow-exile and victim, the Frenchman. It
was this that made them have recourse to the device of
the heliograph.

So three or four days passed before Muriel dared to
approach M. Peyron's cottage. When she did at last go
there with Felix, it was in the early morning, before the
fierce tropical sun, that beat full on the island, had begun
to exert its midday force and power. The path that led
there lay through the thick and tangled mass of brushwood which covered the greater part of the island with its
dense vegetation; it was overhung by huge tree-ferns and
broad-leaved Southern bushes, and abutted at last on the
little wind-swept knoll where the King of the Birds had
his appropriate dwelling-place. The Frenchman received
them with studied Parisian hospitality. He had decorated
his arbor with fresh flowers for the occasion, and bright

tropical fruits, with their own green leaves, did duty for the coffee or the absinthe of his fatherland on his home-made rustic table. Yet in spite of all the rudeness of the physical surroundings, they felt themselves at home again with this one exiled European ; the faint flavor of civili-zation pervaded and permeated the Frenchman's hut, after the unmixed savagery to which they had now been so long accustomed.

Muriel's curiosity, however, centred most about the mys-terious old parrot, of whose strange legend so much had been said to her. After they had sat for a little under the shade of the spreading banyan, to cool down from their walk—for it was an oppressive morning—M. Peyron led her round to his aviary at the back of the hut, and introduced her, by their native names, to all his sub-jects. " I am responsible for their lives," he said, gravely, "for their welfare, for their happiness. If I were to let one of them grow old without a successor in the field to follow him up and receive his soul—as in the case of my friend Methuselah here, who was so neglected by my predecessors—the whole species would die out for want of a spirit, and my own life would atone for that of my peo-ple. There you have the central principle of the theology of Boupari. Every race, every element, every power of nature, is summed up for them in some particular person or thing ; and on the life of that person or thing depends, as they believe, the entire health of the species, the se-quence of events, the whole order and succession of natural phenomena."

Felix approached the mysterious and venerable bird with somewhat incautious fingers. " It looks very old," he said, trying to stroke its head and neck with a friendly gesture. " You do well, indeed, in calling it Methuselah."

As he spoke, the bird, alarmed at the vague conscious-ness of a hand and voice which it did not recognize, and mindful of Tu-Kila-Kila's recent attack, made a vicious peck at the fingers outstretched to caress it, " Take care !"

the Frenchman cried, in a warning voice. "The patriarch's temper is no longer what it was sixty or seventy
years ago. He grows old and peevish. His humor is
soured. He will sing no longer the lively little scraps of
Offenbach I have taught him. He does nothing but sit
still and mumble now in his own forgotten language.
And he's dreadfully cross—so crabbed—*mon Dieu*, what a
character! Why, the other day, as I told you, he bit Tu-
Kila-Kila himself, the high god of the island, with a good
hard peck, when that savage tried to touch him; you'd
have laughed to see his godship sent off bleeding to his
hut with a wounded finger! I will confess I was by no
means sorry at the sight myself. I do not love that god,
nor he me; and I was glad when Methuselah, on whom he
is afraid to revenge himself openly, gave him a nice smart
bite for trying to interfere with him."

"He's very snappish, to be sure," Felix said, with a
smile, trying once more to push forward one hand to
stroke the bird cautiously. But Methuselah resented all
such unauthorized intrusions. He was growing too old
to put up with strangers. He made a second vicious attempt to peck at the hand held out to soothe him, and
screamed, as he did so, in the usual discordant and unpleasant voice of an angry or frightened parrot.

"Why, Felix," Muriel put in, taking him by the arm
with a girlish gesture—for even the terrors by which they
were surrounded hadn't wholly succeeded in killing out
the woman within her—"how clumsy you are! You don't
understand one bit how to manage parrots. I had a parrot of my own at my aunt's in Australia, and I know their
ways and all about them. Just let me try him." She held
out her soft white hand toward the sulky bird with a
fearless, caressing gesture. "Pretty Poll, pretty Poll!"
she said, in English, in the conventional tone of address
to their kind. "Did the naughty man go and frighten her
then? Was she afraid of his hand? Did Polly want a
lump of sugar?"

On a sudden the bird opened its eyes quickly with an awakened air, and looked her back in the face, half blindly, half quizzingly. It preened its wings for a second, and crooned with pleasure. Then it put forward its neck, with its head on one side, took her dainty finger gently between its beak and tongue, bit it for pure love with a soft, short pressure, and at once allowed her to stroke its back and sides with a very pleased and surprised expression. The success of her skill flattered Muriel. "There! it knows me!" she cried, with childish delight; "it understands I'm a friend! It takes to me at once! Pretty Poll! Pretty Poll! Come, Poll, come and kiss me!"

The bird drew back at the words, and steadied itself for a moment knowingly on its perch. Then it held up its head, gazed around it with a vacant air, as if suddenly awakened from a very long sleep, and, opening its mouth, exclaimed in loud, clear, sharp, and distinct tones—and in English—"Pretty Poll! Pretty Poll! Polly wants a buss! Polly wants a nice sweet bit of apple!"

For a moment M. Peyron couldn't imagine what had happened. Felix looked at Muriel. Muriel looked at Felix. The Englishman held out both his hands to her in a wild fervor of surprise. Muriel took them in her own, and looked deep into his eyes, while tears rose suddenly and dropped down her cheeks, one by one, unchecked. They couldn't say why, themselves; they didn't know wherefore; yet this unexpected echo of their own tongue, in the mouth of that strange and mysterious bird, thrilled through them instinctively with a strange, unearthly tremor. In some dim and unexplained way, they felt half unconsciously to themselves that this discovery was, perhaps, the first clue to the solution of the terrible secret whose meshes encompassed them.

M. Peyron looked on in mute astonishment. He had heard the bird repeat that strange jargon so often that it had ceased to have even the possibility of a meaning for him. It was the way of Methuselah—just his language

that he talked; so harsh! so guttural! "Pretty Poll!
Pretty Poll!" he had noticed the bird harp upon those
quaint words again and again. They were part, no doubt,
of that old primitive and forgotten Pacific language the
creature had learned in other days from some earlier
bearer of the name and ghastly honors of Tu-Kila-Kila.
Why should these English seem so profoundly moved by
them ?

"Mademoiselle doesn't surely understand the barbarous dialect which our Methuselah speaks!" he exclaimed
in surprise, glancing half suspiciously from one to the
other of these incomprehensible Britons. Like most other
Frenchmen, he had been brought up in total ignorance of
every European language except his own ; and the words
the parrot pronounced, when delivered with the well-
known additions of parrot harshness and parrot volubility,
seemed to him so inexpressibly barbaric in their clicks
and jerks that he hadn't yet arrived at the faintest inkling
of the truth as he observed their emotion.

Felix seized his new friend's hand in his and wrung it
warmly. "Don't you see what it is?" he exclaimed, half
beside himself with this vague hope of some unknown
solution. "Don't you realize how the thing stands?
Don't you guess the truth? This isn't a Polynesian dialect
at all. It's our own mother tongue. The bird speaks
English!"

"English!" M. Peyron replied, with incredulous scorn.
"What! Methuselah speak English! Oh, no, monsieur,
impossible. *Vous vous trompez, j'en suis sûr.* I can never
believe it. Those harsh, inarticulate sounds to belong to
the noble language of Shaxper and Newtowne! *Ah, monsieur, incroyable! vous vous trompez ; vous vous trompez!*"

As he spoke, the bird put its head on one side once
more, and, looking out of its half-blind old eyes with a
crafty glance round the corner at Muriel, observed again,
in not very polite English, "Pretty Poll! Pretty Poll!
Polly wants some fruit! Polly wants a nut! Polly wants

to go to bed! . . . God save the king! To hell with all papists!"

"Monsieur," Felix said, a certain solemn feeling of surprise coming over him slowly at this last strange clause, "it is perfectly true. The bird speaks English. The bird that knows the secret of which we are all in search—the bird that can tell us the truth about Tu-Kila-Kila—can tell us in the tongue which mademoiselle and I speak as our native language. And what is more—and more strange—I gather from his tone and the tenor of his remarks, he was taught, long since—a century ago, or more—and by an English sailor!"

Muriel held out a bit of banana on a sharp stick to the bird. Methuselah-Polly took it gingerly off the end, like a well-behaved parrot? "God save the king!" Muriel said, in a quiet voice, trying to draw him on to speak a little further.

Methuselah twisted his eye sideways, first this way, then that, and responded in a very clear tone, indeed, "God save the king! Confound the Duke of York! Long live Dr. Oates! And to hell with all papists!"

CHAPTER XXII.

TANTALIZING, VERY.

They looked at one another again with a wild surmise. The voice was as the voice of some long past age. Could the parrot be speaking to them in the words of seventeenth-century English?

Even M. Peyron, who at first had received the strange discovery with incredulity, woke up before long to the importance of this sudden and unexpected revelation. The Tu-Kila-Kila who had taught Methuselah that long poem or sermon, which native tradition regarded as containing the central secret of their creed or its mysteries, and which the cruel and cunning Tu-Kila-Kila of to-day believed to be of immense importance to his safety—that Tu-Kila-Kila of other days was, in all probability, no other than an English sailor. Cast on these shores, perhaps, as they themselves had been, by the mercy of the waves, he had managed to master the language and religion of the savages among whom he found himself thrown; he had risen to be the representative of the cannibal god; and, during long months or years of tedious exile, he had beguiled his leisure by imparting to the unconscious ears of a bird the weird secret of his success, for the benefit of any others of his own race who might be similarly treated by fortune in future. Strange and romantic as it all sounded, they could hardly doubt now that this was the real explanation of the bird's command of English words. One problem alone remained to disturb their souls. Was the bird really in possession of any local secret and mystery at all, or was this the whole burden of the message he had brought down across the vast abyss of time—"God save the king, and to hell with all papists?"

Felix turned to M. Peyron in a perfect tumult of suspense. "What he recites is long?" he said, interrogatively, with profound interest. "You have heard him say much more than this at times? The words he has just uttered are not those of the sermon or poem you mentioned?"

M. Peyron opened his hands expansively before him. "Oh, *mon Dieu*, no, monsieur," he answered, with effusion. "You should hear him recite it. He's never done. It is whole chapters—whole chapters; a perfect Henriade in parrot-talk. When once he begins, there's no possibility of checking or stopping him. On, on he goes. Farewell to the rest; he insists on pouring it all forth to the very last sentence. Gabble, gabble, gabble; chatter, chatter, chatter; pouf, pouf, pouf; boum, boum, boum; he runs ahead eternally in one long discordant sing-song monotone. The person who taught him must have taken entire months to teach him, a phrase at a time, paragraph by paragraph. It is wonderful a bird's memory could hold so much. But till now, taking it for granted he spoke only some wild South Pacific dialect, I never paid much attention to Methuselah's vagaries."

"Hush. He's going to speak," Muriel cried, holding up, in alarm, one warning finger.

And the bird, his tongue-strings evidently loosened by the strange recurrence after so many years of those familiar English sounds, "Pretty Poll! Pretty Poll!" opened his mouth again in a loud chuckle of delight, and cried, with persistent shrillness, "God save the king! A fig for all arrant knaves and roundheads!"

A creepier feeling than ever came over the two English listeners at those astounding words. "Great heavens!" Felix exclaimed to the unsuspecting Frenchman, "he speaks in the style of the Stuarts and the Commonwealth!"

The Frenchman started. "*Époque Louis Quatorze!*" he murmured, translating the date mentally into his own more familiar chronology. "Two centuries since! Oh, incredible! incredible! Methuselah is old, but not quite so much of a patriarch as that. Even Humboldt's parrot could hardly have lived for two hundred years in the wilds of South America."

Felix regarded the venerable creature with a look of almost superstitious awe. "Facts are facts," he answered shortly, shutting his mouth with a little snap. "Unless this bird has been deliberately taught historical details in an archaic diction—and a shipwrecked sailor is hardly likely to be antiquarian enough to conceive such an idea —he is undoubtedly a survival from the days of the Commonwealth or the Restoration. And you say he runs on with his tale for an hour at a time! Good heavens, what a thought! I wish we could manage to start him now. Does he begin it often?"

"Monsieur," the Frenchman answered, "when I came

here first, though Methuselah was already very old and feeble, he was not quite a dotard, and he used to recite it all every morning regularly. That was the hour, I suppose, at which the master, who first taught him this lengthy recitation, used originally to impress it upon him. In those days his sight and his memory were far more clear than now. But by degrees, since my arrival, he has grown dull and stupid. The natives tell me that fifty years ago, while he was already old, he was still bright and lively, and would recite the whole poem whenever anybody presented him with his greatest dainty, the claw of a moora-crab. Nowadays, however, when he can hardly eat, and hardly mumble, he is much less persistent and less coherent than formerly. To say the truth, I have discouraged him in his efforts, because his pertinacity annoyed me. So now he seldom gets through all his lesson at one bout, as he used to do at the beginning. The best way to get him on is for me to sing him one of my French songs. That seems to excite him, or to rouse him to rivalry. Then he will put his head on one side, listen critically for a while, smile a superior smile, and finally begin—jabber, jabber, jabber—trying to talk me down, as if I were a brother parrot."

"Oh, do sing now !" Muriel cried, with intense persuasion in her voice. "I do so want to hear it." She meant, of course, the parrot's story.

But the Frenchman bowed, and laid his hand on his heart. "Ah, mademoiselle," he said, "your wish is almost a royal command. And yet, do you know, it is so long since I have sung, except to please myself—my music is so rusty, old pieces you have heard—I have no accompaniment, no score—*mais enfin*, we are all so far from Paris !"

Muriel didn't dare to undeceive him as to her meaning, lest he should refuse to sing in real earnest, and the chance of learning the parrot's secret might slip by them irretrievably. "Oh, monsieur," she cried, fitting herself to his humor at once, and speaking as ceremoniously as if she were assisting at a musical party in the Avenue Victor Hugo, "don't decline, I beg of you, on those accounts. We are both most anxious to hear your song. Don't disappoint us, pray. Please begin immediately."

" Ah, mademoiselle," the Frenchman said, "who could resist such an appeal? You are altogether too flattering." And then, in the same cheery voice that Felix had heard on the first day he visited the King of Birds' hut, M. Peyron began, in very decent style, to pour forth the merry sounds of his rollicking song :

> "Quand on conspi-re,
> Quand sans frayeur
> On peut se di-re
> Conspirateur—
> Pour tout le mon-de
> Il faut avoir
> Perruque blon-de
> Et collet noir.'

He had hardly got as far as the end of the first stanza, however, when Methuselah, listening, with his ear cocked up most knowingly, to the Frenchman's song, raised his head in opposition, and, sitting bolt upright on his perch, began to scream forth a voluble stream of words in one unbroken flood, so fast that Muriel could hardly follow them. The bird spoke in a thick and very harsh voice, and, what was more remarkable still, with a distinct and extremely peculiar North Country accent. "In the nineteenth year of the reign of his most gracious majesty, King Charles the Second," he blurted out, viciously, with an angry look at the Frenchman, "I, Nathaniel Cross, of the borough of Sunderland, in the county of Doorham, in England, an able-bodied mariner, then sailing the South Seas in the good bark Martyr Prince, of the Port of Great Grimsby, whereof one Thomas Wells, gent., under God, was master——"

"Oh, hush, hush!" Muriel cried, unable to catch the parrot's precious words through the emulous echo of the

Frenchman's music. "Whereof one Thomas Wells, gent.,
under God, was master—go on, Polly."

> " Perruque blonde
> Et collet noir,"

the Frenchman repeated, with a half-offended voice, finish-
ing his stanza.

But just as he stopped, Methuselah stopped too, and,
throwing back his head in the air with a triumphant look,
stared hard at his vanquished and silenced opponent out
of those blinking gray eyes of his. " I thought I'd be too
much for you ! " he seemed to say, wrathfully.

"Whereof one Thomas Wells, gent., under God, was
master," Muriel suggested again, all agog with excitement.
"Go on, good bird ! Go on, pretty Polly."

But Methuselah was evidently put off the scent now by
the unseasonable interruption.   Instead of continuing, he
threw back his head a second time with a triumphant air
and laughed aloud boisterously. " Pretty Polly," he cried.
" Pretty Polly wants a nut. Tu-Kila-Kila maroo! Pretty
Poll! Pretty Polly ! "

"Sing again, for Heaven's sake ! " Felix exclaimed, in
a profoundly agitated mood, explaining briefly to the
Frenchman the full significance of the words Methuselah
had just begun to utter.

The Frenchman struck up his tune afresh to give the
bird a start ; but all to no avail. Methuselah was evidently
in no humor for talking just then.   He listened with a
callous, uncritical air, bringing his white eyelids down
slowly and sleepily over his bleared gray eyes.   Then he
nodded his head slowly. " No use," the Frenchman murmured, pursing his lips up gravely. "The bird won't
talk. It's going off to sleep now. Methuselah gets visibly
older every day, monsieur and mademoiselle. You are
only just in time to catch his last accents."

CHAPTER XXIII.

A MESSAGE FROM THE DEAD.

Early next morning, as Felix lay still in his hut, dozing,
and just vaguely conscious of a buzz of a mosquito close
to his ear, he was aroused by a sudden loud cry outside—
a cry that called his native name three times, running:
" O King of the Rain, King of the Rain, King of the Rain,
awake ! High time to be up ! The King of the Birds
sends you health and greeting ! "

Felix rose at once ; and his Shadow, rising before him,
and unbolting the loose wooden fastener of the door, went
out in haste to see who called beyond the white taboo-line
of their sacred precincts.

A native woman, tall, lithe, and handsome, stood there
in the full light of morning, beckoning. A strange glow
of hatred gleamed in her large gray eyes. Her shapely
brown bosom heaved and panted heavily. Big beads glist-
ened moistly on her smooth, high brow. It was clear she
had run all the way in haste. She was deeply excited and
full of eager anxiety.

"Why, what do you want here so early, Ula?" the
Shadow asked, in surprise—for it was indeed she. "How
have you slipped away, as soon as the sun is risen, from
the sacred hut of Tu-Kila-Kila?"

"Ula's gray eyes flashed angry fire as she answered. "He
has beaten me again," she cried, in revengeful tones ; "see
the weals on my back ! See my arms and shoulders ! He
has drawn blood from my wounds. He is the most
hateful of gods. I should love to kill him. Therefore I
slipped away from him with the early dawn and came to
consult with his enemy, the King of the Birds, because I
heard the words that the Eyes of Tu-Kila-Kila, who per-
vade the world, report to their master. The Eyes have

II

told him that the King of the Rain, the Queen of the Clouds, and the King of the Birds are plotting together in secret against Tu-Kila-Kila. When I heard that, I was glad ; I went to the King of the Birds to warn him of his danger ; and the King of the Birds, concerned for your safety, has sent me in haste to ask his brother gods to go at once to him.

In a minute Felix was up and had called out Mali from the neighboring hut. "Tell Missy Queenie," he cried, "to come with me to see the man-a-oui-oui ! The man-a-oui-oui has sent me for us to come. She must make great haste. He wants us immediately."

With a word and a sign to Toko, Ula glided away stealthily, with the cat-like tread of the native Polynesian woman, back to her hated husband.

Felix went out to the door and heliographed with his bright metal plate, turned on the Frenchman's hill, "What is it ?"

In a moment the answer flashed back, word by word, "Come quick, if you want to hear. Methuselah is reciting !"

A few seconds later Muriel emerged from her hut, and the two Europeans, closely followed, as always, by their inseparable Shadows, took the winding side-path that led through the jungle by a devious way, avoiding the front of Tu-Kila-Kila's temple, to the Frenchman's cottage.

They found M. Peyron very much excited, partly by Ula's news of Tu-Kila-Kila's attitude, but more still by Methuselah's agitated condition. "The whole night through, my dear friends," he cried, seizing their hands, "that bird has been chattering, chattering, chattering. *Oh, mon Dieu, quel oiseau !* It seems as though the words heard yesterday from mademoiselle had struck some lost chord in the creature's memory. But he is also very feeble. I can see that well. His garrulity is the garrulity of old age in its last flickering moments. He mumbles and mutters. He chuckles to himself. If you don't hear his message now and at once, it's my solemn conviction you will never hear it."

He led them out to the aviary, where Methuselah, in effect, was sitting on his perch, most tremulous and woebegone. His feathers shuddered visibly ; he could no longer preen himself. "Listen to what he says," the Frenchman exclaimed, in a very serious voice. "It is your last, last chance. If the secret is ever to be unravelled at all, by Methuselah's aid, now is, without doubt, the proper moment to unravel it."

Muriel put out her hand and stroked the bird gently. "Pretty Poll," she said, soothingly, in a sympathetic voice. "Pretty Poll ! Poor Poll ! Was he ill ! Was he suffering ? "

At the sound of those familiar words, unheard so long till yesterday, the parrot took her finger in his beak once more, and bit it with the tenderness of his kind in their softer moments. Then he threw back his head with a sort of mechanical twist, and screamed out at the top of his voice, for the last time on earth, his mysterious message :

"Pretty Poll ! Pretty Poll ! God save the king ! Confound the Duke of York ! Death to all arrant knaves and roundheads !

"In the nineteenth year of the reign of his most gracious majesty, King Charles the Second, I, Nathaniel Cross, of the borough of Sunderland, in the county of Doorham, in England, an able-bodied mariner, then sailing the South Seas in the good bark Martyr Prince, of the Port of Great Grimsby, whereof one Thomas Wells, gent., under God, was master, was, by stress of weather, wrecked and cast away on the shores of this island, called by its gentile inhabitants by the name of Boo Parry. In which wreck, as it befell, Thomas Wells, gent., and his equipment were, by divine disposition, killed and drowned, save and except three mariners, whereof I am one, who in God's good providence swam safely through an exceeding great flood of waves and landed at laast on this island. There my two companions, Owen Williams, of Swansea, in the parts of Wales, and Lewis le Pickard, a French Hewgenott refugee, were at once, by the said gentiles, cruelly entreated, and after great torture cooked and eaten at the temple of their chief god, Too-Keela-Keela. But I, myself, having through God's grace found favor in their eyes, was promoted to the post which in their speech is called Korong, the nature of which this bird, my mouthpiece, will hereafter, to your ears, more fully discover."

Having said so much, in a very jerky way, Methuselah paused, and blinked his eyes wearily.

"What does he say?" the Frenchman began, eager to know the truth. But Felix, fearful lest any interruption might break the thread of the bird's discourse and cheat them of the sequel, held up a warning finger, and then laid it on his lips in mute injunction. Methuselah threw back his head at that and laughed aloud. "God save the king!" he cried again, in a still feebler way, "and to hell with all papists!"

It was strange how they all hung on the words of that unconscious messenger from a dead and gone age, who himself knew nothing of the import of the words he was uttering. Methuselah laughed at their earnestness, shook his head once or twice, and seemed to think to himself. Then he remembered afresh the point he had broken off at.

"More fully discover. For seven years have I now lived on this island, never having seen or h'ard Christian face or voice; and at the end of that time, feeling my health feail, and being apprehensive lest any of my fellow-countrymen should hereafter suffer the same fate as I have done, I began to teach this parrot his message, a few words at a time, impressing it duly and fully on his memory.

"Larn, then, O wayfarer, that the people of Boo Parry are most arrant gentiles, heathens, and carribals. And this, as I discover, is the nature and method of their vile faith. They hold that the gods are each and several in-

carnate in some one particular human being. This human
being they worship and reverence with all ghostly respect
as his incarnation. And chiefly, above all, do they revere
the great god Too-Keela-Keela, whose representative
(may the Lord in Heaven forgive me for the same) I myself am at this present speaking. Having thus, for my
sins, attained to that impious honor.

"God save the king! Confound the Duke of York!
To hell with all papists!

"It is the fashion of this people to hold that their gods
must always be strong and lusty. For they argue to themselves thus : that the continuance of the rain must needs
depend upon the vigor and subtlety of its Soul, the rain-
god. So the continuance and fruitfulness of the trees and
plants which yield them food must needs depend upon
the health of the tree-god. And the life of the world, and
the light of the sun, and the well-being of all things that in
them are, must depend upon the strength and cunning of
the high god of all, Too-Keela-Keela.. Hence they take
great care and woorship of their gods, surrounding them
with many rules which they call Taboo, and restricting
them as to what they shall eat, and what drink, and where-
withal they shall seemly clothe themselves. For they
think that if the King of the Rain at' anything that might
cause the colick, or like humor or distemper, the weather
will thereafter be stormy and tempestuous ; but so long
as the King of the Rain fares well and retains his health,
so long will the weather over their island of Boo Parry be
clear and prosperous.

"Furthermore, as I have larned from their theologians,
being myself, indeed, the greatest of their gods, it is evident that they may not let any god die, lest that depart-
ment of nature over which he presideth should wither
away and feail, as it were, with him. But reasonably no
care that mortal man can exercise will prevent the possibility of their god—seeing he is but one of themselves—
growing old and feeble and dying at laast. To prevent

which calamity, these gentile folk have invented (as I believe by the aid and device of Sathan) this horrid and
most onnatural practice. The man-god must be killed so
soon as he showeth in body or mind that his native powers
are beginning to feail. And it is necessary that he be
killed, according to their faith, in this ensuing fashion.

" If the man-god were to die slowly by a death in the
course of nature, the ways of the world might be stopped
altogether. Hence these savages catch the soul of their
god, as it were, ere it grow old and feeble, and transfer it
betimes, by a magic device, to a suitable successor. And
surely, they say, this suitable successor can be none other
than him that is able to take it from him. This, then, is
their horrid counsel and device—that each one of their
gods should kill his antecessor. In doing thus, he taketh
the old god's life and soul, which thereupon migrates and
dwells within him. And by this tenure—may Heaven be
merciful to me, a sinner—do I, Nathaniel Cross, of the
county of Doorham, now hold this dignity of Too-Keela-
Keela, having slain, therefor, in just quarrel, my antecessor in the high godship."

As he reached these words Methuselah paused, and
choked in his throat slightly. The mere mechanical effort
of continuing the speech he had learned by heart two
hundred years before, and repeated so often since that it
had become part of his being, was now almost too much
for him. The Frenchman was right. They were only
just in time. A few days later, and the secret would have
died with the bird that preserved it.

CHAPTER XXIV.

AN UNFINISHED TALE.

For a minute or two Methuselah mumbled inarticulately to himself. Then, to their intense discomfiture, he began once more : "In the nineteenth year of the reign of his most gracious majesty, King Charles the Second, I, Nathaniel Cross——"

"Oh, this will never do," Felix cried. "We haven't got yet to the secret at all. Muriel, do try to set him right. He must waste no breath. We can't afford now to let him go all over it."

Muriel stretched out her hand and soothed the bird gently as before. "Having slain, therefore, my predecessor in the high godship," she suggested, in the same singsong voice as the parrot's.

To her immense relief, Methuselah took the hint with charming docility.

"In the high godship," he went on, mechanically, where he had stopped. "And this here is the manner whereby I obtained it. The Too-Keela-Keela from time to time doth generally appoint any castaway stranger that comes to the island to the post of Korong—that is to say, an annual god or victim. For, as the year doth renew itself at each change of seasons, so do these carribals in their gentilisme believe and hold that the gods of the seasons—to wit, the King of the Rain, the Queen of the Clouds, the Lord of Green Leaves, the King of Fruits, and others—must needs be sleain and renewed at the diverse solstices. Now, it so happened that I, on my arrival in the island, was appointed Korong, and promoted to the post of King of the Rain, having a native woman assigned me as Queen of the Clouds, with whom I might keep company. This woman being, after her kind, enamored of me, and anxious to escape her own fate, to be sleain by my side, did betray to me that secret which they call in their tongue the Great Taboo, and which had been betrayed to herself in turn by a native man, her former lover. For the men are instructed in these things in the mysteries when they coom of age, but not the women.

"And the Great Taboo is this : No man can becoom a Too-Keela-Keela unless he first sleay the man in whom the high god is incarnate for the moment. But in order that he may sleay him, he must also himself be a full Korong, only those persons who are already gods being capable for the highest post in their hierarchy ; even as with ourselves, none but he that is a deacon may become a priest, and none but he that is a priest may be made a bishop. For this reason, then, the Too-Keela-Keela prefers to advance a stranger to the post of Korong, seeing that such a person will not have been initiated in the mysteries of the island, and therefore will not be aware of those sundry steps which must needs be taken of him that would inherit the godship.

"Furthermore, even a Korong can only obtain the highest rank of Too-Keela-Keela if he order all things according to the forms and ceremonies of the Taboo parfectly. For these gentiles are very careful of the levitical parts of their religion, deriving the same, as it seems to me, from the polity of the Hebrews, the fame of whose tabernacle must sure have gone forth through the ends of the woorld, and the knowledge of whose temple must have been yet more wide dispersed by Solomon, his ships, when they came into these parts to fetch gold from Ophir. And the ceremony is, that before any man may sleay the 'arthly tenement of Too-Keela-Keela and inherit his soul, which is in very truth, as they do think the god himself, he must needs fight with the person in whom Too-Keela-Keela doth then dwell, and for this reason : If the holder of the soul can defend himself in fight, then it is clear that his strength is not one whit decayed, nor is his vigor feailing ; nor yet has his assailant been able to take his soul from him. But if the Korong in open fight do sleay the person in whom Too-Keela-Keela dwells, he becometh at once a Too-Keela-Keela himself—that is to say, in their tongue, the Lord of Lords, because he hath taken the life of him that preceded him.

"Yet so intricate is the theology and practice of these loathsome savages, that not even now have I explained it in full to you, O shipwrecked mariner, for your aid and protection. For a Korong, though it be a part of his privilege to contend, if he will, with Too-Keela-Keela for the high godship and princedom of this isle, may only do so at certain appointed times, places, and seasons. Above all things, it is necessary that he should first find out the hiding-place of the soul of Too-Keela-Keela. For though the Too-Keela-Keela for the time that is, be animated by the god, yet, for greater security, he doth not keep his soul in his own body, but, being above all things the god of fruitfulness and generation, who causes women to bear children, and the plant called taro to bring forth its increase, he keepeth his soul in the great sacred tree behind his temple, which is thus the Father of All Trees, and the chiefest abode of the great god Too-Keela-Keela.

"Nor does Too-Keela-Keela's soul abide equally in every part of this aforesaid tree ; but in a certain bough of it, resembling a mistletoe, which hath yellow leaves, and, being broken off, groweth ever green and yellow afresh ; which is the central mystery of all their Sathanic religion. For in this very bough—easy to be discerned by the eye among the green leaves of the tree—" the bird paused and faltered.

Muriel leaned forward in an agony of excitement. "Among the green leaves of the tree—" she went on soothing him.

Her voice seemed to give the parrot a fresh impulse to speak. "—Is contained, as it were," he continued, feebly, "the divine essence itself, the soul and life of Too-Keela-Keela. Whoever, then, being a full Korong, breaks this

off, hath thus possessed himself of the very god in person.
This, however, he must do by exceeding stealth ; for Too-
Keela-Keela, or rather the man that bears that name, being the guardian and defender of the great god, walks
ever up and down, by day and by night, in exceeding
great cunning, armed with a spear and with a hatchet of
stone, around the root of the tree, watching jealously over
the branch which is, as he believes, his own soul and being.
I, therefore, being warned of the Taboo by the woman
that was my consort, did craftily, near the appointed time
for my own death, creep out of my hut, and my consort,
having induced one of the wives of Too-Keela-Keela to
make him drunken with too much of that intoxicating
drink which they do call kava, did proceed—did proceed—
did proceed—In the nineteenth year of the reign of his
most gracious majesty, King Charles the Second—"

Muriel bent forward once more in an agony of suspense.
" Oh, go on, good Poll ! " she cried. " Go on. Remember it. Did proceed to—"

The single syllable helped Methuselah's memory. "—
Did proceed to stealthily pluck the bough, and, having
shown the same to Fire and Water, the guardians of the
Taboo, did boldly challenge to single combat the bodily
tenement of the god, with spear and hatchet, provided
for me in accordance with ancient custom by Fire and
Water. In which combat, Heaven mercifully befriending
me against my enemy, I did coom out conqueror ; and
was thereupon proclaimed Too-Keela-Keela myself, with
ceremonies too many and barbarous to mention, lest I raise
your gorge at them. But that which is most important to
tell you for your own guidance and safety, O mariner, is
this—that being the sole and only end I have in imparting
this history to so strange a messenger—that after you have
by craft plucked the sacred branch, and by force of arms
over-coom Too-Keela-Keela, it is by all means needful,
whether you will or not, that submitting to the hateful
and gentile custom of this people—of this people—Pretty

Poll! Pretty Poll! God save—God save the king! Death to the nineteenth year of the reign of all arrant knaves and roundheads."

He dropped his head on his breast, and blinked his white eyelids more feebly than ever. His strength was failing him fast. The Soul of all dead parrots was wearing out. M. Peyron, who had stood by all this time, not knowing in any way what might be the value of the bird's disclosures, came forward and stroked poor Methuselah with his caressing hand. But Methuselah was incapable now of any further effort. He opened his blind eyes sleepily for the last, last time, and stared around him with a blank stare at the fading universe. "God save the king!" he screamed aloud with a terrible gasp, true to his colors still. "God save the king, and to hell with all papists!"

Then he fell off his perch, stone dead, on the ground. They were never to hear the conclusion of that strange, quaint message from a forgotten age to our more sceptical century.

Felix looked at Muriel, and Muriel looked at Felix. They could hardly contain themselves with awe and surprise. The parrot's words were so human, its speech was so real to them, that they felt as though the English Tu-Kila-Kila of two hundred years back had really and truly been speaking to them from that perch; it was a human creature indeed that lay dead before them. Felix raised the warm body from the ground with positive reverence. "We will bury it decently," he said in French, turning to M. Peyron. "He was a plucky bird, indeed, and he has carried out his master's intentions nobly."

As they spoke, a little rustling in the jungle hard by attracted their attention. Felix turned to look. A stealthy brown figure glided away in silence through the tangled brushwood. M. Peyron started. "We are observed, monsieur," he said. "We must look out for squalls! It is one of the Eyes of Tu-Kila-Kila!"

"Let him do his worst!" Felix answered. "We know his secret now, and can protect ourselves against him. Let us return to the shade, monsieur, and talk this all over. Methuselah has indeed given us something to-day very serious to think about."

CHAPTER XXV.

TU-KILA-KILA STRIKES.

And yet, when all was said and done, knowledge of Tu-Kila-Kila's secret didn't seem to bring Felix and Muriel much nearer a solution of their own great problems than they had been from the beginning. In spite of all Methuselah had told them, they were as far off as ever from securing their escape, or even from the chance of sighting an English steamer.

This last was still the main hope and expectation of all three Europeans. M. Peyron, who was a bit of a mathematician, had accurately calculated the time, from what Felix told him, when the Australasian would pass again on her next homeward voyage ; and, when that time arrived, it was their united intention to watch night and day for the faintest glimmer of her lights, or the faintest wreath of her smoke on the far eastern horizon. They had ventured to confide their design to all three of their Shadows ; and the Shadows, attached by the kindness to which they were so little accustomed among their own people, had in every case agreed to assist them with the canoe, if occasion served them. So for a time the two doomed victims subsided into their accustomed calm of mingled hope and despair, waiting patiently for the expected arrival of the much-longed-for Australasian.

If she took that course once, why not a second time ? And if ever she hove in sight, might they not hope, after

all, to signal to her with their rudely constructed heliograph, and stop her ?

As for Methuselah's secret, there was only one way,
Felix thought, in which it could now prove of any use to
them. When the actual day of their doom drew nigh, he
might, perhaps, be tempted to try the fate which Nathaniel
Cross, of Sunderland, had successfully courted. That
might gain them at least a little respite. Though even so
he hardly knew what good it could do him to be elevated
for a while into the chief god of the island. It might not
even avail him to save Muriel's life ; for he did not doubt
that when the awful day itself had actually come the natives would do their best to kill her in spite of him, unless
he anticipated them by fulfilling his own terrible, yet merciful, promise.

Week after week went by—month after month passed—
and the date when the Australasian might reasonably be
expected to reappear drew nearer and nearer. They
waited and trembled. At last, a few days before the time
M. Peyron had calculated, as Felix was sitting under the
big shady tree in his garden one morning, while Muriel,
now worn out with hope deferred, lay within her hut alone
with Mali, a sound of tom-toms and beaten palms was
heard on the hill-path. The natives around fell on their
faces or fled. It announced the speedy approach of Tu-
Kila-Kila.

By this time both the castaways had grown comparatively accustomed to that hideous noise, and to the
hateful presence which it preceded and heralded. A dozen
temple attendants tripped on either side down the hill-
path, to guard him, clapping their hands in a barbaric
measure as they went ; Fire and Water, in the midst,
supported and flanked the divine umbrella. Felix rose
from his seat with very little ceremony, indeed, as the
great god crossed the white taboo-line of his precincts,
followed only beyond the limit by Fire and Water.

Tu-Kila-Kila was in his most insolent vein. He glanced

around with a horrid light of triumph dancing visibly in his eyes. It was clear he had come, intent upon some grand theatrical *coup*. He meant to take the white-faced stranger by surprise this time. "Good-morning, O King of the Rain," he exclaimed, in a loud voice and with boisterous familiarity. "How do you like your outlook now? Things are getting on. Things are getting on. The end of your rule is drawing very near, isn't it? Before long I must make the seasons change. I must make my sun turn. I must twist round my sky. And then, I shall need a new Korong instead of you, O pale-faced one!"

Felix looked back at him without moving a muscle.

"I am well," he answered shortly, restraining his anger. "The year turns round whether you will or not. You are right that the sun will soon begin to move southward on its path again. But many things may happen to all of us meanwhile *I* am not afraid of you."

As he spoke, he drew his knife, and opened the blade, unostentatiously, but firmly. If the worst were really coming now, sooner than he expected, he would at least not forget his promise to Muriel.

Tu-Kila-Kila smiled a hateful and ominous smile. "I am a great god," he said, calmly, striking an attitude as was his wont. "Hear how my people clap their hands in my honor! I order all things. I dispose the course of nature in heaven and earth. If I look at a cocoa-nut tree, it dies; if I glance at a bread-fruit, it withers away. We will see before long whether or not you are afraid of me. Meanwhile, O Korong, I have come to claim my dues at your hands. Prepare for your fate. To-morrow the Queen of the Clouds must be sealed my bride. Fetch her out, that I may speak with her. I have come to tell her so."

It was a thunderbolt from a clear sky, and it fell with terrible effect on Felix. For a moment the knife trembled in his grasp with an almost irresistible impulse. He could hardly restrain himself, as he heard those horrible, incredible words, and saw the loathsome smirk on the speaker's face by which they were accompanied, from leaping then and there at the savage's throat, and plunging his blade to the haft into the vile creature's body. But by a violent effort he mastered his indignation and wrath for the present. Planting himself full in front of Tu-Kila-Kila, and blocking the way to the door of that sacred English girl's hut—oh, how horrible it was to him even to think of her purity being contaminated by the vile neighborhood, for one minute, of that loathsome monster! He looked full into the wretch's face, and answered very distinctly, in low, slow tones, "If you dare to take one step toward the place where that lady now rests, if you dare to move your foot one inch nearer, if you dare to ask to see her face again, I will plunge the knife hilt-deep into your vile heart, and kill you where you stand without one second's deliberation. Now you hear my words and you know what I mean. My weapon is keener and fiercer than any you Polynesians ever saw. Repeat those words once more, and by all that's true and holy, before they're out of your mouth I leap upon you and stab you."

Tu-Kila-Kila drew back in sudden surprise. He was unaccustomed to be so bearded in his own sacred island. "Well, I shall claim her to-morrow," he faltered out, taken aback by Felix's unexpected energy. He paused for a second, then he went on more slowly: "To-morrow I will come with all my people to claim my bride. This afternoon they will bring her mats of grass and necklets of nautilus shell to deck her for her wedding, as becomes Tu-Kila-Kila's chosen one. The young maids of Boupari will adorn her for her lord, in the accustomed dress of Tu-Kila-Kila's wives. They will clap their hands; they will sing the marriage song. Then early in the morning I will come to fetch her—and woe to him who strives to prevent me!"

Felix looked at him long, with a fixed and dogged look.

"What has made you think of this devilry?" he asked at last, still grasping his knife hard, and half undecided whether or not to use it. "You have invented all these ideas. You have no claim, even in the horrid customs of your savage country, to demand such a sacrifice."

Tu-Kila-Kila laughed loud, a laugh of triumphant and discordant merriment. "Ha, ha!" he cried, "you do not understand our customs, and will you teach *me*, the very high god, the guardian of the laws and practices of Boupari? You know nothing; you are as a little child. I am absolute wisdom. With every Korong, this is always our rule. Till the moon is full, on the last month before we offer up the sacrifice, the Queen of the Clouds dwells apart with her Shadow in her own new temple. So our fathers decreed it. But at the full of the moon, when the day has come, the usage is that Tu-Kila-Kila, the very high god, confers upon her the honor of making her his bride. It is a mighty honor. The feast is great. Blood flows like water. For seven days and nights, then, she lives with Tu-Kila-Kila in his sacred abode, the threshold of Heaven; she eats of human flesh; she tastes human blood; she drinks abundantly of the divine kava. At the end of that time, in accordance with the custom of our fathers, those great dead gods, Tu-Kila-Kila performs the high act of sacrifice. He puts on his mask of the face of a shark, for he is holy and cruel; he brings forth the Queen of the Clouds before the eyes of all his people, attired in her wedding robes, and made drunk with kava. Then he gashes her with knives; he offers her up to Heaven that accepted her; and the King of the Rain he offers after her; and all the people eat of their flesh, Korong! and drink of their blood, so that the body of gods and goddesses may dwell within all of them. And when all is done, the high god chooses a new king and queen at his will (for he is a mighty god), who rule for six moons more, and then are offered up, at the end, in like fashion."

As he spoke, the ferocious light that gleamed in the

savage's eye made Felix positively mad with anger. But he answered nothing directly. "Is this so?" he asked, turning for confirmation to Fire and Water. "Is it the custom of Boupari that Tu-Kila-Kila should wed the Queen of the Clouds seven days before the date appointed for her sacrifice?"

The King of Fire and the King of Water, tried guardians of the etiquette of Tu-Kila-Kila's court, made answer at once with one accord, "It is so, O King of the Rain. Your lips have said it. Tu-Kila-Kila speaks the solemn truth. He is a very great god. Such is the custom of Boupari."

Tu-Kila-Kila laughed his triumph in harsh, savage outbursts.

But Felix drew back for a second, irresolute. At last he stood face to face with the absolute need for immediate action. Now was almost the moment when he must redeem his terrible promise to Muriel. And yet, even so, there was still one chance of life, one respite left. The mystic yellow bough on the sacred banyan! the Great Taboo! the wager of battle with Tu-Kila-Kila! Quick as lightning it all came up in his excited brain. Time after time, since he heard Methuselah's strange message from the grave, had he passed Tu-Kila-Kila's temple enclosure and looked up with vague awe at that sacred parasite that grew so conspicuously in a fork of the branches. It was easy to secure it, if no man guarded. There still remained one night. In that one short night he must do his best— and worst. If all then failed, he must die himself with Muriel!

For two seconds he hesitated. It was hateful even to temporize with so hideous a proposition. But for Muriel's sake, for her dear life's sake, he must meet these savages with guile for guile. "If it be, indeed, the custom of Boupari," he answered back, with pale and trembling lips, "and if I, one man, am powerless to prevent it, I will give your message, myself, to the Queen of the Clouds, and you may send, as you say, your wedding decorations. But

come what will—mark this—you shall not see her yourself
to-day. You shall not speak to her. There I draw a line
—so, with my stick in the dust. If you try to advance one
step beyond, I stab you to the heart. Wait till to-morrow
to take your prey. Give me one more night. Great god
as you are, if you are wise, you will not drive an angry
man to utter desperation."

Tu-Kila-Kila looked with a suspicious side glance at
the gleaming steel blade Felix still fingered tremulously.
Though Boupari was one of those rare and isolated small
islands unvisited as yet by European trade, he had, nevertheless, heard enough of the sailing gods to know that
their skill was deep and their weapons very dangerous. It
would be foolish to provoke this man to wrath too soon.
To-morrow, when taboo was removed, and all was free
license, he would come when he willed and take his bride,
backed up by the full force of his assembled people.
Meanwhile, why provoke a brother god too far? After all,
in a little more than a week from now the pale-faced Korong would be eaten and digested!

"Very well," he said, sulkily, but still with the sullen
light of revenge gleaming bright in his eye. "Take my
message to the queen. You may be my herald. Tell her
what honor is in store for her—to be first the wife and
then the meat of Tu-Kila-Kila! She is a very fair woman.
I like her well. I have longed for her for months. To-
morrow, at the early dawn, by the break of day, I will
come with all my people and take her home by main force
to me."

He looked at Felix and scowled, an angry scowl of revenge. Then, as he turned and walked away, under
cover of the great umbrella, with its dangling pendants on
either side, the temple attendants clapped their hands in
unison. Fire and Water marched slow and held the umbrella over him. As he disappeared in the distance, and
the sound of his tom-toms grew dim on the hills, Toko, the
Shadow, who had lain flat, trembling, on his face in the

hut while the god was speaking, came out and looked anxiously and fearfully after him.

"The time is ripe," he said, in a very low voice to Felix. "A Korong may strike. All the people of Boupari murmur among themselves. They say this fellow has held the spirit of Tu-Kila-Kila within himself too long. He waxes insolent. They think it is high time the great God of Heaven should find before long some other fleshly tabernacle."

CHAPTER XXVI.

A RASH RESOLVE.

The rest of that day was a time of profound and intense anxiety. Felix and Muriel remained alone in their huts, absorbed in plans of escape, but messengers of many sorts from chiefs and gods kept continually coming to them. The natives evidently regarded it as a period of preparation. The Eyes of Tu-Kila-Kila surrounded their precinct; yet Felix couldn't help noticing that they seemed in many ways less watchful than of old, and that they whispered and conferred very much in a mysterious fashion with the people of the village. More than once Toko shook his head, sagely, "If only any one dared break the Great Taboo," he said, with some terror on his face, "our people would be glad. It would greatly please them. They are tired of this Tu-Kila-Kila. He has held the god in his breast far, far too long. They would willingly see some other in place of him."

Before noon, the young girls of the village, bringing native mats and huge strings of nautilus shells, trooped up to the hut, like bridesmaids, with flowers in their hands, to deck Muriel for her approaching wedding. Before them they carried quantities of red and brown tappa-cloth and very fine net-work, the dowry to be presented by the royal bride to her divine husband. Within the hut, they decked out the Queen of the Clouds with garlands of flowers and necklets of shells, in solemn native fashion, bewailing her fate all the time to a measured dirge in their own language. Muriel could see that their sympathy, though partly conventional, was largely real as well. Many of the young girls seized her hand convulsively from time to time, and kissed it with genuine feeling. The gentle young English woman had won their savage hearts by her purity and innocence. "Poor thing, poor thing," they said, stroking her hand tenderly. "She is too good for Korong! Too good for Tu-Kila-Kila! If only we knew the Great Taboo like the men, we would tell her everything. She is too good to die. We are sorry she is to be sacrificed!"

But when all their preparations were finished, the chief among them raised a calabash with a little scented oil in it, and poured a few drops solemnly on Muriel's head. "Oh, great god!" she said, in her own tongue, "we offer this sacrifice, a goddess herself, to you. We obey your words. You are very holy. We will each of us eat a portion of her flesh at your feast. So give us good crops, strong health, many children!"

"What does she say?" Muriel asked, pale and awe-struck, of Mali.

Mali translated the words with perfect *sang-froid*. At that awful sound Muriel drew back, chill and cold to the marrow. How inconceivable was the state of mind of these terrible people! They were really sorry for her; they kissed her hand with fervor; and yet they deliberately and solemnly proposed to eat her!

Toward evening the young girls at last retired, in regular order, to the clapping of hands, and Felix was left alone with Muriel and the Shadows.

Already he had explained to Muriel what he intended to do; and Muriel, half dazed with terror and paralyzed by these awful preparations, consented passively. "But how if you never come back, Felix?" she cried at last, clinging to him passionately.

Felix looked at her with a fixed look. "I have thought of that," he said. "M. Peyron, to whom I sent a message by flashes, has helped me in my difficulty. This bowl has poison in it. Peyron sent it to me to-day. He prepared it himself from the root of the kava bean. If by sunrise to-morrow you have heard no news, drink it off at once. It will instantly kill you. You shall *not* fall alive into that creature's clutches."

By slow degrees the evening wore on, and night approached—the last night that remained to them. Felix had decided to make his attempt about one in the morning. The moon was nearly full now, and there would be plenty of light. Supposing he succeeded, if they gained nothing else, they would gain at least a day or two's respite.

As dusk set in, and they sat by the door of the hut, they were all surprised to see Ula approach the precinct stealthily through the jungle, accompanied by two of Tu-Kila-Kila's Eyes, yet apparently on some strange and friendly message. She beckoned imperiously with one finger to Toko to cross the line. The Shadow rose, and without one word of explanation went out to speak to her. The woman gave her message in short, sharp sentences. "We have found out all," she said, breathing hard. "Fire and Water have learned it. But Tu-Kila-Kila himself knows nothing. We have found out that the King of the Rain has discovered the secret of the Great Taboo. He heard it from the Soul of all dead parrots. Tu-Kila-Kila's Eyes saw, and learned, and understood. But they said nothing to Tu-Kila-Kila. For my counsel was wise; I planned that they should not, with Fire and Water. Fire and Water and all the people of Boupari think, with me, the time has come that there should arise among us a new Tu-Kila-Kila. This one let his blood fall out upon the dust of the ground. His luck has gone. We have need of another."

"Then for what have you come?" Toko asked, all awe-struck. It was terrible to him for a woman to meddle in such high matters.

"I have come," Ula answered, laying her hand on his arm, and holding her face close to his with profound solemnity—"I have come to say to the King of the Rain, 'Whatever you do, that do quickly.' To-night I will en-gage to keep Tu-Kila-Kila in his temple. He shall see nothing. He shall hear nothing. I know not the Great Taboo ; but I know from him this much—that if by wile or guile I keep him alone in his temple to-night, the King of the Rain may fight with him in single combat ; and if the King of the Rain conquers in the battle, he becomes him-self the home of the great deity."

She nodded thrice, with her hands on her forehead, and withdrew as stealthily as she had come through the jungle. The Eyes of Tu-Kila-Kila, falling into line, remained be-hind, and kept watch upon the huts with the closest ap-parent scrutiny.

More than ever they were hemmed in by mystery on mystery.

The Shadow went back and reported to Felix. Felix, turning it over in his own mind, wondered and debated Was this true, or a trap to lure him to destruction ?

As the night wore on, and the hour drew nigh, Muriel sat beside her friend and lover, in blank despair and agony. How could she ever allow him to leave her now? How could she venture to remain alone with Mali in her hut in this last extremity ? It was awful to be so girt with mys-terious enemies. "I must go with you, Felix ! I must go, too !" she cried over and over again. "I daren't remain behind with all these awful men. And then, if he kills either of us, he will kill us at least both together."

But Felix knew he might do nothing of the sort. A more terrible chance was still in reserve. He might spare Muriel. And against that awful possibility he felt it his duty now to guard at all hazard.

"No, Muriel," he said, kissing her, and holding her pale hand, "I must go alone. You can't come with me. If I return, we will have gained at least a respite, till the

Australasian may turn up. If I don't, you will at any rate have strength of mind left to swallow the poison, before Tu-Kila-Kila comes to claim you."

Hour after hour passed by slowly, and Felix and the Shadow watched the stars at the door, to know when the hour for the attempt had arrived. The eyes of Tu-Kila-Kila, peering silent from just beyond the line, saw them watching all the time, but gave no sign or token of disapproval. With heads bent low, and tangled hair about their faces, they stood like statues, watching, watching sullenly. Were they only waiting till he moved, Felix wondered ; and would they then hasten off by short routes through the jungle to warn their master of the impending conflict?

At last the hour came when Felix felt sure there was the greatest chance of Tu-Kila-Kila sleeping soundly in his hut, and forgetting the defence of the sacred bough on the holy banyan-tree. He rose from his seat with a gesture for silence, and moved forward to Muriel. The poor girl flung herself, all tears, into his arms. "Oh, Felix, Felix," she cried, "redeem your promise now! Kill us both here together, and then, at least, I shall never be separated from you! It wouldn't be wrong! It can't be wrong! We would surely be forgiven if we did it only to escape falling into the hands of these terrible savages!"

Felix clasped her to his bosom with a faltering heart. "No, Muriel," he said, slowly. "Not yet. Not yet. I must leave no opening on earth untried by which I can possibly or conceivably save you. It's as hard for me to leave you here alone as for you to be left. But for your own dear sake, I must steel myself. I must do it."

He kissed her many times over. He wiped away her tears. Then, with a gentle movement, he untwined her clasping arms. "You must let me go, my own darling," he said, "You must let me go, without crossing the bor-

der. If you pass beyond the taboo-line to-night, Heaven
only knows what, perhaps, may happen to you. We must
give these people no handle of offence. Good-night, Muriel, my own heart's wife ; and if I never come back, then
good-by forever."

She clung to his arm still. He disentangled himself,
gently. The Shadow rose at the same moment, and followed in silence to the open door. Muriel rushed after
them, wildly. " Oh, Felix, Felix, come back," she cried,
bursting into wild floods of hot, fierce tears. " Come
back and let me die with you ! Let me die ! Let me die
with you ! "

Felix crossed the white line without one word of reply,
and went forth into the night, half unmanned by this effort.
Muriel sank, where she stood, into Mali's arms. The girl
caught her and supported her. But before she had fainted
quite away, Muriel had time vaguely to see and note one
significant fact. The Eyes of Tu-Kila-Kila, who stood
watching the huts with lynx-like care, nodded twice to
Toko, the Shadow, as he passed between them ; then they
stealthily turned and dogged the two men's footsteps afar
off in the jungle.

Muriel was left by herself in the hut, face to face with
Mali.

" Let us pray, Mali," she cried, seizing her Shadow's
arm.

And Mali, moved suddenly by some half-obliterated impulse, exclaimed in concert, in a terrified voice, " Let us
pray to Methodist God in heaven ! "

For her life, too, hung on the issue of that rash endeavor.

CHAPTER XXVII.

A STRANGE ALLY.

In Tu-Kila-Kila's temple-hut, meanwhile, the jealous, revengeful god, enshrined among his skeletons, was having in his turn an anxious and doubtful time of it. Ever since his sacred blood had stained the dust of earth by the Frenchman's cottage and in his own temple, Tu-Kila-Kila, for all his bluster, had been deeply stirred and terrified in his inmost soul by that unlucky portent. A savage, even if he be a god, is always superstitious. Could it be that his own time was, indeed, drawing nigh ? that he, who had remorselessly killed and eaten so many hundreds of human victims, was himself to fall a prey to some more successful competitor ? Had the white-faced stranger, the King of the Rain, really learned the secrets of the Great Taboo from the Soul of all dead parrots ? Did that mysterious bird speak the tongue of these new fire-bearing Korongs, whose doom was fixed for the approaching solstice ? Tu-Kila-Kila wondered and doubted. His suspicions were keen, and deeply aroused. Late that night he still lurked by the sacred banyan-tree, and when at last he retired to his own inner temple, white with the grinning skulls of the victims he had devoured, it was with strict injunctions to Fire and Water, and to his Eyes that watched there, to bring him word at once of any projected aggression on the part of the stranger.

Within the temple-hut, however, Ula awaited him. That was a pleasant change. The beautiful, supple, satin-skinned Polynesian looked more beautiful and more treacherous than ever that fateful evening. Her great brown limbs, smooth and glossy as pearl, were set off by a narrow girdle or waistband of green and scarlet leaves, twined spirally around her. Armlets of nautilus shell threw up the dainty plumpness of her soft, round forearm.

A garland hung festooned across one shapely shoulder; her bosom was bare or but half hidden by the crimson hibiscus that nestled voluptuously upon it. As Tu-Kila-Kila entered, she lifted her large eyes, and, smiling, showed two even rows of pearly white teeth. "My master has come!" she cried, holding up both lissome arms with a gesture to welcome him. "The great god relaxes his care of the world for a while. All goes on well. He leaves his sun to sleep and his stars to shine, and he retires to rest on the unworthy bosom of her, his mate, his meat, that is honored to love him."

Tu-Kila-Kila was scarcely just then in a mood for dalliance. "The Queen of the Clouds comes hither to-morrow," he answered, casting a somewhat contemptuous glance at Ula's more dusky and solid charms. "I go to seek her with the wedding gifts early in the morning. For a week she shall be mine. And after that—" he lifted his tomahawk and brought it down on a huge block of wood significantly.

Ula smiled once more, that deep, treacherous smile of hers, and showed her white teeth even deeper than ever. "If my lord, the great god, rises so early to-morrow," she said, sidling up toward him voluptuously, "to seek one more bride for his sacred temple, all the more reason he should take his rest and sleep soundly to-night. Is he not a god? Are not his limbs tired? Does he not need divine silence and slumber?"

Tu-Kila-Kila pouted. "I could sleep more soundly," he said, with a snort, "if I knew what my enemy, the Korong, is doing. I have set my Eyes to watch him, yet I do not feel secure. They are not to be trusted. I shall be happier far when I have killed and eaten him." He passed his hand across his bosom with a reflective air. You have a great sense of security toward your enemy, no doubt, when you know that he slumbers, well digested, within you.

Ula raised herself on her elbow, and gazed snake-like into his face, "My lord's Eyes are everywhere," she said, reverently, with every mark of respect. "He sees and knows all things. Who can hide anything on earth from his face? Even when he is asleep, his Eyes watch well for him. Then why should the great god, the Measurer of Heaven and Earth, the King of Men, fear a white-faced stranger? To-morrow the Queen of the Clouds will be yours, and the stranger will be abased : ha, ha, he will grieve at it! To-night, Fire and Water keep guard and watch over you. Whoever would hurt you must pass through Fire and Water before he reach your door. Fire would burn, Water would drown. This is a Great Taboo. No stranger dare face it."

Tu-Kila-Kila lifted himself up in his thrasonic mood. "If he did," he cried, swelling himself, "I would shrivel him to ashes with one flash of my eyes. I would scorch him to a cinder with one stroke of my lightning."

Ula smiled again, a well-satisfied smile. She was working her man up. "Tu-Kila-Kila is great," she repeated, slowly. "All earth obeys him. All heaven fears him."

The savage took her hand with a doubtful air. "And yet," he said, toying with it, half irresolute, "when I went to the white-faced stranger's hut this morning, he did not speak fair; he answered me insolently. His words were bold. He talked to me as one talks to a man, not to a great god. Ula, I wonder if he knows my secret?"

Ula started back in well-affected horror. "A white-faced stranger from the sun know your secret, O great king!" she cried, hiding her face in a square of cloth. "See me beat my breast! Impossible! Impossible! No one of your subjects would dare to tell him so great a taboo. It would be rank blasphemy. If they did, your anger would utterly consume them!"

"That is true," Tu-Kila-Kila said, practically, "but I might not discover it. I am a very great god. My Eyes are everywhere. No corner of the world is hid from my gaze. All the concerns of heaven and earth are my care, And therefore, sometimes, I overlook some detail."

"No man alive would dare to tell the Great Taboo!" Ula repeated, confidently. "Why, even I myself, who am the most favored of your wives, and who am permitted to bask in the light of your presence—even I, Ula—I do not know it. How much less, then, the spirit from the sun, the sailing god, the white-faced stranger!"

Tu-Kila-Kila pursed up his brow and looked preternaturally wise, as the savage loves to do. "But the parrot," he cried, "the Soul of all dead parrots! *He* knew the secret, they say :—I taught it him myself in an ancient day, many, many years ago—when no man now living was born, save only I—in another incarnation—and *he* may have told it. For the strangers, they say, speak the language of birds ; and in the language of birds did I tell the Great Taboo to him."

Ula pooh-poohed the mighty man-god's fears. "No, no," she cried, with confidence ; "he can never have told them. If he had, would not your Eyes that watch ever for all that happens on heaven or earth, have straightway reported it to you? The parrot died without yielding up the tale. Were it otherwise, Toko, who loves and worships you, would surely have told me."

The man-god puckered his brows slightly, as if he liked not the security. "Well, somehow, Ula," he said, feeling her soft brown arms with his divine hand, slowly, "I have always had my doubts since that day the Soul of all dead parrots bit me. A vicious bird! What did he mean by his bite?" He lowered his voice and looked at her fixedly. "Did not his spilling my blood portend," he asked, with a shudder of fear, "that through that ill-omened bird I, who was once Lavita, should cease to be Tu-Kila-Kila?"

Ula smiled contentedly again. To say the truth, that was precisely the interpretation she herself had put on that terrific omen. The parrot had spilled Tu-Kila-Kila's sacred blood upon the soil of earth. According to her simple natural philosophy, that was a certain sign that through the parrot's instrumentality Tu-Kila-Kila's life would be forfeited to the great eternal earth-spirit. Or, rather, the earth-spirit would claim the blood of the man Lavita, in whose body it dwelt, and would itself migrate to some new earthly tabernacle.

But for all that, she dissembled. "Great god," she cried, smiling, a benign smile, "you are tired! You are thirsty! Care for heaven and earth has wearied you out. You feel the fatigue of upholding the sun in heaven. Your arms must ache. Your thews must give under you. Drink of the soul-inspiring juice of the kava! My hands have prepared the divine cup. For Tu-Kila-Kila did I make it—fresh, pure, invigorating!"

She held the bowl to his lips with an enticing smile. Tu-Kila-Kila hesitated and glanced around him suspiciously. "What if the white-faced stranger should come to-night?" he whispered, hoarsely. "He may have discovered the Great Taboo, after all. Who can tell the ways of the world, how they come about? My people are so treacherous. Some traitor may have betrayed it to him."

"Impossible," the beautiful, snake-like woman answered, with a strong gesture of natural dissent. "And even if he came, would not kava, the divine, inspiriting drink of the gods, in which dwell the embodied souls of our fathers—would not kava make you more vigorous, strong for the fight? Would it not course through your limbs like fire? Would it not pour into your soul the divine, abiding strength of your mighty mother, the eternal earth-spirit?"

"A little," Tu-Kila-Kila said, yielding, "but not too much. Too much would stupefy me. When the spirits, that the kava-tree sucks up from the earth, are too strong within us, they overpower our own strength, so that even I, the high god—even I can do nothing."

Ula held the bowl to his lips, and enticed him to drink with her beautiful eyes. "A deep draught, O supporter of the sun in heaven," she cried, pressing his arm tenderly.

"Am I not Ula? Did I not brew it for you? Am I not the chief and most favored among your women? I will sit at the door. I will watch all night. I will not close an eye. Not a footfall on the ground but my ear shall hear it."

"Do," Tu-Kila-Kila said, laconically. "I fear Fire and Water. Those gods love me not. Fain would they make me migrate into some other body. But I myself like it not. This one suits me admirably. Ula, that kava is stronger than you are used to make it."

"No, no," Ula cried, pressing it to his lips a second time, passionately. "You are a very great god. You are tired; it overcomes you. And if you sleep, I will watch. Fire and Water dare not disobey your commands. Are you not great? Your Eyes are everywhere. And I, even I, will be as one of them."

The savage gulped down a few more mouthfuls of the intoxicating liquid. Then he glanced up again suddenly with a quick, suspicious look. The cunning of his race gave him wisdom in spite of the deadly strength of the kava Ula had brewed too deep for him. With a sudden resolve, he rose and staggered out. "You are a serpent, woman!" he cried angrily, seeing the smile that lurked upon Ula's face. "To-morrow I will kill you. I will take the white woman for my bride, and she and I will feast off your carrion body. You have tried to betray me, but you are not cunning enough, not strong enough. No woman shall kill me. I am a very great god. I will not yield. I will wait by the tree. This is a trap you have set, but I do not fall into it. If the King of the Rain comes, I shall be there to meet him."

He seized his spear and hatchet and walked forth, erect, without one sign of drunkenness. Ula trembled to herself as she saw him go. She was playing a deep game. Had she given him only just enough kava to strengthen and inspire him?

CHAPTER XXVIII.

WAGER OF BATTLE.

Felix wound his way painfully through the deep fern-brake of the jungle, by no regular path, so as to avoid exciting the alarm of the natives, and to take Tu Kila-Kila's palace-temple from the rear, where the big tree, which overshadowed it with its drooping branches, was most easily approachable. As he and Toko crept on, bending low, through that dense tropical scrub, in deathly silence, they were aware all the time of a low, crackling sound that rang ever some paces in the rear on their trail through the forest. It was Tu-Kila-Kila's Eyes, following them stealthily from afar, footstep for footstep, through the dense undergrowth of bush, and the crisp fallen leaves and twigs that snapped light beneath their footfall. What hope of success with those watchful spies, keen as beagles and cruel as bloodhounds, following ever on their track ? What chance of escape for Felix and Muriel, with the cannibal man-gods toils laid round on every side to insure their destruction ?

Silently and cautiously the two men groped their way on through the dark gloom of the woods, in spite of their mute pursuers. The moonlight flickered down athwart the trackless soil as they went ; the hum of insects innumerable droned deep along the underbrush. Now and then the startled scream of a night jar broke the monotony of the buzz that was worse than silence ; owls boomed from the hollow trees, and fireflies darted dim through the open spaces. At last they emerged upon the cleared area of the temple. There Felix, without one moment's hesitation, with a firm and resolute tread, stepped over the white coral line that marked the taboo of the great god's precincts. That was a declaration of open war ; he had crossed the Rubicon of Tu-Kila-Kila's empire. Toko stood trembling on the far side ; none might pass that mystic line unbidden and live, save the Korong alone who could succeed in breaking off the bough "with yellow leaves, resembling a mistletoe," of which Methuselah, the parrot, had told Felix and Muriel, and so earn the right to fight for his life with the redoubted and redoubtable Tu-Kila-Kila.

As he stepped over the taboo-line, Felix was aware of many native eyes fixed stonily upon him from the surrounding precinct. Clearly they were awaiting him. Yet not a soul gave the alarm ; that in itself would have been to break taboo. Every man or woman among the temple attendants within that charmed circle stood on gaze curiously. Close by, Ula, the favorite wife of the man-god, crouched low by the hut, with one finger on her treacherous lips, bending eagerly forward, in silent expectation of what next might happen. Once, and once only, she glanced at Toko with a mute sign of triumph ; then she fixed her big eyes on Felix in tremulous anxiety ; for to her as to him, life and death now hung absolutely on the issue of his enterprise. A little farther back the King of Fire and the King of Water, in full sacrificial robes, stood smiling sardonically. For them it was merely a question of one master more or less, one Tu-Kila-Kila in place of another. They had no special interest in the upshot of the contest, save in so far as they always hated most the man who for the moment held by his own strong arm the superior godship over them. Around, Tu-Kila-Kila's Eyes kept watch and ward in sinister silence. Taboo was stronger than even the commands of the high god himself. When once a Korong had crossed that fatal line, unbidden and unwelcomed by Tu-Kila-Kila, he came as Tu-Kila-Kila's foe and would-be successor ; the duty of every guardian of the temple was then to see fair play between the god that was and the god that might be—the Tu-Kila-Kila of the hour and the Tu-Kila-Kila who might possibly supplant him.

"Let the great spirit itself choose which body it will

inhabit," the King of Fire murmured in a soft, low voice, glancing toward a dark spot at the foot of the big tree. The moonlight fell dim through the branches on the place where he looked. The glibbering bones of dead victims rattled lightly in the wind. Felix's eyes followed the King of Fire's, and saw, lying asleep upon the ground, Tu-Kila-Kila himself, with his spear and tomahawk.

He lay there, huddled up by the very roots of the tree, breathing deep and regularly. Right over his head projected the branch, in one part of whose boughs grew the fateful parasite. By the dim light of the moon, straggling through the dense foliage, Felix could see its yellow leaves distinctly. Beneath it hung a skeleton, suspended by invisible cords, head downward from the branches. It was the skeleton of a previous Korong who had tried in vain to reach the bough, and perished. Tu-Kila-Kila had made high feast on the victim's flesh ; his bones, now collected together and cunningly fastened with native rope, served at once as a warning and as a trap or pitfall for all who might rashly venture to follow him.

Felix stood for one moment, alone and awe-struck, a solitary civilized man, among those hideous surroundings. Above, the cold moon ; all about, the grim, stolid, half-hostile natives ; close by, that strange, serpentine, savage wife, guarding, cat-like, the sleep of her cannibal husband ; behind, the watchful Eyes of Tu-Kila-Kila, waiting ever in the background, ready to raise a loud shout of alarm and warning the moment the fatal branch was actually broken, but mute, by their vows, till that moment was accomplished. Then a sudden wild impulse urged him on to the attempt. The banyan had dropped down rooting offsets to the ground, after the fashion of its kind, from its main branches. Felix seized one of these and swung himself lightly up, till he reached the very limb on which the sacred parasite itself was growing.

To get to the parasite, however, he must pass directly above Tu-Kila-Kila's head, and over the point where that ghastly grinning skeleton was suspended, as by an unseen hair, from the fork that bore it.

He walked along, balancing himself, and clutching, as he went, at the neighboring boughs, while Tu-Kila-Kila, overcome with the kava, slept stolidly and heavily on beneath him. At last he was almost within grasp of the parasite. Could he lunge out and clutch it? One try— one effort! No, no.; he almost lost footing and fell over in the attempt. He couldn't keep his balance so. He must try farther on. Come what might, he must go past the skeleton.

The grisly mass swung again, clanking its bones as it swung, and groaned in the wind ominously. The breeze whistled audibly through its hollow skull and vacant eye-sockets. Tu-Kila-Kila turned uneasily in his sleep below. Felix saw there was not one instant of time to be lost now. He passed on boldly; and as he passed, a dozen thin cords of paper mulberry, stretched every way in an invisible network among the boughs, too small to be seen in the dim moonlight, caught him with their toils and almost overthrew him. They broke with his weight, and Felix himself, tumbling blindly, fell forward. At the cost of a sprained wrist and a great jerk on his bruised fingers, he caught at a bough by his side, but wrenched it away suddenly. It was touch and go. At the very same moment, the skeleton fell heavily, and rattled on the ground beside Tu-Kila-Kila.

Before Felix could discover what had actually happened, a very great shout went up all round below, and made him stagger with excitement. Tu-Kila-Kila was awake, and had started up, all intent, mad with wrath and kava. Glaring about him wildly, and brandishing his great spear in his stalwart hands, he screamed aloud, in a perfect frenzy of passion and despair: "Where is he, the Korong? Bring him on, my meat! Let me devour his heart! Let me tear him to pieces. Let me drink of his blood! Let me kill him and eat him!"

Sick and desperate at the accident, Felix, in turn, clinging hard to his bough with one hand, gazed wildly about
him to look for the parasite. But it had gone as if by
magic. He glanced around in despair, vaguely conscious
that nothing was left for it now but to drop to the ground
and let himself be killed at leisure by that frantic savage.
Yet even as he did so, he was aware of that great cry—a
cry as of triumph—still rending the air. Fire and Water
had rushed forward, and were holding back Tu-Kila-Kila,
now black in the face from rage, with all their might. Ula
was smiling a malicious joy. The Eyes were all agog with
interest and excitement. And from one and all that wild
scream rose unanimous to the startled sky : " He has it !
He has it ! The Soul of the Tree ! The Spirit of the
World ! The great god's abode. Hold off your hands,
Lavita, son of Sami ! Your trial has come. He has it !
He has it ! "

Felix looked about him with a whirling brain. His eye
fell suddenly. There, in his own hand, lay the fateful
bough. In his efforts to steady himself, he had clutched
at it by pure accident, and broken it off unawares with the
force of his clutching. As fortune would have it, he grasped
it still. His senses reeled. He was almost dead with excitement, suspense, and uncertainty, mingled with pain of
his wrenched wrist. But for Muriel's sake he pulled himself together. Gazing down and trying hard to take it all
in—that strange savage scene—he saw that Tu-Kila-Kila
was making frantic attempts to lunge at him with the spear,
while the King of Fire and the King of Water, stern and
relentless, were holding him off by main force, and striving
their best to appease and quiet him.

There was an awful pause. Then a voice broke the still-
ness from beyond the taboo-line :

"The Shadow of the King of the Rain speaks," it said,
in very solemn, conventional accents. " Korong ! Korong !
The Great Taboo is broken. Fire and Water, hold him in
whom dwells the god till my master comes. He has the

Soul of all the spirits of the wood in his hands. He will fight for his right. Taboo! Taboo! I, Toko, have said it."

He clapped his hands thrice.

Tu-Kila-Kila made a wild effort to break away once more. But the King of Fire, standing opposite him, spoke still louder and clearer. "If you touch the Korong before the line is drawn," he said, with a voice of authority, "you are no Tu-Kila-Kila, but an outcast and a criminal. All the people will hold you with forked sticks, while the Korong burns you alive slowly, limb by limb, with me, who am Fire, the fierce, the consuming. I will scorch you and bake you till you are as a bamboo in the flame. Taboo! Taboo! Taboo! I, Fire, have said it."

The King of Water, with three attendants, forced Tu-Kila-Kila on one side for a moment. Ula stood by and smiled pleased compliance. A temple slave, trembling all over at this conflict of the gods, brought out a calabash full of white coral-sand. The King of Water spat on it and blessed it. By this time a dozen natives, at least, had assembled outside the taboo-line, and stood eagerly watching the result of the combat. The temple slave made a long white mark with the coral-sand on one side of the cleared area. Then he handed the calabash solemnly to Toko. Toko crossed the sacred precinct with a few inaudible words of muttered charm, to save the Taboo, as prescribed in the mysteries. Then he drew a similar line on the ground on his side, some twenty yards off. "Descend, O my lord!" he cried to Felix; and Felix, still holding the bough tight in his hand, swung himself blindly from the tree, and took his place by Toko.

"Toe the line!" Toko cried, and Felix toed it.

"Bring up your god!" the Shadow called out aloud to the King of Water. And the King of Water, using no special ceremony with so great a duty, dragged Tu-Kila-Kila helplessly along with him to the farther taboo-line.

The King of Water brought a spear and tomahawk. He

handed them to Felix. "With these weapons," he said, "fight, and merit heaven. I hold the bough meanwhile —the victor takes it."

The King of Fire stood out between the lists. "Korongs and gods," he said, "the King of the Rain has plucked the sacred bough, according to our fathers' rites, and claims trial which of you two shall henceforth hold the sacred soul of the world, the great Tu-Kila-Kila. Wager of Battle decides the day. Keep toe to line. At the end of my words, forth, forward, and fight for it. The great god knows his own, and will choose his abode. Taboo, Taboo, Taboo! I, Fire, have spoken it."

Scarcely were the words well out of his mouth, when, with a wild whoop of rage, Tu-Kila-Kila, who had the advantage of knowing the rules of the game, so to speak, dashed madly forward, drunk with passion and kava, and gave one lunge with his spear full tilt at the breast of the startled and unprepared white man. His aim, though frantic, was not at fault. The spear struck Felix high up on the left side. He felt a dull thud of pain ; a faint gurgle of blood. Even in the pale moonlight his eye told him at once a red stream was trickling out over his flannel shirt. He was pricked, at least. The great god had wounded him.

CHAPTER XXIX.

VICTORY—AND AFTER ?

The great god had wounded him. But not to the heart. Felix, as good luck would have it, happened to be wearing buckled braces. He had worn them on board, and, like the rest of his costume, had, of course, never since been able to discard them. They stood him in good stead now. The buckle caught the very point of the bone-tipped spear, and broke the force of the blow, as the great god lunged forward. The wound was but a graze ; and Tu-Kila-Kila's light shaft snapped short in the middle.

Madder and wilder than ever, the savage pitched it away, yelling, rushed forward with a fierce curse on his angry tongue, and flung himself, tooth and nail, on his astonished opponent.

The suddenness of the onslaught almost took the Englishman's breath away. By this time, however, Felix had pulled together his ideas and taken in the situation. Tu-Kila-Kila was attacking him now with his heavy stone axe. He must parry those deadly blows. He must be alert, but watchful. He must put himself in a posture of defence at once. Above all, he must keep cool and have his wits about him.

If he could but have drawn his knife, he would have stood a better chance in that hand-to-hand conflict. But there was no time now for such tactics as those. Besides, even in close fight with a bloodthirsty savage, an English gentleman's sense of fair play never for one moment deserts him. Felix felt, if they were to fight it out face to face for their lives, they should fight at least on a perfect equality. Steel against stone was a mean advantage. Parrying Tu-Kila-Kila's first desperate blow with the haft of his own hatchet, he leaped aside half a second to gain breath and strength. Then he rushed on, and dealt one deadly downstroke with the ponderous weapon.

For a minute or two they closed, in perfectly savage single combat. Fire and Water, observant and impartial, stood by like seconds to see the god himself decide the issue, which of the two combatants should be his living representative. The contest was brief but very hard-fought. Tu-Kila-Kila, inspired with the last frenzy of despair, rushed wildly on his opponent with hands and fists, and teeth and nails, dealing his blows in blind fury, right and left, and seeking only to sell his life as dearly as possible. In this last extremity, his very superstitions told against him. Everything seemed to show his hour had

come. The parrot's bite—the omen of his own blood that
stained the dust of earth—Ula's treachery—the chance by
which the Korong had learned the Great Taboo—Felix's
accidental or providential success in breaking off the
bough—the length of time he himself had held the divine
honors—the probability that the god would by this time
begin to prefer a new and stronger representative—all these
things alike combined to fire the drunk and maddened
savage with the energy of despair. He fell upon his enemy
like a tiger upon an elephant. He fought with his tomahawk and his feet and his whole lithe body ; he foamed at
the mouth with impotent rage ; he spent his force on the
air in the extremity of his passion.

Felix, on the other hand, sobered by pain, and nerved
by the fixed consciousness that Muriel's safety now depended absolutely on his perfect coolness, fought with the
calm skill of a practised fencer. Happily he had learned
the gentle art of thrust and parry years before in England ;
and though both weapon and opponent were here so different, the lesson of quickness and calm watchfulness he
had gained in that civilized school stood him in good stead,
even now, under such adverse circumstances. Tu-Kila-
Kila, getting spent, drew back for a second at last, and
panted for breath. That faint breathing-space of a moment's duration sealed his fate. Seizing his chance with
consummate skill, Felix closed upon the breathless monster, and brought down the heavy stone hammer point
blank upon the centre of his crashing skull. The weapon
drove home. It cleft a great red gash in the cannibal's
head. Tu-Kila-Kila reeled and fell. There was an infini-
tesimal pause of silence and suspense. Then a great shout
went up from all round to heaven, " He has killed him !
He has killed him ! We have a new-made god ! Tu-Kila-
Kila is dead ! Long live Tu-Kila-Kila ! "

Felix drew back for a moment, panting and breathless,
and wiped his wet brow with his sleeve, his brain all whirling. At his feet, the savage lay stretched like a log. Felix

gazed at the blood-bespattered face remorsefully.   It is an awful thing, even in a just quarrel, to feel that 'you have really taken a human life!   The responsibility is enough to appal the bravest of us.   He stooped down and examined the prostrate body with solemn reverence.   Blood was flowing in torrents from the wounded head.   But Tu-Kila-Kila was dead—stone-dead forever.

Hot tears of relief welled up into Felix's eyes.   He touched the body cautiously with a reverent hand.   No life.   No motion.

Just as he did so, the woman Ula came forward, bare-limbed and beautiful, all triumph in her walk, a proud, insensitive savage.   One second she gazed at the great corpse disdainfully.   Then she lifted her dainty foot, and gave it a contemptuous kick.   " The body of Lavita, the son of Sami," she said, with a gesture of hatred.   " He had a bad heart.   We will cook it and eat it."   Next turning to Felix, " Oh, Tu-Kila-Kila," she cried, clapping her hands three times and bowing low to the ground, " you are a very great god.   We will serve you and salute you. Am not I, Ula, one of your wives, your meat ?   Do with me as you will.   Toko, you are henceforth the great god's Shadow ! "

Felix gazed at the beautiful, heartless creature, all horrified.   Even on Boupari, that cannibal island, he was hardly prepared for quite so low a depth of savage insensibility.   But all the people around, now a hundred or more, standing naked before their new god, took up the shout in concert.   " The body of Lavita, the son of Sami," they cried.   "A carrion corpse !   The god has deserted it. The great soul of the world has entered the heart of the white-faced stranger from the disk of the sun ; the King of the Rain ; the great Tu-Kila-Kila.   We will cook and eat the body of Lavita, the son of Sami.   He was a bad man.   He is a worn-out shell.   Nothing remains of him now.   The great god has left him."

They clapped their hands in a set measure as they recited this hymn. The King of Fire retreated into the temple. Ula stood by, and whispered low with Toko. There was a ceremonial pause of some fifteen minutes. Presently, from the inner recesses of the temple itself, a low noise issued forth as of a rising wind. For some seconds it buzzed and hummed, droningly. But at the very first note of that holy sound Ula dropped her lover's hand, as one drops a red-hot coal, and darted wildly off at full speed, like some frightened wild beast, into the thick jungle. Every other woman near began to rush away with equally instantaneous signs of haste and fear. The men, on the other hand, erect and naked, with their hands on their foreheads, crossed the taboo-line at once. It was the summons to all who had been initiated at the mysteries —the sacred bull-roarer was calling the assembly of the men of Boupari.

For several minutes it buzzed and droned, that mystic implement, growing louder and louder, till it roared like thunder. One after another, the men of the island rushed in as if mad or in flight for their lives before some fierce beast pursuing them. They ran up, panting, and dripping with sweat ; their hands clapped to their foreheads ; their eyes starting wildly from their staring sockets ; torn and bleeding and lacerated by the thorns and branches of the jungle, for each man ran straight across country from the spot where he lay asleep, in the direction of the sound, and never paused or drew breath, for dear life's sake, till he stood beside the corpse of the dead Tu-Kila-Kila.

And every moment the cry pealed louder and louder still. "Lavita, the son of Sami, is dead, praise Heaven ! The King of the Rain has slain him, and is now the true Tu-Kila-Kila !"

Felix bent irresolute over the fallen savage's blood-stained corpse. What next was expected of him he hardly knew or cared. His one desire now was to return to Muriel—to Muriel, whom he had rescued from something worse than death at the hateful hands of that accursed creature who lay breathless forever on the ground beside him.

Somebody came up just then, and seized his hand warmly. Felix looked up with a start. It was their friend, the Frenchman. "Ah, my captain, you have done well," M. Peyron cried, admiring him. "What courage! What coolness! What pluck! What soldiership! I couldn't see all. But I was in at the death! And oh, *mon Dieu*, how I admired and envied you!"

By this time the bull-roarer had ceased to bellow among the rocks. The King of Fire stood forth. In his hands he held a length of bamboo-stick with a lighted coal in it. "Bring wood and palm-leaves," he said, in a tone of command. "Let me light myself up, that I may blaze before Tu-Kila-Kila."

He turned and bowed thrice very low before Felix. "The accepted of Heaven," he cried, holding his hands above him. "The very high god! The King of all Things! He sends down his showers upon our crops and our fields. He causes his sun to shine brightly over us. He makes our pigs and our slaves bring forth their increase. All we are but his meat. We, his people, praise him."

And all the men of Boupari, naked and bleeding, bent low in response. "Tu Kila-Kila is great," they chanted, as they clapped their hands. "We thank him that he has chosen a fresh incarnation. The sun will not fade in the heavens overhead, nor the bread-fruits wither and cease to bear fruit on earth. Tu-Kila-Kila, our god, is great. He springs ever young and fresh, like the herbs of the field. He is a most high god. We, his people, praise him."

Four temple attendants brought sticks and leaves, while Felix stood still, half dazed with the newness of these strange preparations. The King of Fire, with his torch, set light to the pile. It blazed merrily on high. "I, Fire, salute you," he cried, bending over it toward Felix.

"Now cut up the body of Lavita, the son of Sami," he went on, turning toward it contemptuously. "I will cook it in my flame, that Tu-Kila-Kila the great may eat of it."

Felix drew back with a face all aglow with horror and disgust. "Don't touch that body!" he cried, authoritatively, putting his foot down firm. "Leave it alone at once. I refuse to allow you." Then he turned to M. Peyron. "The King of the Birds and I," he said, with calm resolve, "we two will bury it."

The King of Fire drew back at these strange words, nonplussed. This was, indeed, an ill-omened break in the ceremony of initiation of a new Tu-Kila-Kila, to which he had never before in his life been accustomed. He hardly knew how to comport himself under such singular circumstances. It was as though the sovereign of England, on coronation-day, should refuse to be crowned, and intimate to the archbishop, in his full canonicals, a confirmed preference for the republican form of Government. It was a contingency that law and custom in Boupari had neither, in their wisdom, foreseen nor provided for.

The King of Water whispered low in the new god's ear. "You must eat of his body, my lord," he said. "That is absolutely necessary. Every one of us must eat of the flesh of the god; but you, above all, must eat his heart, his divine nature. Otherwise you can never be full Tu-Kila-Kila."

"I don't care a straw for that," Felix cried, now aroused to a full sense of the break in Methuselah's story and trembling with apprehension. "You may kill me if you like; we can die only once; but human flesh I can never taste; nor will I, while I live, allow you to touch this dead man's body. We will bury it ourselves, the King of the Birds and I. You may tell your people so. That is my last word." He raised his voice to the customary ceremonial pitch. "I, the new Tu Kila-Kila," he said, "have spoken it."

The King of Fire and the King of Water, taken aback at his boldness, conferred together for some seconds privately. The people meanwhile looked on and wondered. What could this strange hitch in the divine proceedings mean? Was the god himself recalcitrant? Never in their lives had the oldest men among them known anything like it.

And as they whispered and debated, awe-struck but discordant, a shout arose once more from the outer circle —a mighty shout of mingled surprise, alarm, and terror. "Taboo! Taboo! Fence the mysteries. Beware! Oh, great god, we warn you. The mysteries are in danger! Cut her down! Kill her! A woman! A woman!"

At the words, Felix was aware of somebody bursting through the dense crowd and rushing wildly toward him. Next moment, Muriel hung and sobbed on his shoulder, while Mali, just behind her, stood crying and moaning.

Felix held the poor startled girl in his arms and soothed her. And all around another great cry arose from five hundred lips : "Two women have profaned the mysteries of the god. They are Tu-Kila-Kila's trespass-offering. Let us kill them and eat them !"

CHAPTER XXX.

SUSPENSE.

In a moment, Felix's mind was fully made up. There was no time to think ; it was the hour for action. He saw. how he must comport himself toward this strange wild people. Seating Muriel gently on the ground, Mali beside her, and stepping forward himself, with Peyron's hand in his, he beckoned to the vast and surging crowd to bespeak respectful silence.

A mighty hush fell at once upon the people. The King of Fire and the King of Water stood back, obedient to his nod. They waited for the upshot of this strange new development.

"Men of Boupari," Felix began, speaking with a marvellous fluency in their own tongue, for the excitement itself supplied him with eloquence; "I have killed your late god in the prescribed way; I have plucked the sacred bough, and fought in single combat by the established rules of your own religion. Fire and Water, you guardians of this holy island, is it not so? You saw all things done, did you not, after the precepts of your ancestors?"

The King of Fire bowed low and answered: "Tu-Kila-Kila speaks, indeed, the truth. Water and I, with our own eyes, have seen it."

"And now," Felix went on, "I am myself, by your own laws, Tu-Kila-Kila."

The King of Fire made a gesture of dissent. "Oh, great god, pardon me," he murmured, "if I say aught, now, to contradict you; but you are not a full Tu-Kila-Kila yet till you have eaten of the heart of the god, your predecessor."

"Then where is now the spirit of Tu-Kila-Kila, the very high god, if I am not he?" Felix asked, abruptly, thus puzzling them with a hard problem in their own savage theology.

The King of Fire gave a start, and pondered. This was a detail of his creed that had never before so much as occurred to him. All faiths have their *cruces.* "I do not well know," he answered, "whether it is in the heart of Lavita, the son of Sami, or in your own body. But I feel sure it must now be certainly somewhere, though just where our fathers have never told us."

Felix recognized at once that he had gained a point. "Then look to it well," he said, austerely. "Be careful how you act. Do nothing rash. For either the soul of the god is in the heart of Lavita, the son of Sami; and then, since I refuse to eat it, it will decay away, as Lavita's body decays, and the world will shrivel up, and all things will perish, because the god is dead and crumbled to dust forever. Or else it is in my body, who am god in his place ; and then, if anybody does me harm or hurt, he will be an impious wretch, and will have broken taboo, and Heaven knows what evils and misfortunes may not, therefore, fall on each and all of you."

A very old chief rose from the ranks outside. His hair was white and his eyes bleared. "Tu-Kila-Kila speaks well," he cried, in a loud but mumbling voice. "His words are wise. He argues to the point. He is very cunning. I advise you, my people, to be careful how you anger the white-faced stranger, for you know what he is ; he is cruel; he is powerful. There was never any storm in my time—and I am an old man—so great in Boupari as the storm that rose when the King of the Rain ate the storm-apple. Our yams and our taros even now are suffering from it. He is a mighty strong god. Beware how you tamper with him ! "

He sat down, trembling. A younger chief rose from a nearer rank, and said his say in turn. "I do not agree with our father," he cried, pointing to the chief who had just spoken. "His word is evil ; he is much mistaken. I have another thought. My thought is this. Let us kill and eat the white-faced stranger at once, by wager of battle ; and let whosoever fights and overcomes him receive his honors, and take to wife the fair woman, the Queen of the Clouds, the sun-faced Korong, whom he brought from the sun with him."

"But who will then be Tu-Kila-Kila ?" Felix asked, turning round upon him quickly. Habituation to danger had made him unnaturally alert in such utmost extremities.

"Why, the man who slays you," the young chief answered, pointedly, grasping his heavy tomahawk with profound expression.

"I think not," Felix answered. "Your reasoning is bad. For if I am not Tu-Kila-Kila, how can any man become Tu-Kila-Kila by killing me ? And if I am Tu-Kila-Kila, how dare you, not being yourself Korong, and not having broken off the sacred bough, as I did, venture to attack me ? You wish to set aside all the customs of Boupari. Are you not ashamed of such gross impiety ? "

"Tu-Kila-Kila speaks well," the King of Fire put in, for he had no cause to love the aggressive young chief, and he thought better of his chances in life as Felix's minister. "Besides, now I think of it, he *must* be Tu-Kila-Kila, because he has taken the life of the last great god, whom he slew with his hands ; and therefore the life is now his—he holds it."

Felix was emboldened by this favorable opinion to strike out a fresh line in a further direction. He stood forward once more, and beckoned again for silence. "Yes, my people," he said calmly, with slow articulation, "by the custom of your race and the creed you profess I am now indeed, and in every truth, the abode of your great god, Tu-Kila-Kila. But, furthermore, I have a new revelation to make to you. I am going to instruct you in a fresh way. This creed that you hold is full of errors. As Tu-Kila-Kila, I mean to take my own course, no islander hindering me. If you try to depose me, what great gods have you now got left ? None, save only Fire and Water, my ministers. King of the Rain there is none ; for I, who was he, am now Tu-Kila-Kila. Tu-Kila-Kila there is none, save only me ; for the other, that was, I have fought and conquered. The Queen of the Clouds is with me. The King of the Birds is with me. Consider, then, O friends, that if you kill us all, you will have nowhere to turn ; you will be left quite godless."

"It is true," the people murmured, looking about them, half puzzled. "He is wise. He speaks well. He is indeed a Tu-Kila-Kila."

Felix pressed his advantage home at once. "Now listen," he said, lifting up one solemn forefinger. "I come from a country very far away, where the customs are better by many yams than those of **Boupari.** And now that I am indeed Tu-Kila-Kila—your god, your master—I will change and alter some of your customs that seem to me here and now most undesirable. In the first place—hear this!—I will put down all cannibalism. No man shall eat of human flesh on pain of death. And to begin with, no man shall cook or eat the body of Lavita, the son of Sami. On that I am determined—I, Tu-Kila-Kila. The King of the Birds and I, we will dig a pit, and we will bury in it the corpse of this man that was once your god, and whom his own wickedness compelled me to fight and slay, in order to prevent more cruelty and bloodshed."

The young chief stood up, all red in his wrath, and interrupted him, brandishing a coral-stone hatchet. "This is blasphemy," he said. "This is sheer rank blasphemy. These are not good words. They are very bad medicine. The white-faced Korong is no true Tu-Kila-Kila. His advice is evil—and ill-luck would follow it. He wishes to change the sacred customs of Boupari. Now, that is not well. My counsel is this : let us eat him now, unless he changes his heart, and amends his ways, and partakes, as is right, of the body of Lavita, the son of Sami."

The assembly swayed visibly, this way and that, some inclining to the conservative view of the rash young chief, and others to the cautious liberalism of the gray-haired warrior. Felix noted their division, and spoke once more, this time still more authoritatively than ever.

"Furthermore," he said, "my people, hear me. As I came in a ship propelled by fire over the high waves of the sea, so I go away in one. We watch for such a ship to pass by Boupari. When it comes, the Queen of the Clouds—upon whose life I place a great Taboo ; let no man dare to touch her at his peril ; if he does, I will rush upon him and kill him as I killed Lavita, the son of Sami. When it comes, the Queen of the Clouds, the King of the Birds, and I, we will go away back in it to the land whence we came, and be quit of Boupari. But we will not leave it fireless or godless. When I return back home again to my own far land, I will send out messengers, very good men, who will tell you of a God more powerful by much than any you ever knew, and very righteous. They will teach you great things you never dreamed of. Therefore, I ask you now to disperse to your own homes, while the King of Birds and I bury the body of Lavita, the son of Sami."

All this time Muriel had been seated on the ground, listening with profound interest, but scarcely understanding a word, though here and there, after her six months' stay in the island, a single phrase was dimly intelligible to her. But now, at this critical moment she rose, and, standing upright by Felix's side in her spotless English purity among those assembled savages, she pointed just once with her uplifted finger to the calm vault of heaven, and then across the moonlit horizon of the sea, and last of all to the clustering huts and villages of Boupari. " Tell them," she said to Felix, with blanched lips, but without one sign of a tremor in her fearless voice, " I will pray for them to Heaven, when I go across the sea, and will think of the children that I loved to pat and play with, and will send out messengers from our home beyond the waves, to make them wiser and happier and better."

Felix translated her simple message to them in its pure womanly goodness. Even the natives were touched. They whispered and hesitated. Then after a time of much murmured debate, the King of Fire stood forward as a mediator. "There is an oracle, O Korong," he said, "not to prejudge the matter, which decides all these things— a great conch-shell at a sacred grove in the neighboring island of Aloa Mauna. It is the holiest oracle of all our holy religion. We gods and men of Boupari have taken counsel together, and have come to a conclusion. We will put forth a canoe and send men with blood on their faces to inquire at Aloa Mauna of the very great oracle. Till then, you are neither Tu-Kila-Kila, nor not Tu-Kila-Kila.

14

It behooves us to be very careful how we deal with gods. Our people will stand round your precinct in a row, and guard you with their spears. You shall not cross the taboo-line to them, nor they to you: all shall be neutral. Food shall be laid by the line, as always, morn, noon, and night; and your Shadows shall take it in; but you shall not come out. Neither shall you bury the body of Lavita, the son of Sami. Till the canoe comes back it shall lie in the sun and rot there."

He clapped his hands twice.

In a moment a tom-tom began to beat from behind, and the people all crowded without the circle. The King of Fire came forward ostentatiously and made taboo. "If, any man cross this line," he said in a droning sing-song, "till the canoe return from the great oracle of our faith on Aloa Mauna, I, Fire, will scorch him into cinder and ashes. If any woman transgress, I will pitch her with palm oil, and light her up for a lamp on a moonless night to lighten this temple."

The King of Water distributed shark's-tooth spears. At once a great serried wall hemmed in the Europeans all round, and they sat down to wait, the three whites together, for the upshot of the mission to Aloa Mauna.

And the dawn now gleamed red on the eastern horizon.

CHAPTER XXXI.

AT SEA: OFF BOUPARI.

Thirteen days out from Sydney, the good ship Australasian was nearing the equator.

It was four of the clock in the afternoon, and the captain (off duty) paced the deck, puffing a cigar, and talking idly with a passenger on former experiences.

Eight bells went on the quarter-deck; time to change watches.

"This is only our second trip through this channel," the captain said, gazing across with a casual glance at the palm-trees that stood dark against the blue horizon. "We used to go a hundred miles to eastward, here, to avoid the reefs. But last voyage I came through this way quite safely—though we had a nasty accident on the road—unavoidable—unavoidable! Big sea was running free over the sunken shoals; caught the ship aft unawares, and stove in better than half a dozen portholes. Lady passenger on deck happened to be leaning over the weather gunwale; big sea caught her up on its crest in a jiffy, lifted her like a baby, and laid her down again gently, just so, on the bed of the ocean. By George, sir, I was annoyed. It was quite a romance, poor thing; quite a romance; we all felt so put out about it the rest of that voyage. Young fellow on board, nephew of Sir Theodore Thurstan, of the Colonial Office, was in love with Miss Ellis —girl's name was Ellis—father's a parson somewhere down in Somersetshire—and as soon as the big sea took her up on its crest, what does Thurstan go and do, but he ups on the taffrail, and, before you could say Jack Robinson, jumps over to save her."

"But he didn't succeed?" the passenger asked, with languid interest.

"Succeed, my dear sir? and with a sea running twelve feet high like that? Why, it was pitch dark, and such a surf on that the gig could hardly go through it." The captain smiled, and puffed away pensively. "Drowned," he said, after a brief pause, with complacent composure. "Drowned. Drowned. Drowned. Went to the bottom, both of 'em. Davy Jones's locker. But unavoidable, quite. These accidents *will* happen, even on the best-regulated liners. Why, there was my brother Tom, in the Cunard service—same that boast they never lost a passenger; there was my brother Tom, he was out one day off the Newfoundland banks, heavy swell setting in from the nor'-nor'-east, icebergs ahead, passengers battened down—

Bless my soul, how that light seems to come and go, don't it ? "

It was a reflected light, flashing from the island straight in the captain's eyes, small and insignificant as to size, but strong for all that in the full tropical sunshine, and glittering like a diamond from a vague elevation near the centre of the island.

"Seems to come and go in regular order," the passenger observed, reflectively, withdrawing his cigar. "Looks for all the world just like naval signalling."

The captain paused, and shaded his eyes a moment. "Hanged if that isn't just what it *is*," he answered, slowly. "It's a rigged-up heliograph, and they're using the Morse code ; dash my eyes if they aren't. Well, this *is* civilization ! What the dickens can have come to the island of Boupari ? There isn't a darned European soul in the place, nor ever has been. Anchorage unsafe ; no harbor ; bad reef ; too small for missionaries to make a living, and natives got nothing worth speaking of to trade in."

"What do they say ?" the passenger asked, with suddenly quickened interest.

"How the devil should I tell you yet, sir ?" the captain retorted with choleric grumpiness. "Don't you see I'm spelling it out, letter by letter ? O, r, e, s, c, u, e, u, s, c, o, m, e, w, e, l, l, a, r, m, e, d— Yes, yes, I twig it." And the captain jotted it down in his note-book for some seconds, silently.

"Run up the flag there," he shouted, a moment later, rushing hastily forward. "Stop her at once, Walker. Easy, easy. Get ready the gig. Well, upon my soul, there *is* a rum start anyway."

"What does the message say ?" the passenger inquired, with intense surprise.

"Say ? Well, there's what I make it out," the captain answered, handing him the scrap of paper on which he had jotted down the letters. "I missed the beginning, but the end's all right. Look alive there, boys, will you.

Bring out the Winchester. Take cutlasses, all hands. I'll go along myself in her."

The passenger took the piece of paper on which he read, "and send a boat to rescue us. Come well armed. Savages on guard. Thurstan, Ellis."

In less than three minutes the boat was lowered and manned, and the captain, with the Winchester six-shooter by his side, seated grim in the stern, took command of the tiller.

On the island it was the first day of Felix and Muriel's imprisonment in the dusty precinct of Tu-Kila-Kila's temple. All the morning through, they had sat under the shade of a smaller banyan in the outer corner ; for Muriel could neither enter the noisome hut nor go near the great tree with the skeletons on its branches ; nor could she sit where the dead savage's body, still festering in the sun, attracted the buzzing blue flies by thousands, to drink up the blood that lay thick on the earth in a pool around it. Hard by, the natives sat, keen as lynxes, in a great circle just outside the white taboo-line, where, with serried spears, they kept watch and ward over the persons of their doubtful gods or victims. M. Peyron, alone preserving his equanimity under these adverse circumstances, hummed low to himself in very dubious tones ; even he felt his French gayety had somewhat forsaken him ; this revolution in Boupari failed to excite his Parisian ardor.

About one o'clock in the day, however, looking casually seaward—what was this that M. Peyron, to his great surprise, descried far away on the dim southern horizon ? A low black line, lying close to the water ? No, no ; not a steamer !

Too prudent to excite the natives' attention unnecessarily, the cautious Frenchman whispered, in the most commonplace voice on earth to Felix : "Don't look at once ; and when you do look, mind you don't exhibit any agitation in your tone or manner. But what do you make that out to be—that long black haze on the horizon to southward ? "

Felix looked, disregarding the friendly injunction, at once. At the same moment, Muriel turned her eyes quickly in the self-same direction. Neither made the faintest sign of outer emotion ; but Muriel clenched her white hands hard, till the nails dug into the palm, in her effort to restrain herself, as she murmured very low, in an agitated voice, "*Un vapeur, un vapeur !* "

" So I think," M. Peyron answered, very low and calm. " It is, indeed, a steamer !"

For three long hours those anxious souls waited and watched it draw nearer and nearer. Slowly the natives, too, began to perceive the unaccustomed object. As it drew abreast of the island, and the decisive moment arrived for prompt action, Felix rose in his place once more and cried aloud, " My people, I told you a ship, propelled by fire, would come from the far land across the sea to take us. The ship has come ; you can see for yourselves the thick black smoke that issues in huge puffs from the mouth of the monster. Now, listen to me, and dare not to disobey me. My word is law ; let all men see to it. I am going to send a message of fire from the sun to the great canoe that walks upon the water. If any man ventures to stop me from doing it the people from the great canoe will land on this isle and take vengeance for his act, and kill with the thunder which the sailing gods carry ever about with them."

By this time the island was alive with commotion. Hundreds of natives, with their long hair falling unkempt about their keen brown faces, were gazing with open eyes at the big black ship that ploughed her way so fast against wind and tide over the surface of the waters. Some of them shouted and gesticulated with panic fear ; others seemed half inclined to waste no time on preparation or doubt, but to rush on at once, and immolate their captives before a rescue was possible. But Felix, keeping ever his cool head undisturbed, stood on the dusty mound by Tu-Kila-Kila's house, and taking in his hand the little mirror he had made from the match-box, flashed the light from the sun full in their eyes for a moment, to the astonishment and discomfiture of all those gaping savages. Then he focussed it on the Australasian, across the surf and the waves, and with a throbbing heart began to make his last faint bid for life and freedom.

For four or five minutes he went flashing on, uncertain of the effect, whether they saw or saw not. Then a cry from Muriel burst at once upon his ears. She clasped her hands convulsively in an agony of joy. " They see us! They see us!"

And sure enough, scarcely half a minute later, a British flag ran gayly up the mainmast, and a boat seemed to drop down over the side of the vessel.

As for the natives, they watched these proceedings with considerable surprise and no little discomfiture—Fire and Water, in particular, whispering together, much alarmed, with many superstitious nods and taboos, in the corner of the enclosure.

Gradually, as the boat drew nearer and nearer, divided counsels prevailed among the savages. With no certainly recognized Tu-Kila-Kila to marshal their movements, each man stood in doubt from whom to take his orders. At last, the King of Fire, in a hesitating voice, gave the word of command. " Half the warriors to the shore to repel the enemy; half to watch round the taboo-line, lest the Korongs escape us! Let Breathless Fear, our war-god, go before the face of our troops, invisible!"

And, quick as thought, at his word, the warriors had paired off, two and two, in long lines; some running hastily down to the beach, to man the war-canoes, while others remained, with shark's tooth spears still set in a looser circle, round the great temple-enclosure of Tu-Kila-Kila.

For Muriel, this suspense was positively terrible. To feel one was so close to the hope of rescue, and yet to know that before that help arrived, or even as it came up, those savages might any moment run their ghastly spears through them.

But Felix made the best of his position still. "Remember," he cried, at the top of his voice, as the warriors started at a run for the water's edge, "your Tu-Kila-Kila tells you, these new-comers are his friends. Whoever hurts them, does so at his peril. This is a great Taboo. I bid you receive them. Beware for your lives. I, Tu-Kila-Kila the Great, have said it."

CHAPTER XXXII.

THE DOWNFALL OF A PANTHEON.

The Australasian's gig entered the lagoon through the fringing reef by its narrow seaward mouth, and rowed steadily for the landing place on the main island.

A little way out from shore, amid loud screams and yells, the natives came up with it in their laden war-canoes. Shouting and gesticulating and brandishing their spears with the shark's tooth tips, they endeavored to stop its progress landward by pure noise and bravado.

"We must be careful what we do, boys," the captain observed, in a quiet voice of seamanlike resolution to his armed companions. "We mustn't frighten the savages too much, or show too hostile a front, for fear they should retaliate on our friends on the island." He held up his hand, with the gold braid on the wrist, to command silence; and the natives, gazing open-mouthed, looked and wondered at the gesture. These sailing gods were certainly arrayed in most gorgeous vestments, and their canoe, though devoid of a grinning figure-head, was provided with a most admirable and well-uniformed equipment.

A coral rock jutted high out of the sea to the left hard by. Its summit was crowded with a basking population of sea-gulls and pelicans. The captain gave the word to "easy all." In a second the gig stopped short, as those stout arms held her. He rose in his place and lifted the six-shooter. Then he pointed it ostentatiously at the rock, away from the native canoes, and held up his hand yet again for silence. "We'll give 'em a taste of what we can do, boys," he said, "just to show 'em, not to hurt 'em." At that he drew the trigger twice. His first two chambers were loaded on purpose with duck-shot cartridges. Twice the big gun roared; twice the fire flashed red from its smoking mouth. As the smoke cleared away, the natives, dumb with surprise, and perfectly cowed with terror, saw ten or a dozen torn and bleeding birds float mangled upon the water.

"Now for the dynamite!" the captain said, cheerily, proceeding to lower a small object overboard by a single wire, while he held up his hand a third time to bespeak silence and attention.

The natives looked again, with eyes starting from their heads. The captain gave a little click, and pointed with his finger to a spot on the water's top, a little way in front of him. Instantly, a loud report, and a column of water spurted up into the air, some ten or twelve feet, in a boisterous fountain. As it subsided again, a hundred or so of the bright-colored fish that browse among the submerged coral-groves of these still lagoons, rose dead or dying to the seething, boiling surface.

The captain smiled. Instantly the natives set up a terrified shout. "It is even as he said," they cried. "These gods are his ministers! The white-faced Korong is a very great deity! He is indeed the true Tu-Kila-Kila. These gods have come for him. They are very mighty. Thunder and lightning and waterspouts are theirs. The waves do as they bid. The sea obeys them. They are here to take away our Tu-Kila-Kila from our midst. And what will then become of the island of Boupari? Will it not sink in the waves of the sea and disappear? Will not the

sun in heaven grow dark, and the moon cease to shed its
benign light on the earth, when Tu-Kila-Kila the Great
returns at last to his own far country ? "

"That lot'll do for 'em, I expect," the captain said
cheerily, with a confident smile. "Now forward all,
boys. I fancy we've astonished the natives a trifle."

They rowed on steadily, but cautiously, toward the
white bank of sand which formed the usual landing-place,
the captain holding the six-shooter in readiness all the
time, and keeping an eye firmly fixed on every movement
of the savages. But the warriors in the canoes, thoroughly
cowed and overawed by this singular exhibition of the
strangers' prowess, paddled on in whispering silence,
nearly abreast of the gig, but at a safe distance, as they
thought, and eyed the advancing Europeans with quiet
looks of unmixed suspicion.

At last, the adventurous young chief, who had advised
killing Felix off-hand on the island, mustered up courage
to paddle his own canoe a little nearer, and flung his spear
madly in the direction of the gig. It fell short by ten
yards. He stood eying it angrily. But the captain,
grimly quiet, raising his Winchester to his shoulder without
one second's delay, and marking his man, fired at the
young chief as he stood, still half in the attitude of throwing, on the prow of his canoe, an easy aim for fire-arms.
The ball went clean through the savage's breast, and then
ricochetted three times on the water afar off. The young
chief fell stone dead into the sea like a log, and sank instantly to the bottom.

It was a critical moment. The captain felt uncertain
whether the natives would close round them in force or
not. It is always dangerous to fire a shot at savages.
But the Boupari men were too utterly awed to venture on
defence. "He was Tu-Kila-Kila's enemy," they cried, in
astonished tones. "He raised his voice against the very
high god. Therefore, the very high god's friends have
smitten him with their lightning. Their thunderbolt

went through him, and hit the water beyond. How strong is their hand! They can kill from afar. They are mighty gods. Let no man strive to fight against the friends of Tu-Kila-Kila."

The sailors rowed on and reached the landing-place. There, half of them, headed by the captain, disembarked in good order, with drawn cutlasses, while the other half remained behind to guard, the gig, under the third officer. The natives also disembarked, a little way off, and, making humble signs of submission with knee and arm, endeavored, by pantomime, to express the idea of their willingness to guide the strangers to their friends' quarters.

The captain waved them on with his hand. The natives, reassured, led the way, at some distance ahead, along the paths through the jungle. The captain had his finger on his six-shooter the while; every sailor grasped his cutlass and kept his revolver ready for action. "I don't half like the look of it," the captain observed, partly to himself. "They seem to be leading us into an ambuscade or something. Keep a sharp lookout against surprise from the jungle, boys; and if any native shows fight shoot him down instantly."

At last they emerged upon a clear space in the front, where a great group of savages stood in a circle, with serried spears, round a large wattled hut that occupied the elevated centre of the clearing.

For a minute or two the action of the savages was uncertain. Half of the defenders turned round to face the invaders angrily; the other half stood irresolute, with their spears still held inward, guarding a white line of sand with inflexible devotion.

The warriors who had preceded them from the shore called aloud to their friends by the temple in startled tones. The captain and sailors had no idea what their words meant. But just then, from the midst of the circle, an English voice cried out in haste, "Don't fire! Do nothing rash! We're safe. Don't be frightened. The natives are disposed to parley and palaver. Take care how you act. They're terribly afraid of you."

Just outside the taboo-line the captain halted. The gray-headed old chief, who had accompanied his fellows to the shore, spoke out in Polynesian. "Do not resist them," he said, "my people. If you do, you will be blasted by their lightning like a bare bamboo in a mighty cyclone. They carry thunder in their hands. They are mighty, mighty gods. The white-faced Korong spoke no more than the truth. Let them do as they will with us. We are but their meat. We are as dust beneath their sole, and as driven mulberry-leaves before the breath of the tempest."

The defenders hesitated still a little. Then, suddenly losing heart, they broke rank at last at a point close by where the captain of the Australasian stood, one man after another falling aside slowly and shamefacedly a pace or two. The captain, unhesitatingly, overstepped the white taboo-line. Next instant, Felix and Muriel were grasping his hand hard, and M. Peyron was bowing a polite Parisian reception.

Forthwith, the sailors crowded round them in a hollow square. Muriel and Felix, half faint with relief from their long and anxious suspense, staggered slowly down the seaward path between them. But there was no need now for further show of defence. The islanders, pressing near and flinging away their weapons, followed the procession close, with tears and lamentations. As they went on, the women, rushing out of their huts while the fugitives passed, tore their hair on their heads, and beat their breasts in terror. The warriors who had come from the shore recounted, with their own exaggerative additions, the miracle of the six-shooter and the dynamite cartridge. Gradually they approached the landing-place on the beach. There the third officer sat waiting in the gig to receive them. The lamentations of the islanders now became positively poignant. "Oh, my father," they cried aloud, "my brother, my revered one, you are indeed the true Tu-

Kila-Kila. Do not go away like this and desert us! Oh, our mother, great queen, mighty goddess, stop with us! Take not away your sun from the heavens, nor your rain from the crops. We acknowledge we have sinned; we have done very wrong; but the chief sinner is dead; the wrong-doer has paid; spare us who remain; spare us, great deity; do not make the bright lights of heaven become dark over us. Stay with your worshippers, and we will give you choice young girls to eat every day, we will sacrifice the tenderest of our children to feed you."

It is an awful thing for any race or nation when its taboos fail all at once, and die out entirely. To the men of Boupari, the Tu-Kila-Kila of the moment represented both the Moral Order and the regular sequence of the physical universe. Anarchy and chaos might rule when he was gone. The sun might be quenched, and the people run riot. No wonder they shrank from the fearful consequence that might next ensue. King and priest, god and religion, all at one fell blow were to be taken away from them!

Felix turned round on the shore and spoke to them again. "My people," he said, in a kindly tone—for, after all, he pitied them—"you need have no fear. When I am gone, the sun will still shine and the trees will still bear fruit every year as formerly. I will send the messengers I promised from my own land to teach you. Until they come, I leave you this as a great Taboo. Tu-Kila-Kila enjoins it. Shed no human blood; eat no human flesh. Those who do will be punished when another fire-canoe comes from the far land to bring my messengers."

The King of Fire bent low at the words. "Oh, Tu-Kila-Kila," he said, "it shall be done as you say. Till your messengers come, every man shall live at peace with all his neighbors."

They stepped into the gig. Mali and Toko followed before M. Peyron as naturally as they had always followed their masters on the island before.

"Who are these?" the captain asked, smiling.

"Our Shadows," Felix answered. "Let them come. I will pay their passage when I reach San Francisco. They have been very faithful to us, and they are afraid to remain, lest the islanders should kill them for letting us go or for not accompanying us."

"Very well," the captain answered. "Forward all, there, boys! Now, ahead for the ship. And thank God, we're well out of it!"

But the islanders still stood on the shore and wept, stretching their hands in vain after the departing boat, and crying aloud in piteous tones, "Oh, my father, return! Oh, my mother, come back! Oh, very great gods, do not fly and desert us!"

Seven weeks later Mr. and Mrs. Felix Thurstan, who had been married in the cathedral at Honolulu the very morning the Australasian arrived there, sat in an eminently respectable drawing-room in a London square, where Mrs. Ellis, Muriel's aunt by marriage, was acting as their hostess.

"But how dreadful it is to think, dear," Mrs. Ellis remarked for the twentieth time since their arrival, with a deep-drawn sigh, "how dreadful to think that you and Felix should have been all those months alone on the island together without being married!"

Muriel looked up with a quiet smile toward Felix. "I think, Aunt Mary," she said, dreamily, "if you'd been there yourself, and suffered all those fears, and passed through all those horrors that we did together, you'd have troubled your head very little indeed about such conventionalities, as whether or not you happened to be married. . . . Besides," she added, after a pause, with a fine perception of the inexorable stringency of Mrs. Grundy's law, "we weren't quite without chaperons, either, don't you know; for our Shadows, of course, were always with us."

Whereat Felix smiled an equally quiet smile. "And terrible as it all was," he put in, "I shall never regret it, because it made Muriel know how profoundly I loved her, and it made me know how brave and trustful and pure a woman could be under such awful conditions."

But Mrs. Ellis sat still in her chair and smiled uncomfortably. It affected her spirits. Taboos, after all, are much the same in England as in Boupari.

THE END.

BURT'S HOME LIBRARY.

Comprising two hundred and fifty titles of standard works, embracing fiction, essays, poetry, history, travel, etc., selected from the world's best literature, written by authors of world-wide reputation. Printed from large type, on good paper, and bound in handsome cloth binding, uniform with this volume, Price, 75 cents per copy.

www.ingramcontent.com/pod-product-compliance
Lightning Source LLC
Chambersburg PA
CBHW021244260626
47155CB00004BA/1315